Tomyris

"Never underestimate the hate of a woman."

~ Atossa

I

The red sands of Khorasan were unforgivably cold on the first days of winter. One could see their breath steaming out before their face as the first gold bursts of sun tried to stab through the black darkness of morning. Not many people dared bear the early cold if they didn't have to. Most decided to stoke the fires beside their hide tents and pray to the gods for a clearing in the heavy clouds rolling over the hills. The Persians were cursing their latest round of northern exploits. Their infamous unitor, Cyrus the Great, was an old, and vain man. He was short and fat, with a large white beard that fluffed around his chubby face. Bushy brows towered over his deep, inset eyes that were caked in dark circles of exhaustion anymore. He was a busy man whose ambition seemed to know no bounds. His lust for conquest was insatiable. No tribe could withstand him, though many had tried. He had dreams of grandeur, set down to him by the gods, or so he said. No one would question him, out loud. This morning he was in his tent, fighting back the frost with a roaring fire in the center of his blood red tent, big enough for twelve men though he only shared it with his son and heir, Cambysses. The heir was in his prime, young twenties, with the best education a man could buy, and Cyrus could afford to buy most of the known world. Cambysses didn't understand the luxury he had been given in life, the sheer privilege of being a first-born son. He was naïve and simple in thought. His training was highly selective and protective. Despite his age, he knew very little of the world, and cared not to learn more. He was a content soul, eager to be bought a native wife from the new conquests in the north. Cyrus had promised him that as a means to manipulate his son out of the comforts of home and to earn some respect on the battlefield. He wouldn't be fighting of course, too dangerous for a man of political promise, but it was important he be there, overseeing things. No one in the cities needed to know anything more particular than that. Cyrus was a living legend, and so, some stories wrote themselves.

While servants attended the royal Persian's fire, and set up a decadent breakfast that could make the soldiers whimper in jealousy, Cambysses could hardly be roused. Cyrus was already up, an early riser, drinking his wine and rocking back and forth on bended knee to pray to the gods. Cambysses wasn't much for religion, or routine. He stirred half asleep, only because a servant had accidentally dropped a tray of freshly baked flatbread on the frozen ground. The dirt was hard here, scraped clear of the surrounding red sand by the heavy winds. Cambysses hated it here, it was an arid and unforgiving landscape. The people weren't much different. The prince had met some of the reluctant new recruits, ones who had reluctantly chosen to join Persia over death. They seemed crude, and crass. Hygiene was not important, nor common courtesy. The languages differed, the clothing and customs seemed startingly counterintuitive. Cambysses envied these people not in the least, and he was unsure what bride could come of this, but his father insisted it must be done. The old leader beckoned his son come sit with him on his rug, finely woven with gorgeous colors of lilac and saffron. It was finer than most rugs revered in people's homes, and here, it was just good enough for a king to sit on in the dirt of some godforsaken harsh land. Cambysses was slow to wipe the sleep out of his eyes. His black beard was messy and unkempt, much like the rest of his appearance. His right eye wandered, to which Cyrus would click his tongue in disapproval. There was a lengthy lecture hanging in midair about duty and sacrifice but the elderly father was interrupted by the raucous screaming of a wild black horse running through the center of the Persian camp. Cambysses rushed out into the gusty winds to see the animal. Free. The prince was envious of the wild horse as it wreaked havoc amongst his countrymen and forced conscripts. And as quickly as the animal had come into the camp, it was gone, running along the sandy hillsides without a care in the world.

Deeper into the red sands the Massagetae tribe was undergoing training. One of the few Saka people left to remain unconquered, it was a pressing matter to properly alert the youth to understand the gravity of what it meant to maintain their sovereignty. The Massagetae were led by Tomyris, a fierce woman in her own right, despite being the sole child and daughter of a mighty tribal chief. Having no brothers or siblings, Tomyris had been raised to defend herself, and as such had become as much a queen and soldier, as she had been a mother and horse rider. The Saka people prided themselves on their horsemanship and independence. Persia was threatening to take away all of that in the name of slavery and taxes. All Cyrus represented to them was death, and the Massagetae were some of the proudest of them all, which is why Tomyris assumed they were among the last free people in the area. She would do everything in her power to keep it that way. This morning, despite the bite in the air and the darkness of the clouds, she was overlooking the training of her soldiers. The general in charge was her sixteen-year-old son, her only child, Spargapeithes. She named him after her father though the boy had taken after his father, mostly a stranger to Tomyris. It was the gangly boy's first assignment on his own. While the queen wanted to project trust in her child, she couldn't help but be nosy and perch herself on the hillside to keep eye on him, and occasionally snicker at the crack in his voice as he tried to find a proper tone. Beside the queen on her rare white horse was her advisor and best friend, Skunkha. The man was pale skinned with a curly head of hair, and an untamable beard. He was thin and quick witted, and somewhat of a father figure for the boy general in the valley below. Skunkha's father Homarges had been Tomyris' father's advisor, so the successorship seemed only natural to the young queen of thirty-two. Her long brown hair was braided tight this morning to combat the harsh weather, but she relished the uncomfortable temperatures. She was the only one in day's ride who could be seen smiling in such freezing wind. There was a bit of a tear in her eye, to watch her son commanding soldiers for the first time. But before her tears could betray her tough exterior, a wild black horse, a few hands taller than her own white mare, came bolting across her position. Skunkha nearly fell back off of his own horse as the black buck came barging through. Tomyris had no idea where the beast had come from, or why it was running so quickly. Nothing was chasing it, but it had come from the hills where smoke was rising. Persians. It was the closest the young queen had ever seen them. She hung her head in disappointment. It had been such a fine morning up until then. Skunkha got himself back upright on his horse, and pulled up close beside his friend. His horse didn't like the cold, and was comically unsettled on its hooves.

"Did you pick the youngest horse of the bunch this morning, Skunkha?"

"You left without warning. This one's still early in its training. Had you told me you were coming out, I'd have saddled a more preferrable horse."

"I didn't want to come out this morning, but I couldn't help it. It's a big day for Sparga. Will you look at him down there?"

"He sounds like his father."

"It's been so long now since I lost him; I don't even remember the sound of his voice."

"You've done a good job raising that boy on your own."

"I've hardly been alone. I've always had you by my side, and the whole of the tribe. The Massagetae have raised that boy. He will make a fine general, don't you think?"

"I wish we didn't have to have a boy general."

"Oh, come now, Skunkha, I know you see the smoke of the Persian's fires as clear as I do."

"Will we send scouts out to keep an eye on them today?"

"Tomorrow."

"Why the wait?"

"Today is my son's day."

"The only reason he's even down there right now is because that fat man Cyrus is right over those hills. *Our* hills."

"Is he really as fat as everyone says?"

"I don't know, I've never seen him with my own two eyes."

"Perhaps it is just because he is a king that they say he is fat."

"You are queen, and no one dares say such a thing about you."

"That's because I am thin."

"You could be as big as three women and still, no one would dare say you were fat. Your people love you."

"Do you think Cyrus' people don't love him?"

"They are told to love him or die. That's not love."

"It's something. I have heard that he commands ten thousand men. They're called Immortals. I wonder why? Is it their arrogance that keeps them alive?"

"I don't know, Tomyris, but they've taken thirty-six tribes over the past several years. They've taken the Dahae just this summer. I never thought the gods would allow such a thing. Even if Cyrus is fat, the man must know what he is doing."

"I know what I am doing too."

"We have a sixteen-year-old barking orders as a general."

"But he's not just any sixteen-year-old. He's *mine*."

"Just because he shares your blood, it's not enough to keep him alive. Thirty-six tribes have fallen. Most were twice our size, if not larger, with *real* generals."

"Spargapeithes *will* be a real general."

"You see what I see right now. You are no liar, Tomyris. Be honest with me."

"I am worried for my son, but all mothers are the same."

"And as a queen?"

"As a leader of my people, I must trust that our soldiers will protect the tribe. I must honor their sacrifices."

"I'd feel better about all of this if you'd allow me to send scouts to the Persian camp."

"What good do you expect to get out of that? We know we are outnumbered. I don't need to know how hard this winter will be for us. It will not make the fighting any easier."

"What if we didn't fight?"

"Are you suggesting we run from the only home we've ever known like a bunch of cowards? Cyrus would only follow us like a wolf hunting its prey. I am not prey. I will not be hunted. I will not allow my people to believe the fight is over before it's begun."

"But running could save lives."

"What life is worth living if you never feel safe?"

"Just a suggestion. You're the queen, not me."

"That's good. You'd make a terrible queen. There aren't enough horses to race to find you a suitable husband, Skunkha!"

"You tease."

"I must. You are the only person I trust with my insecurities. When we are away like this, I can take the weight of being a queen off of my shoulders and just be myself. I wish I could do this more often."

"You are a good queen though."

"You are biased."

"That may be, but I have eyes too, and ears. The people love you. You do a good job at protecting them."

"I lean on you to make so many of my decisions. You deserve half of the praise in my name."

"I can't take it."

"But you deserve it. You are a fine man, Skunkha, and a good friend. I am so glad Sparga has had you in his life. You said you heard his father when he barked orders down there, but *I* heard *you*. He makes the men laugh, and puts them at ease. That will earn him respect, and even if a man is faulty on his horse, and uneasy with a sword, he will get men to follow him off the edge of a cliff if he has their respect. My son is like you, and that's why I know he will be a good general."

"No, it's the similarities he shares with you, Tomyris. All that your father taught you, and his father before him. So many leader's lessons are in that boy. His strength and tenacity, that's all you. Men will die for him because they will die for you. I don't know a person who has met you who wouldn't give their life."

"Perhaps I should arrange a meeting with Cyrus then, the old fat man. If all it took was meeting me to save our tribe…"

"You know it can't be that way. The only thing that man understands is bloodshed. People sing his praises like he is as worthy of devotion as the gods themselves. I'd like to shake those people."

"Are the men in camp worried, Skunkha?"

"They're too proud to be scared. I don't know that that is a good thing. At night, I hear them around the campfires talking about the spoils of war, and how all the other tribes must have failed."

"I never hear such talk."

"You disapprove of it, and they know that, so they hold their tongues in your presence. It's a matter of respect."

"Why can't all men respect women as their equals?"

"I don't know, Tomyris."

"I heard Cyrus has our people's wives as his own. That's how he takes over, he marries everyone, forces children on them. I'd die before I ever let that happen to me."

"Don't worry. It'll never come to that."

"I'd never make a good wife, anyway."

"Why do you say that?"

"I wouldn't know the first thing about being dependent on another soul for my day-to-day happiness."

"I think you might be surprised. If the right man ran across your path, you could make a very fine wife."

"Says the man who's never been married."

"I am married to my position. Serving you is my life's purpose."

"I wouldn't keep you from marriage, you know."

"I am not built to be a husband."

"Why not?"

"No woman could ever be more important in my life than you, and I sense that would be a source of never-ending conflict."

"I can see how that might cause an argument or two."

"It's a good thing the two of us have each other, isn't it, Tomyris?"

"If you really think it's wise to send scouts out to the Persian camp, then I'll permit a party of four this evening, just after the sun sets."

"Why so late? With such heavy clouds, we could go now and no one over those hills would be any the wiser."

"I don't want Sparga to volunteer."

"You think he would? Scouting is beneath a general's duties."

"I've never seen a boy so eager to get his sword bloody before. If he got near a Persian, he'd kill them before he realized what he was doing. I don't need to start a war with such a petty altercation. You will go tonight, and Sparga is to know nothing until you return."

"Alright. As you wish. Queen knows best."

"I'll keep him distracted."

"And how will you do that?"

"I need to speak with him about the horse race coming up."

"Ah. The finding of a wife."

"Any general worth his weight in gold has a woman who loves him and sends him off to battle with tears in her eyes and a baby in her belly. It is a duty as much as it is an honor."

"And what lucky girl have you set your sights on for your son?"

"Many men have come to me trying to sell their daughters. I've heard tales of hollow accomplishments, and impossible promises."

"Let me guess, no one is good enough for your boy?"

"It's not that. I just want him to be happy. I didn't know his father at all. I never loved the man. I was just doing what I was told, and he was doing the same. If at all possible, I want more for my son. I want him to marry for love. Is that too much to ask for?"

"You're a queen. You can ask for anything you want."

"But the race is tradition. And he's been sixteen for the better part of a year. I can't stall anymore. I can't keep him from becoming a man anymore than I can stop this war with Cyrus."

"Which bothers you more, the Persians, or Sparga growing up?"

"War is easier than losing a child."

"You're not losing him, Tomyris."

"I can't watch this anymore. My thoughts grow dark. Where is that stupid black horse that ran through here a few minutes ago?"

"Why does it matter?"

"I need to chase something."

"It looked like it was headed to the burning grounds."

"Perfect."

Tomyris sat in the burning grounds until dark consumed her. It was the only place she could commune with the gods. It was a strongly held belief that because the Massagetae burned their dead in these sands for generations, that this particular valley nestled between a pair of steep hills, was sacred. No one liked coming here if they didn't have to. It was an uncomfortably long walk from camp, and the thick ash deposits from the dead burned people's eyes something fierce. The young queen combatted that simply by tying a strip of cloth around her face, and tugging the flaps of her pointed cap out over her forehead. The gods very rarely gave her any indication that the help or advice she was looking for was promised, yet she visited anyway time and time again in her hour of need. As Spargapeithes grew, and her fellow Saka tribes around her fell, she came out to the burning grounds more and more. She was not to be disturbed. Skunkha was on a scouting mission to spy on the Persian camps sprawled on the edge of the Massagetae's territory. No good news was coming to Tomyris. Heavy hooves behind her though had her looking for a godlike sign for her next course of action. It was that foul black beast again, the large buck who had nearly spooked her off her horse this morning. But this time he wasn't alone. A man's voice was shouting in the night. Tomyris drew her bow and arrow from her back and pulled the string back to strike. She took a defensive position just beneath the crest of the outer sand dune for the burning grounds. The man didn't appear familiar with the area. He was coughing from the ash and dust swirling in the air. Only an outsider would come this far out and not wear the proper protection. The young queen assumed this visitor must be a Persian, perhaps a scout for Cyrus. She must strike before he made it any further into her lands. As soon as a shadow crested the dune, she let the arrow fly and watched the figure tumble into the ground. It lied still long enough for her to assume she killed the intruder. Carefully, she crept up to retrieve her arrow, and was ambushed by two men lying in wait on the outside of the dune. They tackled her from behind. They smelled foreign. Persians. Tomyris wriggled and fought as her arrows were stripped from her back with force and the shadow began to laugh. The young queen's feet were kicked out from under her and she was pressed onto her knees for observation. The shadow came close to her face and she spit at him. She could tell it was a man. The black horse ran up now, much calmer than before, and the shadowed man took its reins. It was a tame in progress. His skin was darker, so Tomyris assumed the man was Persian, but he spoke her language and knelt down in front of her. His light eyes and teeth caught the moonlight in flickers.

"Who are you, woman?"

"I'm on my own land. I don't owe you any answers. Who are *you*?"

"My name is Ariomardus. Last soldier of the Dahae."

"The Dahae have fallen. I was told Cyrus took all their soldiers or killed those who refused to submit to him."

"You heard wrong. Though, you are well informed. That means you must be a woman of some importance. But, if that were true, you wouldn't be out here in the sands all alone."

"No man owns me. I come and go as I please."

"A widow then?"

"Yes."

"Newly widowed?"

"No. Sixteen years."

"You don't sound old enough to be so long unmarried."

"What do you care?"

"Just trying to get to know the woman who nearly killed me."

"I want my arrows back."

"I'll give them to you. But I want the one that bloodied me."

"To remember me by?"

"Something like that. I don't often get taken by surprise."

"That makes two of us."

"I heard of a queen in the red sands. A widowed queen. Daughter of a mighty man, and an ally to my tribe. Are these Massagetae lands?"

"Yes. These are our burning grounds."

"Explains the ash. That must make you...*Tomyris*?"

"You're quite well informed for being nothing more than a soldier of the Dahae."

"I was their *best* soldier."

"If you were their best, you'd have died for them."

"I almost did. But someone carried me away and I lived."

"How fortunate."

"That is yet to be determined. Stand her up. No queen deserves to spend any time on her knees, unless she wills it herself."

"Thank you. Now why don't you ask them to let me go?"

"I don't trust you yet."

"You think I'll attack you again, Ariomardus? With what?"

"I know better than to think that Queen Tomyris would come out alone in the dead of night armed with only a bow and a few arrows. Even the Dahae women with nothing to their name kept knives on their person."

"Smart man."

"I have my moments."

"If you are so smart, then why are you here?"

"My horse here, seems to have a mind of his own."

"This beast is yours?"

"I'm trying to make him be."

"He's been running my lands since sunrise. You aren't very good with horses, are you?"

"I do well enough. Never met a horse I couldn't break, or a person for that matter. Though I wonder if my luck may be running out."

"Were you out tonight looking for shelter from the Massagetae, or from the Persians?"

"I have a deal with Cyrus."

"Then get on with it, and leave me be."

"You don't want an escort back to your camp?"

"Any Dahae willing to make a deal with Cyrus is no ally of mine.
You are not welcome in my camp, Ariomardus."

"I am sorry to hear that. Come on men, I think it's time we leave this
young woman alone. Your arrows, Queen Tomyris."

As soon as the men loosened their grip on the young queen's
arms, she jerked herself free and stood up on her feet. Ariomardus
was kind in his promise to return her arrows, but he was clever
enough to snap her wooden bow over his knee so she couldn't shoot
them as they walked for the Persian camp all aglow in golden fire
over the hillsides. If the Dahae man was going to smirk and be petty,
then Tomyris would level herself to his games, and tapped him on
the shoulder for the return of her final arrow. He flinched at her
touch, and he was embarrassed when she smirked back at him. He
had already tucked the bloody arrow into the waist of his pants, and
was reluctant to return it, but as a Saka, he could not refuse the
request of a queen. She may not have been his leader, but she was
more authority over him than Cyrus, who was dragging his heels to
go and see. He was late enough by three days as it was, a few more
minutes wouldn't hurt. Tomyris reached out for the final arrow as
Ariomardus extended it out towards her. She had to step closer to
him for it to be within reach, but once she had her hands around the
shaft, there was resistance. The Dahae soldier smothered a laugh at
the base of his throat. He wasn't going to just let go. Tomyris ran
her fist up and down the arrow for leverage. The tip was sticky with
his blood. The man was injured, but it wasn't something that
couldn't be repaired. In the daylight, his confidence might be more
deceived, but as it was in the darkness, he could keep up a charade
that kept the queen guessing. She tugged, and he stepped in, closing
the distance between them. While he stared down at her face, she
would not rise her eyes to meet him, and instead noticed his free
hand holding the glint of a knife in his waistband. He was close
enough to stab her and kill her right there, drag her body to Cyrus.

It might have been the deal all along. Tomyris let the arrow go in anger, and stepped back so she couldn't feel Ariomardus' breath on her neck any longer. The Dahae soldier seemed pleased with himself, and hopped up onto the back of his black horse which didn't seem too keen to be ridden. The young queen couldn't be content with losing the higher ground in this interaction, so with a swift lunge she drove one of her arrows into the hind of the black buck and sent the man running wildly without control into the dead of night with the two Persians scrambling to try and catch him.

Cyrus was waiting impatiently in his large, blood red tent in the center of the Persian camp. Scouts had already told him that Ariomardus was coming in to see him finally. The old man was quite pleased with himself. The Dahae soldier's reputation preceded him as a stubborn yet highly skilled hand. Ariomardus had been the personal guard for the King of the Dahae, and now he was to be the personal guard for Cyrus' heir Cambysses. The Persian prince already had one guard, Darius, but one was not enough for Cyrus' legacy. In his elder years the leader was growing paranoid, and there were never enough precautions which could be taken. Darius wasn't fond of getting a partner either. He thought it somewhat insulting that an outsider who couldn't be trusted was getting assigned to one of the most important positions in the fledgling empire, but he had no room to state his opinion. Darius was Cyrus' son-in-law, and ambitious in his own right. A young man of twenty, he already had seven years of fighting experience, and had been instrumental in taking down most of the thirty-six tribes across central Asia. Ariomardus was filling an expendable role. No harm could come to Cambysses, or Darius. Ariomardus' black horse came bolting through camp, similar to how it had left this morning. Again, Cambysses ran from his tent to admire the beast's freedom, and gave a pout to see a ride upon it's back. Ariomardus was out of breath and bleeding badly from his neck. Blood had soaked down the shoulder and chest of his brown shirt, but nerves had made him oblivious to the pain and appearance of the injury. His two Persian escorts were not permitted to come inside Cyrus' tent, so the interaction with Tomyris was his story, and his alone to tell or keep private. After taking one look about the tent, Ariomardus would not be volunteering any extra information if he didn't have to. He didn't want to be here, nor on a friendly basis with the old man who was solely responsible for subduing his people, but here he was. Sitting on a lilac and saffron carpet, Cyrus would not stand to greet his new guard. On his left, Cambysses walked over to take a seat with a judging and wandering eye that Ariomardus couldn't help but stare at in confusion. Darius cleared his throat loudly, taking the Dahae soldier forcefully by the shoulder and directing him to Cyrus' immediate audience. Darius shoved the Dahae soldier down to his knees, then kept pressing lower until Ariomardus was finally in a bow with his forehead to the dirt. A tsk of the tongue and Darius removed his pressure, taking his seat on Cyrus' other side, though in the dirt, not on a carpet. Ariomardus was slow to raise his head and sit back on his behind, legs crossed in an uneasy manner that would still allow him to lunge out at the Persian royals if necessary. Darius was waiting for this too, his dark-skinned hand ever ready on an axe at his waist. The young man had a sharp beard and even sharper eyes. To be so young and full of hate, Ariomardus thought of himself and eased the muscles in his body. Cyrus was slowly stroking his fluffy white beard. It covered so much of his face it was hard to read his expressions. What the beard didn't hide, the bushy eyebrows did.

"You took your time coming to me, Ariomardus."

"The sands can be difficult to navigate this time of year."

"Did you get into trouble tonight?"

"Oh! The blood, it's nothing. I'm fine."

"You don't look fine. Who did this to you?"

"No one. I overestimated my abilities is all. It won't happen again."

"I hope not. I'd hate to lose you before I could be of service to you. You know, being a guard for my son, there is no higher office in my empire that a man can hold."

"I appreciate the offer, Cyrus."

"I am giving you the rank of Lieutenant General in my army, like my son-in-law here, Darius. Each of you will command a thousand men a piece."

"A thousand?!"

"Is that a problem?"

"The Dahae barely had two hundred soldiers to our name, and that was after calling in favors."

"Which is why the Dahae have fallen. Now, if you feel that you can't command a thousand men, please tell me now so I can make different arrangements for…"

"I can handle the assignment, Cyrus."

"Good. I like to hear that. Tomorrow morning there will be an inspection of the army and you can meet your men. It would be wise of you to clean yourself up by then. A tent has been set up for you already, stocked with everything an officer might need. If for some reason I overlooked something, please do not hesitate to tell Darius. Do you have any questions, Ariomardus?"

"These men in my command, are they part of the force I've heard about, the ten thousand Immortals?"

"Yes."

"If I might ask, if the men are immortal, why bother with all of the shields then?"

"Conscripts never bleed dry, Ariomardus. If one of my men ever falls in battle, there is no shortage of men willing to take his place. And so, in a way, my army can never die, never wither even."

"I understand."

"Do you? Do you understand that anyone who fails to do what I ask of them *can* and *will* be replaced?"

"Yes. I understand."

"Good! Darius, show your fellow officer his new living quarters."

Darius was an obedient son-in-law. Ariomardus wondered if it was age or ambition that explained the swiftness of the young man's moves. Perhaps it was a bit of both. Again, Darius placed a heavy hand on the Dahae soldier's shoulder, and led him out of the tent with force. Once clear of the old leader's eyes Ariomardus shrugged out of Darius' hold, and the men locked eyes to come to an understanding. Ariomardus was thirty-two, hardly ready or willing to take orders as a subordinate from Darius, a man who could practically be his son as far as age was concerned. They were equal in rank and command. Their positions, identical. Ariomardus kept a ready hand on his golden knife at his waist, and Darius knew it, but his heavyset black brows unfurrowed, and a smile spread sharply across his bearded face. It was an act of obedience, out of fear. Ariomardus could set back on his heels somewhat easier because of this. His fist loosened on his blade, and let his eyes survey the new camp that was to be his home for the cold season ahead. It was comical seeing the Persians swarming their campfires for relief. The Saka conscripts from the varying thirty-six fallen tribes fared much better here in Khorasan. As much as Ariomardus pained to find a friendly and familiar Dahae face, there was none to be found. Darius assumed this much, and so when they stepped into Ariomardus' own blood red tent, all games fell to the wayside. Darius helped himself to some of the soup sitting in a pot over the private campfire tended to by a meek and beaten servant boy who scurried out of the tent as soon as the two officers walked in. Ariomardus couldn't apologize before the boy fled. Darius seemed amused, sloppily slurping the soup and warming himself in the sweet relief of the golden flames. A wash basin was beside him, and Darius picked up a rag to throw at his new best friend, smiling at a bloody arrow in his hands.

"Cyrus was right, you know. If the men see blood on you for the inspection tomorrow, they'll never listen to a thing you say. It'll be hard enough to get any respect out of them as it is."

"And why is that?"

"Old man gave you the hardest battalion. The Aspiciae."

"I know them. Very difficult if you're Persian, very forgiving if you're a fellow Saka."

"We'll see tomorrow morning. Can I ask you something, Ariomardus?"

"I don't see why not."

"What really happened with that cut on your neck?"

"You wouldn't believe me if I told you."

"Try me."

"A woman happened."

"Did you at least have your way with her first?!"

"I'd *never* try such a thing."

"What is this?!"

"I know her. Well, we've never met before tonight, but I know *of* her. And I'd never force myself on her. She's too important."

"Important? A woman?"

"I told you; you wouldn't believe me. But if you knew this woman, you would understand. She could have killed me tonight, and I'd have been happy to die by her hand, *lucky* even."

Despite the desert terrain, the Massagetae enjoyed a homeland barricaded on two sides by the Araxes and Jaxartes rivers. Both were sizable water resources in their own right, and provided excellent protection for the desert tribes. The Persian camp sat on the far side of the Araxes, where the red sands were especially shifty. This afternoon, Spargapeithes was on a scouting mission along the river's edge. His mother Tomyris thought it wise to make the scouting painfully obvious so the Persians knew they weren't welcome or wanted. Cyrus was not intimidated by the sixteen-year-old boy on his horse, or his two young friends who often rode with him. Had the Persians understood that Spargapeithes was a prince, and a general, perhaps the scouting might have been taken more seriously, but as of today, the queen's son was merely an amusement on the hillside. Spargapeithes and his friends were slaves to their age however, and could not resist the harmless trap that Cyrus had laid out for them at a bend in the river. The sands built up and made a shallow area prime for bathing where the current was not as strong. Cyrus' harem of wives, consorts, and officer's wives had been sent down in all their glory to draw the attention of the enemy scouts, and it didn't even take long. Joining the group of thirty or so women, some of Persia's finest, was Cyrus' twenty-year-old daughter, Atossa, his true pride and joy. She was often considered the brains of the family, excelling in every sphere of life that her older brother

Cambysses had failed. She had a mind for politics, and a sweet talent for manipulation. Her husband Darius was her father's most trusted officer. Together, the couple was untouchable and very well connected. Cyrus loved his daughter's ambition, but feared it all the same. He was hoping marriage might tame her a bit, get her to better understand her place in the world as a woman, settle down and start having a handful of children. All that would come in time. Atossa was not about to be sidelined in life so young and become a man's subordinate for the rest of her years. Perhaps one day, but today was not that day. She was eager to meet these scouts on the hillside, and have a little fun at their expense.

Spargapeithes and his two friends had tied their horses back behind the crest of the sand dune nearest the Araxes riverside. After crawling down for prime spying position, they rested on their bellies and hid their faces in haggard sagebrush clinging to the harsh landscape, but providing cover enough for three teenage boys eager to see as much enemy skin as possible. It was something of a novelty to see women so exposed and carefree. They also had darker skin and foreign features that the boys were quick to point out. Different shapes, different languages, customs, and songs. Dress was a big one. These women were important and gorgeous. Their clothes weren't Massagetae custom, where the women often wore pants and shirts indiscernible from the men. These Persians had pretty clothes, fine materials in light colors and flattering forms. The dresses were all hung out on racks and chairs. All sorts of bathing equipment had been brought out, combs, and oils. The wind was blowing away from the teenage boys, so the smells were not hitting them, but their giggles were reaching the women. Most of them cared little to provide a show. Their husbands were officers who never saw them, and barely knew their names. They were left to their own devices more often than not, a night in a shared tent here or there. Their beauty and youth being their biggest leverage in life. Atossa in particular was one of the finest women on the river. She knew it, flaunted it, and took her sweet time making sure Spargapeithes had his eye full. But even then, she disappeared, wrapped herself in a barely there sheet leaving little to the imagination, and came behind the teenage boys on the sand dune without them noticing. Atossa picked up a handful of little pebbles, and proceeded to throw them at the Massagetae scout's heads. The two beside the prince fled in embarrassment at having been found out spying, but Spargapeithes remained, perhaps a little self-inflated and overconfident. There was a saunter in his gangly step which was comical for a sixteen-year-old who couldn't even grow a beard, but attractive on a man twice his age and battle harden. Atossa knew using this boy would be easy to manipulate and hardly a challenge. She strategically let the sheet around her dip around her shoulders, and watched the boy's stare widen. Atossa stepped unusually close to her enemy, and took a fingertip to trace the outline of his shoulder, draped in too large golden armor. Her black hair was braided thickly down her back, but there were loose strands blowing around her face that Spargapeithes eyes were fixated on following. He wanted so badly to reach out and touch this woman in front of him, but he didn't know what to do. Atossa would have to make the first move while the boy struggled to remember how to speak.

"My name is Atossa, what's yours?"

"Sparga. Spargapeithes, I mean. My mother calls me Sparga. But you're not my mother. My name is, Spargapeithes. But, if you wanted to call me Sparga too, I think that'd be alright."

"You're funny, Sparga."

"I am? I mean, thanks. Thank you, Atossa. That's a pretty name."

"You think so? I always hated it."

"Hated it?! Why?"

"It's so old fashioned. I was named after my grandmother. No young woman wants to be named after an old lady."

"I think the name suits you."

"You do?"

"I know what it's like to have to live up to an old name."

"Are you named after somebody too?"

"My grandfather. He was a king, and everyone loved him. Everyone loves my mother too."

"A princess?"

"A queen. *The* queen."

"So, that means you are *Prince* Spargapeithes. You deceived me."

"I didn't mean to!"

"It's alright. I'm a princess myself."

"Figures. As pretty as you are, you must be a princess."

"You think I'm pretty?"

"I know you saw me watching you."

"I saw you watching my father's harem and the officer's wives. But I didn't think I was so lucky to have caught *your* eye."

"Lucky?"

"Uh-huh. It's always nice to be admired by a prince. I wish my husband looked at me the way you are right now."

"And how am I looking at you?"

"Like a man in love."

"I don't know about all that. I'm sure your husband is a fine man, and respected soldier."

"He is a lieutenant general. He commands one thousand men."

"I'm a general."

"And how many men do you command?"

"Not as much as your husband. But we fight well."

"I'm sure you do. And you, an officer, you fight too? Or do you watch from a position on high?"

"I fight. Or, I will be, if your father ever comes to bother us."

"He didn't come all this way to admire the sands. Your mother must know why he is here."

"She does."

"And what does she intend to do about it?"

"Fight to the death."

"And are you prepared to do the same?"

"I am."

"That's a shame. I'm quite fond of you."

"You are?"

"I'd just hate to see anything happen to you."

"I must do what I can to protect my people."

"That's very brave of you."

"I wouldn't have to fight if your father would just leave."

"Or if your mother would bow down, accept my father's proposals."

"My mother doesn't bow down to men, *any* man."

"She sounds too proud for her own good."

"So does your father."

"You don't know my father."

"You don't know my mother."

"I wish we could have met under different circumstances, Sparga. I mean…*Prince* Spargapeithes."

"You can call me, Sparga."

"You sure?"

"Only if I can call you Atossa?"

"Call me whatever you wish. I like the way you say my name."

"I'm not saying it any special way."

"Maybe it's just *you* I like then?"

"You're married."

"So?"

"You shouldn't be speaking to me like this."

"No one will ever know. I won't tell anybody if you won't."

"Our little secret?"

"I'm just fine with that if you are?"

"Why did you come up to speak to me today, Atossa?"

"I was curious."

"But I'm the enemy. I could have killed you, or taken you hostage."

"I'm not afraid of you."

"Why not?"

"I don't know. Something in your eyes. I trust you."

"I trust you too."

"So, it's agreed then?"

"What is?"

"I will be good to you, so long as you are good to me. My father might be in these sands for a while, and I very much look forward to getting to know you better. That is, if I am so lucky to have our paths cross again."

"They'll cross."

"How do you know?"

"I'll make sure they do."

"You can do that?"

"I can do anything I want. I'm a general."

Spargapeithes was feeling himself, reached over for Atossa's hand and kissed the back of it slowly. With her arm draped up and the angle of the sun, there was nothing the young prince could not see of his enemy's petite frame. She had nothing to be ashamed of, and was not ashamed as the sheet stuck to her dark, wet skin. Her cheeks were flushed, and for a genuine minute she could not maintain eye contact. For a boy, Spargapeithes was impressive in his nerves, and it had been quite some time since Atossa had been fawned over. She quite liked the attention, perhaps too much to maintain her political prowess and intelligence gathering, and had to excuse herself. A toothy grin spread across the teenage boy's face. He felt he made real progress on the crest of that dune, and was eager to watch Atossa walk away from him and rejoin the other women in the river. She peered over her dark shoulder more than once to see the prince watching her. He waved, flitted his fingers a bit like a fool, but she could not reciprocate the gesture. She wanted to, and bit her lip out of guilt for using the boy. He was so naïve he didn't even understand what he had done. He had given his name, his rank, position, and alluded to a small army. A sixteen-year-old general. Her father would love to hear that. Atossa admired hearing that Tomyris would prove a worthy opponent. She wasn't, for the first moment since she'd arrived in the red sands, so anxious to leave anymore. But as much as Spargapeithes wanted to press his luck and speak to the princess again, he had to get back to his scouting mission and rejoin his friends who had run off. Skunkha would be back in camp waiting their report on the Persian's activities. Nothing of watching the women bathe could be mentioned. The prince's rendezvous with the enemy princess was quickly congratulated amongst the teenage boys, but all was said and done by the time they were in Skunkha's audience. The curly headed advisor wanted nothing but hard facts, numbers, and statistics. How many tents, how many horses, what weapons were they going to be up against. Spargapeithes conveyed what he could, to which Tomyris was quickly informed. It was the queen's decision to fire a warning strike at sundown, since the scouting missions seemed to provide little relief. The Persian's camp was still growing by the day as forces rode in. Cyrus wanted a landslide battle, an ultimate bloodbath. Skunkha was informed to send runners out to any scattered allies that might still remain in the desert, while fire starters were instructed to gather kindling and fodder for a nice demonstration this evening. A line would be drawn along the crests of dunes that trickled down to the Araxes banks. Oil and animal fat would then soak these lines for a fire that would be hard to extinguish.

As late in the year as it was, darkness fell early. Tomyris hosted a small feast to build up the morale of her people before taking the soldiers and fire dancers out on horseback to the fire line. It was ignited as the Persian's could be seen across the river, gathering around their campfires and cooking dinner, complaining about the chill in the air. The Massagetae loved their fire. There was no fear for the natural phenomenon, but love. Intense love. They would dance and jump through the flames, holler, and howl like wild animals, sing in tongues and chant to the gods. It was primal, and unsettling for Cyrus and his army. The gold of the flames licked up into the black of the sky, allowing the Persians to see that their enemy had painted themselves in sacrificial blood for the night performance. Men, women, children even, could be seen hopping over the fire, running through it, dancing with it like another human, diving in and out of the smoke. Being up on the crests of the sand dunes, the shadows elongated from the Massagetae, stretching down to the water's edge, coming painfully close to the Persian camp's outer limits. Cyrus ordered no response, and for his officers to stand down. Ariomardus however was alerted to keep a weather eye on the enemy. Atossa and Cambysses seemed too entranced with the demonstration for their own good. While Darius tried to keep his wife and son-in-law inside their massive blood red tent, the Dahae soldier was allowed outside. He was posted on guard with the glow of the fire reaching him but none of the warmth. After a few minutes of intense chanting and howling from the Massagetae, Cyrus shuffled out in all of his elderly glory, and grumbled beside his latest, yet one of his most trusted recruits.

"Will you look at that disgusting display, Ariomardus?"

"I'm watching intently. The Massagetae are well known for their fire jumping. It is a sacred art to their people."

"I will enjoy being rid of such filthy customs when I take them."

"You can take people, but you can't take away their customs. Fire is all around us, Cyrus. It's life. Those people, they'll dance in the flames until there isn't a single one of them left."

"Did your people do this, Ariomardus?"

"No. We did not. But I have seen demonstrations like this before. The Massagetae always do this when they prepare for battle."

"Your men could handle it though, yes?"

"My men can handle anything. They're immortal."

"I'll make a Persian of you, yet! Who's that woman in the fire?"

"That's your enemy, Queen Tomyris."

"She's young to be a queen."

"She's suffered much tragedy in her life."

"And she is bound to suffer more should she refuse me."

"Refuse you?"

"I intend to make a wife of her."

"Don't you have enough wives already?"

"A man can always use another wife. And she seems quite strong in spirit. I could use a woman like her."

"And should she refuse to be yours?"

"I'll kill her, and everything she loves. But it usually doesn't come to that. Women know when to stand down. She will not be the obstacle that stops my conquest. This little fire trick, it's amusing, but I'm not afraid. I'm going back in. Will you keep an eye on this for me?"

"Don't worry, Cyrus. I won't take my eyes off her."

For three days the Saka people, what was left of them, had been sending their finest men and horse riders to the Massagetae. This was for two reasons. On the surface, it was a strategic pool of resources to protect against the impending attack by the Persians. But for Tomyris, it was also a deep, ideally lifelong alliance in the works to find her son a wife. She wasn't ready for this, but she was never going to be ready. Spargapeithes had been begging for the traditional wedding festivities since the day he turned sixteen, which was almost a year ago. Tomyris had stalled as long as she could, and with winter and the Persians now pushing her, she couldn't hold out any longer. A general needed a wife. She herself had been married off at sixteen. Any respectable Saka was afforded such stability in life. Skunkha handled much of the messy work, sending out runners, promising favors, and setting up the visitors tents in camp in such a way that the Persian's camp could be seen at night over the hillsides. The threat was there, it was all too real. While it was all fun and games, marriage politics and the like, Cyrus was just a day's ride away. Tomyris tried not to look at his flags hoisted across the horizon, and remain focused on the prospect of losing her son to a naïve little daughter of an important ally. Not many tribes remained, and those that did weren't keen on putting themselves in Cyrus' sights. But for Tomyris, exceptions could be made. Her father was a great leader, and a great soldier in his youth. She was a great leader, and a good soldier in her own right. Her scars from past skirmishes offered her respect. Her humble demeanor also afforded her some favors. Spargapeithes would grow into a great man and a great catch with an impeccable bloodline. Any girl would be lucky to have him and bear him sons. He would be king one day, and she a queen. Tomyris let a shaky smile grace her lips while Skunkha came into her tent to inform her of the arrivals. He was breathless, but genuinely in such a good mood, he could not notice how uncomfortable his friend was right now. He was adorned in a full chest piece of gold armor, with stiff shoulders and arm bands. The sun glinted off him brilliantly.

"Your niece is lucky to have you ride in her name, Skunkha."

"Suraya has made me swear on the gods that I win today."

"From what you have told me, the odds seem to be in your favor. Your niece is a good girl though. I would be more than happy to welcome her into the family. And if I'm not mistaken, Sparga has been known to take notice of her too."

"He's been in an awfully good mood the past few days. I'm happy you decided to finally host this race for him, Tomyris."

"He's a good boy…*man*. I owe him this much."

"Well, the last of the racers have just arrived. So, whenever you are ready to come out and open the games, I'm sure everyone will be excited to see you. I know I am."

"It seems like just yesterday my father was hosting these games for me. But that was over sixteen years ago."

"I was just as nervous then as I am now."

"You rode a valiant race for me."

"Sacephares was better though. Best I've seen, aside from you."

Skunkha hadn't said the name of Tomyris' dead husband out loud in front of her since the man had died. All of Spargapeithes life, Skunkha had tried to tell the boy about his father from what limited friendship they had in their youth, but never was a word spoken in front of Tomyris. She wouldn't allow it, and had actually killed three men over the years for violating that rule at her expense. It was a double-edged sword, the name Sacephares. Tomyris had lost her husband, her father, and her innocence all in the span of three days. She learned how to be a queen on her own, while learning how to be pregnant without a mother, sister, or female confidant. Skunkha envied his friend's strength, but pitied her circumstances all in the same breath. She was too tough for her own good. Today was no different. Skunkha was riding a high right now though, and couldn't be bothered with the weight of negative emotion. His niece was counting on him, and he needed to avenge his own pride. He should have won Tomyris in their youth. He almost did, had Sacephares not fouled him and tripped his horse in the final straightaway of the race. Sacephares wasn't even a Massagetae, but a Dahae, known for their ambition and shifting loyalties and as unpredictable as the red sands. His father had owed Tomyris' father a favor no one knows the specifics of to this day, but it was important enough to sway the tides of the wedding games. Tomyris knew of the deal, but not the specifics. She even attempted, in her teenage angst, to race for her own hand, and had won all of the games but the final race. She'd been absolutely forbidden to ride, and her father had tied up her white horse as punishment. Tomyris was in tears when she was married, and today, she was in tears preparing her son. Spargapeithes had mixed emotions. On the one hand, he'd been begging his mother for these games for months. But on the other hand, he was quite taken with Atossa. If her husband were to be killed in this upcoming war between their people, she could be free to marry him. An alliance which might end things once and for all. A general and a prince was higher in rank than a lieutenant general. And foolishly, he had taken all of her flattering words down by the river as cold hard fact. Surely no girl the Saka had to their names could compete with Atossa. Certainly not Skunkha's niece Suraya, who while funny and suitable for motherhood, was a spitting image of her uncle, curly hair and all. Spargapeithes didn't mind talking to her, but having children with her was stomach turning. The boy general was putting the finishing touches on his golden armor when his mother walked into his tent, and hung in the opening. She was admiring how tall he had gotten, trying to keep tears from falling. When she sniffled, Spargapeithes turned around and rolled his eyes.

"Don't do that mother, please. Today is supposed to be a good day."

"It *will* be a good day. It will be a *wonderful* day. Our family is growing. What's not to celebrate?"

"Am I to understand those are happy tears then?"

"Nevermind my tears. How are you?"

"I'm excited to get this over with."

"Me too."

"Can I ask you something?"

"Of course."

"When my father won you, were you upset that it was him?"

"I was upset before he won. Whoever won me that day, I wasn't going to be happy about it. I wasn't ready to get married. My mother died when I was very young. Your grandfather raised me on his own for most of my life. I felt that I could rule alone like him. I didn't think I needed a husband to lead. And so, when your father won, and he came up to claim me, and he was so happy, I felt so misunderstood. *He* won me, and *I* won nothing. He might have been a nice man. I don't know. I'll never know. I knew him a grand total of three days before the attack that claimed his life and your grandfathers. We had spent *one* night together; a couple of minutes was all it took. He spent the rest of the time drinking with his friends. The truth is, I don't know anything about your father except his name was Sacephares, and that you have his damned light eyes."

"So, you never loved him?"

"I loved my father, and I love you. That's well enough for me."

"And Skunkha?"

"He is a good man."

"He's told me about that race a lot."

"I don't doubt that he has. He was sure he was supposed to win. I saw the foul with my own two eyes. Dirty trick."

"Would you have loved Skunkha if he had won?"

"I don't know. Life would have been much different. I only know him as a subordinate of mine. If *I* had to report to *him* as a wife, it could change the way our friendship has become. But I *like* Skunkha. I'd have *liked* him as a husband. And even *liking* is better than *hating*. Why are you asking me all of this? Are you having doubts after harassing me for these games for months?"

"Skunkha really wants to win this race for his niece."

"Suraya would be a welcomed addition to our family. She would make you a fine wife, Sparga. A very fine wife indeed. She more than likes you already. It could be far worse."

"Her family has been attached to ours for generations. I just feel like we are supposed to be married, whether either of us want it."

"Are you trying to tell me you don't want Skunkha to win today?"

"I don't want to marry Suraya, mother."

"Then Skunkha won't win."

"You would do that for me?"

"I'd do anything for you. You're my baby."

"*Mother*, today I'm getting a *wife*. I'm *not* a *baby*."

"You could be an eighty-year-old man, ancient, haggard, and you would *still* be my baby."

"You're ridiculous sometimes."

"I'm serious. I'll make sure Skunkha doesn't win."

"But he's so excited, and he's your best friend and advisor. He's the only father figure I've ever known."

"And my son deserves to marry a woman he loves. If I can't find that today, or at least a woman you like, then so be it."

"What does that mean?"

"We can hold the games again, assure the woman you like is ridden by a worthy man. We can fix the games."

"Is that honorable? Wouldn't the gods be angry with you for doing such a thing?"

"The gods have taken much from me. Surely, they could allow me this. If I can't have a man to love as my own, *you'll* have a woman."

"Thank you, mother."

"Don't mention it. Seriously, it would break Skunkha's heart. But I am glad you have your doubts. Being uneasy is no way to start a life with someone. You should be sure. And now, I get to keep you to myself a little while longer."

"How are you going to break this to Skunkha?"

"I'm not going to tell him anything."

"I don't understand. He's the best rider I've ever seen aside…"

"From *me*?"

"Are *you* going to race for my hand mother?"

"Let the men try and best me!"

"You know, one of these days, you're going to have to grow up and stop being so petty about these things."

"Why? I have you for that, dear boy! Now come here and give your mother a kiss for good luck!"

"*Mother*!"

Tomyris had her son in a fit of laughs before she left his tent after wrangling him into a chokehold to place a kiss on his cheek. There was a comforting settlement between the two knowing there would be no forced wedding today. But still, there were games, formalities, and business to attend to. The young queen made her grand entrance through her camp and the visitor's quarters by racing through the rows of hide tents on her white horse. She sat sideways, backwards, then stood up on the back of her favored animal. Skunkha led a cheer in his friend's honor as she opened the games with an exhibition. Targets had been set up on the hillsides. A rider had to run as fast as he could and hit as many bullseyes as possible. There was spear throwing contests, sword fights, and wrestling matches. Men raced on foot, and roped young horses. It was an all-day event with laughing, drinking fermented milk, and meeting up with old friends. Many men came up to Tomyris to talk politics, and express concern over the Persians. Thirty-six allied tribes didn't exist anymore. There had been so much death, a weight that Tomyris knew intimately. Then there were promises made, hands shook, blood oaths claimed. Daughters were hosted in Tomyris' personal viewing tent. She treated the girls well, many of them nervous beyond words, most, not ready for marriage, but willing to be obedient to their fathers. The young queen sympathized with them, but kept the tent light hearted knowing full well no wedding would be happening this evening. Secretly, the girls would all be very much relieved. Suraya though, poor curly haired girl that she was, would be devastated. Being a close family friend, Tomyris let the fourteen-year-old sit next to her most of the day.

The Persians were intrigued by this show the Massagetae were putting on. Cyrus was sure this was another demonstration that Tomyris was putting on for his benefit, but sadly he was mistaken. Not everything could be about him. While the ten-thousand-man army still trickled into the red sands, there was much training and building going on in the Persian camps. Bridges needed to be assembled for the Araxes River to transport men and weapons. Observation towers had to be constructed. Darius was in charge of overseeing many of the lower ranking officers in charge of these building crews. This left Ariomardus to watching the Persian heir. Cambysses hated being watched like a child, and in retaliation, was known for running away from his guard any chance he got. Usually, Darius was wise to the prince's schemes and stopped them before they ever got started, but Ariomardus didn't know such things, nor did he expect such childish behavior from a twenty-four-year-old man who was next in line to rule something as substantial as the Persian Empire. Cambysses made his move at daybreak. Ariomardus was a lover of the night, and therefore a late riser. By the time he got up for the day, it was noon, and Cambysses was long gone. Thankfully for the nearly appointed lieutenant general, Cambysses was a sloppy runaway, and painfully easy to predict as well as track. The prince was heavy footed, and made a straight path for the river, from which he swam straight across, made a huge splash landing on the other side, then drug himself up the dunes and into Massagetae territory. Ariomardus knew what Tomyris was doing before he ever arrived. He'd been to Saka wedding games a handful of times before, but never had the social rank to enter. He had no money to his name, no prestige aside from being good at killing and breaking horses. As much as he wanted to enter the games today for humor's sake, he knew he had to keep his head, mingle into the crowds, and play the quiet, invisible observer. Cambysses on the other hand didn't know better, and entered the games. He wasn't half bad at the horse work, being trained since childhood in the ways of patience, but the physical tests he struggled at. It was painful to watch him run. He wasn't a man of rugged nature. He was clean, and soft. Tomyris ran out to help him when he collapsed. She took her horse, made a show of it with her tricks, and almost had the prince back up on his feet when Ariomardus interrupted. He rode in on his rough black buck, still unwilling to heed orders, and pulled a few quick tricks of his own. The crowds roared in applause, begging for more. Tomyris squinted her eyes, trying to figure out what the Dahae soldier was up to. This wasn't about Cambysses anymore. Ariomardus had scolded the young prince, and sent him to the edges of the crowd to be tended to later. When the man cocked a crooked smile his light eyes caught the sun, and shadows shown on his deep cut dimples in his cheeks. Tomyris looked away, and remounted her white horse. The white mare wanted nothing to do with the black buck, but the return could not be said. The young queen was having quiet trouble maintaining her horse much to Ariomardus' delight as the two circled each other.

"Do you need my help with your horse, Queen Tomyris?"

"What are you doing here, Ariomardus? I thought I told you that you weren't welcome in my camp?"

"Even for the wedding games? Aren't all Saka asked to attend?"

"Don't you serve Cyrus now?"

"I serve no one. I get paid by Cyrus now, to watch over his son. But that won't last forever."

"*That* man is Cyrus' son? Lazy eye, weak chest?"

"Are you surprised he was able to walk right into your camp?"

"He's of no threat to me. I just watched him nearly die right before my eyes. But if you are supposed to be watching him, how did he get all the way into my camp? Perhaps *you* are the one who needs *my* help, Ariomardus."

"Fell asleep on the job I guess."

"Well take him and leave. I have the final race to run."

"*Run*? Don't you mean *watch*? Aren't you the host?"

"I'm running for my son's hand. He isn't ready for a wife."

"You can do that?"

"I'm queen. I can make my own rules. Now, if you'll excuse me."

"Can I enter the race?"

"I just told you; *I'm* running."

"So?"

"So…you'd never beat me. Besides, even if the gods did strike me down midrun and allowed you to win, what woman are you riding for? What wife do you have to present to my son?"

"I thought you said he wasn't ready for a wife? You're changing the rules. This is just a race for you to feel better about yourself."

"You don't know what you're talking about."

"Your father tied your horse up when you were sixteen, and kept you from racing for your own hand."

"How do you know that? Unless…"

"Skunkha's father owed my father a favor. Something about an old debt. Sacephares won you before those games ever started."

"How could you possibly…your eyes…"

"Sacephares was my older brother."

Ariomardus hadn't said his brother's name since the day he married Tomyris. He couldn't. It hurt too much. Sacephares wasn't good with horses or weapons, he never had been. It was always Ariomardus who was the soldier, the real talent of the family, the pride of his father. But he was a second born son, a bastard to a woman he was not married to. Sacephares took the better part of a year for Ariomardus to train up. He was at Tomyris' wedding games sixteen years ago purely to watch the fruits of his labor. It was a great insult to him to know his father, and Skunkha's father had already prearranged the games though. The foul was underhanded, and damnable by the gods. They worked swiftly too, striking down Sacephares in a storm three days later. Ariomardus couldn't process the loss for years, it all happened so fast. He wouldn't listen to a word spoken about the Massagetae for years. He had no idea Tomyris had born him a nephew, no idea she'd taken on the role of queen. It was absurd. She was alone, and so young. She had grown so much though. It was a right decision to make. Tomyris was a good leader, and a solid mother. Ariomardus could see that now, up close, in the light of day. He felt embarrassed for trying to banter with her, and pulled away ashamed. He forcefully rounded up Cambysses on the edge of the crowd and tugged on the shoulder of his tunic like scolding a child. The Persian prince had made a drastic error in judgement today. Ariomardus would not explain himself.

He could not find the words, he was just silent as stone, trotting too fast on his black buck for Cambysses to keep up. The young man tripped, faltered, and stumbled into a roll in the sands. Ariomardus jumped down to manhandle him but was interrupted by a whistle. It was Darius, and several Persian officers. Cambysses picked himself up and dusted himself off. Cyrus was here as well, hidden by the pack of officers and his son-in-law. Ariomardus took a knee and bowed his head out of respect while the old man was helped down to the ground to offer his disappointment. Meanwhile, the Massagetae were still confused as to what was going on. Tomyris halted the beginning of the final race to pursue Ariomardus after he so abruptly left her company. She left Skunkha in charge to demonstrate a side show with horse tricks and spear throwing while she went to investigate on foot. The young queen didn't know what to make of the Persian display before her, just steps from her camp. Cyrus seemed a bit startled too, to just see her walking out, alone, not a single guard in sight. He chuckled, and his belly jiggled. Darius smirked. Ariomardus cast a worried glance over his shoulder, and tried to communicate silently for her to stop. They locked eyes. She saw and understood, but kept walking anyways. Cambysses was still cowering by Ariomardus' side. Tomyris came up to stand beside the prince, now knowing who he was, and still feeling pity for his weak showing back in front of her people. Conducting a quick study, she was fitting pieces together. Cambysses feared his father, and Cyrus fed off of people's fear. She planted her boots firmly, and let a smirk of her own grace her lips.

"Cyrus the Great?"

"Queen Tomyris. Seems my son has found his way into your camp."

"Massagetae welcome all souls of the sands for wedding games. I spare no expense for my son."

"You sound upset."

"You've interrupted a happy day. What mother wouldn't be upset?"

"I'll just collect my son and be on my way. Cambysses, come."

"Your son entered my games. He deserves the opportunity to finish, should he so choose. Or…is he not allowed to choose for himself?"

"You speak bravely like a true queen."

"How else would you expect me to speak?"

"Respectful, like a woman. I'm surprised you know my language."

"My people are simple not stupid. You've raided my lands for many years. It was inevitable we'd meet. It's easily assumed you're too proud to learn my language, so I learned yours. I don't trust translators. They can be very…*opportunistic*. The Dahae are known for their changing allegiances. They had many translators. More than once in my life, I've born witness to tragedy because of this."

"My apologies. I will be mindful of the Dahae in my charge. Can I collect my son, now? I hate that I've had to ask twice."

"You strike me as a very hateful man."

"You don't know me, little queen."

"Careful, king of kings. You yourself are still just a man, and an old one at that. All men die someday, even you. If you're not watchful, this little queen might just be enough to knock you off your high horse. I am *so* good with horses after all."

"I knew you were going to be difficult. It doesn't have to be this way. You can submit to me now, spare the games and bloodshed."

"The Massagetae will never submit to you. Not as long as I have anything to say about it."

"That's fine. I've heard that thirty-six times before by your people, and I look forward to the day I hear it from you. It will be glorious."

"What makes you so confident?"

"I am…*unimpressed* by the gathering behind you."

"Wars aren't won by the numbers of men on the field, but rather the size of the hearts of the men fighting. Your men have no heart."

"What do you know of my men?"

"They are more mine than yours. And if you falter, if you even so much as expose an accidental weakness, they will not protect you. They will feed off of you like vultures and scatter into the wind."

"You'd like to think so, wouldn't you?"

"I can see the truth of it in your eyes. You have fears no different than me, old man. Heavy is the head who leads. Right?"

Darius looked back at his father-in-law. No one had expected Tomyris to be so forward and provocative. It was almost as if she was looking for a fight with the Persian leader. She was calling his bluff. No one had ever stood toe to toe with him like this since he was a young man, fighting for his own glory. But he was no longer a young man. There was nothing he could do about that. Unintentionally, he took a step back on his feet to steady himself. There had been no gust of wind, but he cursed it all the same, slipping out of the Persian language into a childhood familial dialect no one, not even Cambysses understood. The prince stepped forward, worried for his father's health. Tomyris looked down at Ariomardus, fearing she might have gone too far in her prowess. He wouldn't look up at her because of his new employment, but she could see a hint of a smile on his face. She hadn't gone too far, but perhaps just far enough. If she knew him better, she'd think she had made him proud, but she had no idea who she was. He wasn't a stranger, but he wasn't family, but he was. Somehow, he was both and neither at the same time. She knew his eyes were different. Something she had only seen in her husband those few brief moments they had together, and her son, every single day of his life.

her son. The games. Skunkha was still keeping the crowds distracted, the guests, visitors, potential military allies, and marriage hopefuls. Tomyris put a gentle hand up on Cambysses' shoulder, and pushed him towards his father. He nodded his head to say thank you, and she smiled in response. But the expression vanished in an instant when she looked upon Darius, who stepped forward to claim the prince, and dug a heavy hand into the back of the prince's neck, muttering something stern under his breath. Cyrus ordered Ariomardus to stand, and the Persians turned to leave without further incident or threat. The Dahae soldier seemed to be hanging back for a few extra seconds. He had something to say, but didn't know how to say it. He didn't want to leave things like this, the way he had just blurted out his ancestry to the young queen. Thankfully, Tomyris was still riding on an adrenaline high, and reached out to grab his boot before he could ride away.

"I'll see you soon, Ariomardus."

Tomyris slapped the hind of the black buck over the same open sore where she had stabbed the horse with her arrow just a couple days prior. Ariomardus was confused. He had no idea what the queen had met in her parting words, and wasn't sure if he should be frightful about it or excited. He repeatedly looked back over his shoulder as she walked back to her wedding games which were all a sham anyways. The crowds cheered when she returned, and it echoed across the red sands all the way to the Araxes River. Cyrus hadn't been this annoyed in a long time. When he returned to his tent, he overturned everything, kicked tables, toppled chairs, and threw serving dishes and water pitchers. The servants were scrambling around on hands and knees like animals to try and appease the old man, but nothing they could do was working. Cambysses had been sat down on his behind by the front tent flaps, like a dog on restriction. He'd been scolded by his father, his brother-in-law, his guard Ariomardus, his father again, and then his sister. When Cyrus seemed at his wit's end, only Atossa could calm him down. Darius sent for his wife where she was out doing laundry with the other female servants at a bend in the river where the sandbars made the waters shallow. The woman could not be upset.

She had learned to shield her emotions from the inside out at a young age from her mother. Women were meant to be pleasing at all times, and so since life was an act, she would be the best actress there ever was. Happy at all times. Supportive and understanding, obliging to a fault, but never stupid or vulnerable. Her mere presence was enough to sit Cyrus down on his lilac and saffron rugs, and finally take a deep breath. She talked nonsense to him on matters she knew nothing of. She reassured his superiority, built back his confidence, and proposed answers to any question he had. Tomyris would be dealt with. Persia would reign on high. Cyrus would die many years from now, at peace in his bed. Atossa knew nothing of the truth or lies she spoke. They were so mixed up together, even she wasn't sure what she was saying, but she cooed all the same, pleasant and mellow. She stroked her father's hands, held them and kissed them goodbye as she left to give orders to her husband, Darius. The lieutenant general had been posted at the tent entrance as well, standing over Cambysses, making sure he didn't even breathe out of place. Atossa was an actress for her husband as well. They weren't so much a married couple as a political alliance. They had similar goals, and were willing to undergo a few personal sacrifices with each other to get there. She whispered particulars in his ear for no one to hear, especially Cambysses at her feet, and then distantly kissed her husband's cheek and sent him on his way. Cambysses watched his brother-in-law trek into camp, straight for Ariomardus' tent on the outskirts near the river's edge where he had moved without approval. Atossa wouldn't answer any of her brother's questions. Instead, she dropped down to her knees and took hold of his face softly with both of her hands.

"If you run like that again, I'll let Darius kill you. You understand?"

"I look forward to the day Darius kills me. It's not a threat, Atossa."

"You really are a sorry excuse for a first-born son, you know that?"

"Father never ceases to remind me, and anymore, neither do you."

"Did you at least learn something about the Massagetae today?"

"There's not a person there who wouldn't die for Tomyris."

"A few hours and you've already fallen in love with their queen?"

"Don't speak of love as if you know what that means, little sister."

"I'm sorry, which sibling is married again?"

"You just married Darius because he's the most ambitious soldier father had in his army. And he married you for the same reason, *power*. As soon as father dies, you'll both make your moves. Tomyris was right, you're all vultures."

Atossa spit in her brother's face. He wasn't wrong, but it wasn't what the princess wanted to hear. She didn't want a hard fight here. She wanted quick submission. She wanted to go home, and spend the cold months on the ocean where it never got too cold and the frost never touched her face. Where people poured her wine for her when she walked into a room, and women couldn't help but want to impress her. None of that happened here in a military camp in the middle of nowhere. She couldn't even understand why her father was fighting to take over these lands so hard, but supported him all the same, because whatever was his today, would be hers in the future. Eventually. And the more land she had, the more taxes she could collect, and the more envy she could attain from her peers back home. One day, one day she would have it all. But there was still a lot of hard work that needed to be done first. She was happy to see her husband ride off with Ariomardus across the river. Cambysses stood up in utter confusion. He knew they were going back to the Massagetae, but couldn't figure out why. Darius had his sword on him, like there was going to be a fight, and in the pit of his stomach, the prince felt like Tomyris was in trouble. She had been so kind to him earlier in the day, and didn't wish any harm to come to her. He had to trust, in his limited time with Ariomardus, that the young queen would fare alright. She would hold her own. And indeed, she would. Scouts for the Massagetae had stopped Darius and Ariomardus after increased patrols had been ordered for the final wedding race. Tomyris had won without issue, and had just recently announced that Spargapeithes would not be taking a wife at this time out of caution for the war with the Persians up ahead. Drawing from her own misfortune, there would be no quick widows made. Another round of festivities would be held in the warmer months, and daughters could be presented then, with more enticing offers. In the meantime, a feast would still be held, and meetings would still continue. Tomyris was in the middle of securing an alliance with a difficult outlying tribe of the Saka in the north when Skunkha rushed in with news from the scouts that the Persians had sent riders. She nodded with an expressionless face, and the mere lack of fear in her eyes was enough for the men to shake hands with her, and promise her men to keep Cyrus at bay. If Tomyris could hold her ground here, in the red sands of Khorasan, it also provided a buffer of protection for thousands of people in the north. It was in the other tribe's best interests to help the Massagetae now. There was no stronger face to put at the front lines than the young queen. Rumors of her interaction with Cyrus this afternoon were already circulating. Skunkha was doing well to embellish where he could, building up his friend and downplaying Cyrus' authority. Campfires were just starting to be lit and gathered around now. Fermented milk was flowing and spirits were high. Tomyris mounted her horse and was quick to see Ariomardus running on the crest of a nearby hillside. Darius had come with him, and was waiting dutifully by the young queen's scouts. She dismissed the men and spoke to Darius directly as he sat stout on his unmoving horse. There was no sense of kindness in the man's voice. Everything was very short, very matter of fact. Skunkha didn't like him, and kept a hand on the hilt of his ax at his waist as he sat beside Tomyris. Ariomardus trotted over to encircle the three before tersely instructing his large black horse to take position beside Darius, opposite of Tomyris. The young queen wouldn't look at him. She thought she saw more and more of Sacephares haunting her every time he smiled. Darius cleared his throat loudly for Ariomardus to take up negotiations.

"Did you think you would see me again so soon, Queen Tomyris?"

"I knew Cyrus would send you back before the night was over. I insulted him too greatly for him to allow me another's night's rest."

"He's tasked me with proposing you an ultimatum. He wants you to be his wife. Form an alliance. Submission without violence."

"I scared him this afternoon, didn't I?"

"What is your answer?!"

"Your name is Darius, yes?"

"How do you know my name, Queen?"

"I know many things. My answer is no. He's as wicked in heart as he is in mind. I'd rather die than be his wife. He'll never own me."

"To refuse his proposal means a duel. First blood or forfeiture."

"I accept. Who am I fighting?"

"You're fighting for your *own* name?"

"Yes. Who has the old man selected to represent himself?"

"Why, Ariomardus, of course."

The Dahae soldier waved uncomfortably. Tomyris was not dissuaded, and slid off the back of her white horse with ease. Skunkha was at odds, trying to convince her to let him fight in her stead, but she wouldn't listen to a thing he had to say. She talked over his reason and arguments, giving him orders to stand back, stand down, and mind the reins of her horse so she wouldn't get spooked. Skunkha had to do as he was told, but as a friend, he hugged her and kissed her cheek for good luck. Ariomardus didn't want to fight, but was intrigued by how ready Tomyris was. He flicked out the gold knife from his waist, and spun it in his hands. The young queen could see he was skilled. He was easily a head taller than her, stronger than her, faster than her, and potentially more skilled in combat. But she could use all of that to her advantage. As the two circled each other in the sand, he realized she was trying to tire him out after multiple dodged lunges. He stopped circling, and she followed. Darius grew restless on his horse, and breathed in deeply through clenched teeth. Neither Tomyris nor Ariomardus had forfeited anything a day in their life, and tonight would be no different. Tomyris couldn't look Ariomardus in the eye. The light irises were too much for her to bear. The Dahae soldier was learning this quickly, and knew distance was her savior, so he took that away. He charged her and she pushed him. Skunkha's ax in her hand, and she pushed him. A real opponent would have cut him, charged back, and fought. She was being evasive. Skunkha was confused, yelling tactics and encouragements. It was like she couldn't hear him. Ariomardus took his hand and seized the young queen's chin, forcing her to look up at him, lock eyes. He was breathing so hard on her face. They were inches apart. Her heartbeat wasn't even fast underneath the Dahae soldier's fingers. He was so worked up, so upset. There was no tension in his hold on her. He couldn't bare the thought of hurting her, not alone drawing blood. He silently begged her to end this. Cut him. Hurt him. Make him feel something. He was being dangerously patient with her. Why was she just standing there? Submitting to his hold. She threw the ax down. He threw his sword away and placed the golden knife back in his waistband. Then he took hold of her chin with both hands. His skin was dark against her paler features in the moonlight. With the lightest of touches, she let her empty hand trail down Ariomardus' shoulder, down his chest, and stomach all the way to his waist where the golden knife had been tucked back. With a swift pull she yanked the knife and slit through the Dahae soldier's chest, right above his heart. He clutched it, as if shocked by the blood on his hand, and held it up to show Darius. They had lost this negotiation. Darius was furious, and began running back for camp to tell Cyrus of the lack of success. The war preparations needed to continue, and quickly. Skunkha was thrilled, and hugged his friend who seemed paralyzed in the sand. Her brown brows furrowed deeply on her face. She was holding the golden knife out for Ariomardus to take, but he wouldn't relieve her of the weapon. Instead, he bowed a way from her, hand over his bleeding heart, eyes lingering on her own.

"Keep it safe for me. Good night…Queen Tomyris."

On the way back into the Massagetae camp a fire caught the eye of the curly headed advisor on the far outskirts of the hills. The hide tent looked old with all of its patchwork colors fixed across the side. Tomyris was riding in a daze on the back of her white horse, the golden knife from Ariomardus still gripped tightly in her hand. She was struggling to make sense of what had just happened, and what the reprisals might be come morning. Skunkha insisted the scouts had been telling him that Cyrus was in no way ready to make a declaration of war in a matter of hours, and that she needed to get some rest after such a long day. She nodded but said nothing. There were more men in her tent, father and military minded alike waiting to speak with her. She couldn't sleep. With a shake of her shoulders Tomyris snapped out of it and tucked the golden knife into the back of her pants, pulling her shirt down over it to keep it hidden. Her role as queen overcame the confusion of being a widow. Skunkha never ceased to be amazed by her emotional control, and asked permission to investigate the mysterious visitor on the far side of camp. She insisted he do, and report back to her at once when he discovered who it was, but he was already pretty sure. The longer he looked at the patches, and the distance the man had took to post himself away from others, it could only be Homarges, his estranged father and Tomyris' father's old advisor. Homarges had been blamed for the death of King Spargapeithes and Prince Sacephares, in addition to a handful of other men who had been caught on the celebratory hunting raid in the storm. Conveniently, Homarges had not been in attendance, though he should have been. It was Tomyris' first decree as queen to exile the sketchy man, and name his son in his place as her advisor. Skunkha was not put out by the decision at all, if anything, he encouraged the forced separation. The way Homarges conducted his affairs, it was hardly praiseworthy. The man got results, but not in a way the gods would ever approve of.

Homarges heard his son ride up on horseback, and snuffed out his campfire with a heap of sand before he arrived. Never mind the light or warmth from the golden flames. Skunkha could see in the dark just fine with the ample moonlight. He silently thanked the gods for that, and asked for the patience to deal with his father. It had been sixteen years since they last spoke, at an event not an all dissimilar to this one. A wedding feast. Pesky mongooses scurried about the outside of the patchwork tent. Homarges had been known to feed the vermin despite everyone else's attempts to kill the little beasts who stole their food and ravaged their tents. The annoying creatures were wily, and difficult to see in the dark with their ruddy brown fur, but Skunkha had no intention of staying here long, just long enough. Homarges could play the blind fool all he wanted with others, but his games never worked well on his son. Without a single word, Homarges' charades dropped to the wayside, and he accepted the disappointment of his son. Skunkha welcomed himself inside, patted a space clear in the sand, and pulled his knees up to his chest like a little boy. Homarges wasn't well. The older man in his sixties now, with scraggly gray hair crowning his pale, bald head that had been sunburned so many times it looked like a painted horse. He was missing most of his teeth, and had an awkward hunch to his shoulders. His breathing was loud and labored. Skunkha almost felt sorry for his father until he began to speak, and upon hearing the familiar tone from his childhood, all sense of empathy abandoned him for good.

"I'm surprised she let you come see me."

"Tomyris and I have a lot of respect for one another. She does not use me as a servant. I told her I was coming out here."

"It should be *you* in those meetings with the tribal chiefs. *You* were meant to be *her* king. I had *everything* arranged! So many years of hard work *wasted*!"

"I'm not having this conversation with you again. If this is all you came here for, then I suggest you leave before the sun rises."

"Wait! Please, Skunkha. It's been so long."

"And yet somehow, not long enough."

"Did you not miss me at all?"

"It is hard to miss a man who disapproved of everything I ever did in life. I was never good enough for you. I wasn't smart enough. I wasn't tall enough. I never rode fast enough. I never shot straight enough. I pushed myself to my absolute limits for you in those wedding games, and it didn't even matter. You made that deal with Sacephares father. I saw you two shaking hands."

"No! No, we made a deal for *you* to win! Sacephares was supposed to throw the race. The boy undermined us all. He was greedy. I was Spargapeithes' advisor. I knew *everything*. I had set it up since the day Tomyris was born. It was all settled. *All* of it. All I ever wanted for you was to be king. I *had* to be hard on you. Kings are put through so many troubles. I wanted to be sure you would have a good life. Better than the life of an advisor, always living his days in the shadows of a greater man. I wanted *you* to be the greater man."

"I am a greater man than you, and that is enough for me."

"I am sure of it."

"And I am happy as an advisor. I have a good life."

"You are happy to be in her shadow."

"Tomyris is a good queen."

"I never had a doubt about that. I had quite a hand in raising her."

"Then you should also know she had every right to exile you."

"Now *that*, I don't agree with. Death would have been a more merciful punishment."

"Why didn't you go on that hunt? Be honest with me, for once."

"I'd have thought you'd learn not to ask questions you don't want to hear the answers to."

"I'm a grown man. I can handle whatever it is you have to say."

"You know the burdens of an advisor, don't you son?"

"Yes, of course I do."

"Knowing everything and keeping the worst from your leader so that they may better handle the rigors of their duty to the Massagetae."

"What are you trying to get at?"

"You don't tell Tomyris everything you learn, do you?"

"It's not helpful for her to know everything."

"Exactly. You are keeping things to yourself, for the betterment of the people, for the betterment of your friend."

"And?"

"I had something to handle the day of the hunt. Something that could not be settled at another point in time."

"What did you do the day the king was killed?"

"Spargapeithes refused to pay Sacephares' father for the wedding."

"I know that. He shouldn't have had to pay. Tomyris was a princess, and Sacephares was just a first-born son to the Dahae."

"Well, when Spargapeithes refused to pay, his life was put in danger. I had to go to the Aspiciae to ask for help, protection. The rains slowed me. I lost my way in the storm. I cursed the gods every day since then. Why, why would they do that to me? Why lead me off course? I was just trying to help, avoid bloodshed."

"Bloodshed? Spargapeithes, Sacephares, and the men drowned. The valley flooded, knocked their horses out from under them. I saw the raging waters with my own two eyes."

"You don't know what you saw. I saw Sacephares' father and several of his men attack Spargapeithes, cut him down from behind."

"I don't understand. This doesn't make sense. Sacephares died. His own father wouldn't kill him."

"Sacephares tried to defend Spargapeithes from his own father. He wanted a life with Tomyris. He wanted to be king. The Dahae weren't enough for him. The whole hunting party was killed. Their dead bodies were thrown into the water, made to look like a simple accident. But it was no accident."

"Why didn't you say any of this when you came back to camp? Tomyris would have understood. *I* would have understood. You didn't need to be exiled."

"The girl was consumed with grief. There was no reasoning with her, or you for that matter. I saw the way that she clung to you, and you to her. I hoped distance might make things clear one day. And I was right. You did so well for yourself. You stayed by her side, helped raise her boy like I raised her. You made yourself irreplaceable. You might as well be king, my dear boy, if only for the title and formal recognition. I am so proud of you. No father could be prouder. You are more than enough for me."

"So many pretty words. You have no idea how badly I want to believe you."

"You think I don't speak the truth?"

"I think you haven't been friendly with the truth in a long time. Lies are all that you know. Lies, and manipulation. You know, I'm not a little boy anymore. I know not to believe a man when what he says seems too good to be true. And what you just told me, it makes you out to be as honorable as the gods themselves. I know that can't be true. It sounds nothing like you. Loyal. Helpful. Kind."

"It *is* the truth son. Every word."

"Why are you here? Why today of all days? Why come to little Sparga's wedding games? You know no one wants you here, least of all, Tomyris."

"I know you're in trouble son."

"You can't help us."

"I know I may not look the best, but my mind is still as good as ever. I can still make deals, and ensure alliances."

"Tomyris exiled you. She'll never listen to a word you say."

"But if I spoke through you, my words could still reach her. I only mean to help, Skunkha, honest."

"We don't need your kind of help. Tomyris has led our people for sixteen years. We have been up against trouble before, and we have gotten through it, and are stronger because of that. We will survive whatever Cyrus thinks he can do to us."

"You don't know what he can do. You haven't seen how far he is willing to go to get what he wants. The man is ruthless."

"You haven't seen Tomyris in a long time. Don't underestimate what she is capable of."

"She might be a smart woman, and she might have a few good tricks up her sleeve, but she just doesn't have the numbers, the weapons, or the manpower. I have seen Cyrus wipe out tribe after tribe from one side of these sands to the other. The Massagetae will not make it through this. Tomyris will not survive. And therefore you, dear boy, will not either."

"You expect me to believe you came back from a sixteen-year exile to keep me from dying at the hands of the Persians?"

"Yes."

"I will need to think about everything that you have said tonight."

"Does that mean you still want me to leave by sunrise?"

"No. You don't need to leave. But I don't need you wandering around camp either, speaking to the chiefs and people. Keep to yourself. You even being here undermines Tomyris' authority, and I will *not* stand for that. Let me think about this."

"Think hard son, because you don't have a lot of time left before Cyrus makes his first move."

"I know we don't have a lot of time. I just have to come up with a way to present all of this to Tomyris."

"Just speak from the heart, Skunkha. If Tomyris has truly grown into the woman you say she is, speak direct, and she will understand. I really *do* want to help."

"You've really seen Cyrus in battle? With your own two eyes?"

"I've seen our people fall. And nothing in this world is more gut wrenching than hearing their screams. It haunts me, nightly."

Skunkha sighed heavily and shook his head. There was no way he could mention his father's name and have Tomyris listen to a word he said. But there was also no way he could keep his father camped here in secret, and not tell his queen. One person was going to be let down. Tomyris was his best friend. She had never done anything to hurt or harm him. His father was another story. A lifetime of hate could not simply be overturned in a single conversation of questionable validity. There was no way to know, no one to ask, if what Homarges said and did that day actually happened. Skunkha never knew his father to go out of his way for anyone. Tomyris' marriage had thrown him into a great depression and rage. He had destroyed their tent that night after the wedding. Skunkha had slept outside because of it. He saw Sacephares leave his wedding bed to go drinking with his friends. And he saw the shadow of Tomyris' shaking body as she cried herself to sleep alone. He heard her sobs. That memory was burned into his mind. Homarges knew nothing of that. Nothing of that pain. He knew nothing of half of Skunkha's life, or Tomyris. On today of all days. The Persians had been wreaking havoc on the sands for years. Why today? The threat from Cyrus was no different today than days past. The old man was still up to something, and he would never tell Skunkha outright. It would be up to the young man to find out on his own. Tomyris could help him, if it was anyone aside from Homarges she would help, but Skunkha couldn't do that to her. He couldn't bring his father's words into the camp, into her tent. He couldn't be trusted. He's never been reliable. Not a day in his life. Skunkha walked back to his tent in the dead of night and just paced back and forth outside. His mind was racing. He couldn't even think of sleeping. Tomyris was up too, making deals, securing alliances. There was a never-ending trek in and out of her tent by one man after the next. One hollow promise after another, and she just had to take their word for it. She needed Skunkha by her side, to help her through this, but he was of no help to anybody right now, least of all her. He was running ragged sweat tracks through his curly hair, tying his fingers up into knots. He couldn't allow his queen to see him like this. By morning he would be better. He had to be. He just needed time, that was all. A few hours. He didn't have a few hours, but he'd take them. Cyrus would not attack in the morning. He couldn't.

The Persian camp was lit up well into the night. Officers were barking orders. Cyrus had moved up the building schedule. The bridges for the river and the observation towers needed to be up by the week's end. The Massagetae needed to feel the pressure, feel their freedom waning with each passing day. Perhaps then, under the stress of an uphill battle, Tomyris would capitulate after all, and Cyrus could have another easy victory to brag about back home. He missed home, the warmth and comradery. The red sands were a hostile environment to a man of his age. But it would all be over soon. It had to be. Darius and Ariomardus came back to the camp in a flutter of this activity. None of the men wanted to be up all night, crafting by fire light or moon light, whichever was better. But they kept their qualms amongst themselves. Chatter quieted when Darius and Ariomardus walked by. Darius' chest puffed a bit when this happened, and the short man walked a little taller. Ariomardus though was not at all impressed by this. It wasn't a behavior to be proud of. That meant the men didn't like you, didn't respect you. When that translated to the battlefield, that ended up with a dead officer. Ariomardus could see it now, Darius speared right through his proud chest. Atossa probably wouldn't even cry. Ariomardus wondered if Tomyris might cry for him, knowing now who he was. He shook his head against the warming though. He was bleeding right now across his heart because of her. His hand was sticky and his shirt torn. Darius put a heavy hand on his shoulder, and stopped the Dahae soldier mid-walk.

"You need to clean yourself up before we go in and tell Cyrus what happened back there with the queen. You're dripping blood all over the damn place."

"Nothing like a trail of blood to find your way back home, huh?"

"Call me crazy, but I can't help but think you *let* her cut you."

"I didn't *let* her do anything. She cut me all on her own."

"From where I was sitting, I saw something much different. You were never going to draw blood on her, were you?"

"I can't hurt her, not if I can help it."

"Why? Who is she to you? I thought you came from the Dahae, not the Massagetae."

"We are all Saka when the day is done. But she is more to me than that. It's difficult to explain."

"Spare me the story tonight. We have to try and come up with some way to spin this to Cyrus in a way that he doesn't order both of our throats slit for Tomyris getting the better of him twice in a matter of only a couple of hours. First, she defends Cambysses, then refuses his marriage proposal, *and* draws blood on his favorite officer."

"I'm his *favorite*?"

"It's annoying how much he talks about you."

"But you married his daughter?"

"Atossa and I are…*complicated*."

"You don't say?"

"Not as complicated as you and that queen."

"There's nothing going on between the queen and I."

"But you *wish* there was."

"You're reading too much into this."

"Why'd you let her keep your knife then?"

"Dahae custom. It's a matter of respect. She bested me with my own weapon. It's hers now."

"*Dahae custom*, huh? You're full of shit, Ariomardus. I like you!"

Night had turned into morning in the Massagetae camp, and still, Tomyris was meeting with men from all over the desert to secure alliances, partnerships, and trade. A few fathers tried pushing their way into their tent begging her to reconsider their daughters for marriage to her son, but those discussions were entirely off the table until the weather warmed next year. She wouldn't even entertain the possibilities. The Persian threat was on the forefront of her mind. As she sat at her table, she kept spinning Ariomardus' golden knife on the tip, slowly but surely digging a divot into the wood. Skunkha came in a couple times to check on her as the hours passed, and advised her to put the knife away for safe keeping. She wasn't listening to much her friend had to say though, she was too inside her head with all of the proposals that had been hurled at her over the course of the day. It was overwhelming, and she didn't want anyone to know she was struggling to figure out a path forward that would benefit the most people. There were people sleeping outside right now that the Persians would kill. Smoke would be billowing from their burning grounds soon enough with all of the deaths in battle. Families would be broken. Fathers and husbands would be killed. Children would know what she knew, what it was like to grow up too fast. She didn't want that; she didn't want any of this. She wanted to protect everyone, and just have Cyrus go away. Why did he want their sands? There was nothing here but them. He didn't want their land, he didn't want their people, it was just a blanket conquest. He was just an insatiable man who always wanted more simply for the sake of having it. He wanted to be able to say he won, he took that land, married that woman, got that victory. But this was her life. These red sands were her world, her son's world. Generals always died in war. She could not lose her son. Her baby. The golden knife spun out of her hand, rolled across the little wooden table in front of her and into the sand beside her feet. It was just out of reach though and she was too tired to stand and go pick it up. Maybe this was it for the night, morning, whatever time it was. It was dark outside. She saw no shadows outside her tent. Perhaps she could close her eyes. She balled her fist up, rested her elbow on her chest, and slumped down in her chair to prop her head up, fist on forehead. It couldn't have been more than a couple of seconds before she heard her tent flap flutter open, and a rush of cold wind rushed straight for her. She could not be more exhausted than she was right now, but she couldn't be angry. Cambysses was standing before her, nervous as ever, offering her the golden knife which had just fallen on the ground. The young queen reached forward and retrieved the weapon, and put on a genuine smile.

"Hello, Cambysses."

"I'm sorry, is this a bad time? I was hoping maybe if I came now, I could avoid an issue with your people."

"Now is a wonderful time. Why have you come to me? Is everything alright? Has something happened?"

"My father is very upset you refused him."

"Men are always upset when a woman tells them no. That does not surprise me."

"He has increased our war preparations."

"I expected he would. Is that why you came? To warn me?"

"I know you won't submit to him, but I do wish you luck."

"Thank you. I will take your well wishes. But you risked a lot to come all this way tonight, Cambysses. Won't your guards be angry with you for running away from them again?"

"They can't be angry with me if they came with me."

"Darius and Ariomardus are *here*?!"

"No, just Ariomardus. Darius is busy barking orders at construction crews. What he doesn't know won't hurt him."

"Construction crews?"

"I told you; my father is increasing war preparations."

"No, I may be tired but I remember you saying that. You came here to wish me luck, yet you won't tell me what to prepare for."

"It's because he doesn't know, Queen Tomyris. Go easy on the young man, will you?"

"Ariomardus! Our paths cross again."

"Seems they keep doing that. The prince wanted to come and express his thanks to you for standing next to him today against his father. He is worried for you, and your people. Cyrus' reputation as a victor precedes him. The truth is, Cambysses has no idea what the old man has planned."

"And *you* do?"

"He's making bridges for the river, so the army can cross faster."

"How big an army?"

"Ten thousand strong. And they've all arrived now."

"How far along are these bridges?"

"Cyrus has ordered them built at all hours of the day and night. He has enough men to keep up production. My best guess is, you might have a couple of days, at the most."

"A *couple*?!"

"He's also building observation towers, to keep an eye on the area. If you run, he'll see where you go and follow."

"So, I'm dead if I stay, dead if I run. Good to know."

"That's just what he wants you to think. But he doesn't know these sands the way you do."

"You sound like you're on my side, Ariomardus."

"I watched my people die. And before the Dahae fell I tried to help four other tribes maintain their lands."

"So, you have failed five times against the Persians, and now you are one of them?"

"I am not a Persian. I will be a Dahae until the day that I die, just like you will be a Massagetae until the day that you die. But I do not want those days to be soon."

"What do you propose I do with all of this information?"

"Pick up camp and move while you can."

"I have nowhere to go. Persian lands surround me. What little in the way of allies I have are already here. *This* is where we have to draw the line. *This* is where we make our stand."

"I figured you'd stay."

"Then why did you bother coming to me?"

"I felt you needed to know what you were up against."

"Well, thank you for telling me how hard this is going to be."

"You knew defending against Cyrus wasn't going to be easy."

"I have heard many stories of fallen men today. I have heard what Cyrus is capable of. Unlike you, I have not seen the horror with my own two eyes, but I see it on your face now. I feel the weight on my shoulders and in my heart. Bloodshed is all Cyrus understands, and so, bloodshed is what I will give him. And if I die protecting my people than so be it. It will be a warrior's death; one my father would be proud of. I can't be upset about that."

"You mean to fight?"

"I would never ask my people to do something I'm not willing to do myself. If *they* fight, *I* fight."

"If it's not too bold of me to say, I think you might just be the most dangerous opponent Cyrus has ever had."

"I'm not the most dangerous, just the most angry. I have a lot I need to speak with Skunkha about now. You two take care of yourselves on your way back to camp, alright? I really appreciate you coming out. And, either one of you is welcome back anytime too."

The young queen stood up from her chair and her eyes were dancing back and forth in her head. Cambysses politely gave a half bow, and let himself out of the tent but Ariomardus wasn't ready to move just yet. He had more to say, but he didn't know if it was appropriate. His golden knife was lying on the queen's table in plain view, as plain as the bloody bandage on his chest. It was eyeline for Tomyris as she stood next to him at the entrance to her tent. It had been such a long day. She wanted to reach up and touch the bandage to apologize, but she couldn't. He didn't seem pained by the injury;

it was only a flesh wound. She wouldn't dare cut him any deeper. She half wished she hadn't done it all, but used her words to negotiate. Skunkha would have handled things better, he was always better with his words. A skill he likely picked up from his father. She was too much like her father, strike first, ask questions later. Tomyris started mumbling to herself under her breath, almost forgetting Ariomardus was still beside her. She was running through lists of men she needed to prepare, warnings to the scouts, special missions for her son to keep him from the front lines, questions for Skunkha. Ariomardus put both of his hands gently on Tomyris' shoulders. She sighed, and hung her head. He still wasn't going anywhere, so she rose her head to meet his gaze. A knot welled up in the base of her throat seeing her husband's light eyes staring down at her. But these also weren't Sacephares' eyes. They were kinder, warmer, and less hollow. They were full of something she didn't have a word for.

"What, Ariomardus?"

"I wish I could tell you that I knew everything was going to be alright, but I am no seer, Tomyris. All I *do* know is that I will do everything in my power to sabotage Cyrus from the inside out."

"Why? You'd risk death if he ever found out you were double crossing him."

"Most of his soldiers aren't loyal to him. Half of the officers I have met are no different than me. We are all just biding our time, waiting for a chance to get back at the old man for what he's taken from us. You give us hope, Tomyris."

"Me? I don't even know what I'm doing half the time."

"If you don't know, then neither does he. You scare him, and he doesn't scare easy. Just stay true to yourself, and let him run himself to ruin. His day will come. I can feel it."

"I just feel sick to my stomach."

"When was the last time you had a good night's rest?"

"How long as Cyrus had his flags posted in my red sands?"

"You must take care of yourself, Tomyris. Our success depends on you keeping yourself together."

"Easier said than done."

"Your advisor will help bear these burdens. And whatever he doesn't help with, I will."

"You want to help me? We're strangers. We should be enemies."

"We're family…kind of. We are Saka."

"Why are you being so kind to me, Ariomardus? I hurt you tonight."

"I feel no pain from the cut. It's a scratch really."

"I cut you. I saw white muscle. Scratches don't bleed this bad."

"A scar to remember you by then."

"Why would you want to remember me?"

"Why wouldn't I?"

"You should get Cambysses back to camp before someone notices that you two have gone."

"Cyrus likes me. I can come and go as I please. I'm a fine enough liar to keep myself safe."

"Don't tell me you're a good liar. I want to trust you."

"Then trust me. Get some rest. Snuff out your fire. Quiet your head, and I'll come back and see you as soon as I have more information."

Like they were old friends who'd known each other their whole lives, Ariomardus pulled the young queen into his chest and held her there until he felt her heart quiet against him. Before stepping away to leave he placed a gentle kiss on the top of her forehead and slipped out of her tent, careful to keep the flap open long enough for a breeze to rush through and knock her smoldering fire out completely. Ariomardus was right, she needed sleep, and she needed to take care of herself. Orders could wait for morning, when the sun rose, which was only a couple of hours away right now at best. But that would be enough. While Tomyris gave into her exhaustion, Skunkha was up tossing and turning in his tent over the troubling conversation he had with his estranged father. Spargapeithes tent was close enough to his mother's advisor that the constant cursing of the gods woke him up, and kept him from getting back to sleep. Wanting to make himself useful, the young general went to grab his horse and go for a ride before the sun came up. The prince hoped to pull off a quick scouting mission and impress his mother for morning reports. He was surprised to see the Persian's camp alive and well, as if they had never closed things down for the night. But he was alarmed at the setting of posts in the river. Pieces of bridge had already been assembled, all that was left to do now was actually set the posts and connect the pieces so the weapons could be transported in their carts. Spargapeithes lost his breath seeing the construction progress. He had naively thought this war was going to take months before a battle was ever fought. A few skirmishes might take place in these colder months, but surely his mother would have time to build up her forces. By the looks of it this morning, the Massagetae had no time to do anything but pray to their gods. He didn't understand. There were scouting missions every day, and somehow overnight so much had been done. There was a sinking feeling in the teenage boy. For the first real time he was feeling fear. There was serious worry racing about his head and a cold sweat spread all across his body. While he was sitting there on his horse, trying to figure out what all of this meant, Atossa had come out of her tent for the morning, and seen him. He wasn't even trying to hide, up on the crest of the sand dune in all his glory, black hair a mess of tangles flowing out to his shoulders. Atossa snuck a wave to him but the boy was so dazed he didn't even respond. She was more than a little hurt by the prospect of being ignored, and decided to go take a walk to investigate further. She took the long way around to a shallower part of the river, allowing her to brave the icy waters and swim across where the current didn't lead her astray too bad. As soon as she was up on the Massagetae side of the Araxes she regretted her decision. Dawn was always the coldest part of the day, and now she was shivering in the shadows of the sand, soaking wet, and not an ounce of help to her name. Spargapeithes was also gone. He was no longer up on the dune in full view of the enemy. Atossa didn't even know what in the world she was doing until she heard a hiss from behind a large pile of boulders. She assumed it was a snake. She didn't know the local area well enough to know snakes were not out in winter, not alone, hissing at her directly. Spargapeithes popped out from the boulders and nearly scared her half to death. She jumped, and he ran out with a warm smile on his face, absolutely innocent of any ill intent at all. He shuffled his fur wrap off his shoulders as he ran, and was eager to help the Persian princess in her time of need. Atossa was used to being doted on hand and foot, but not like this. There was concern on the teenage boy's face. He took care to rub his hands up and down her arms to try and stop the shaking, and before realizing what she was doing again, she leaned in and pressed herself against the enemy prince. It took Spargapeithes a couple of seconds to process this immediate gesture of affection before he was able to let his arms drape around her, and hold her close. She nestled her face into his chest. He was so tall and gangly, he hadn't even grown into himself yet, but he was safe, and kind. Atossa didn't want anything to happen to him. She'd never felt like that about anyone before. No ambition, no logic, no reason. Spargapeithes was just good personified. She felt so guilty for using the boy, but it was in her nature to manipulate. It was as automatic as breathing. As soon as she could stop her shivering and get her back on straight, she slipped right into her old routine of flattering every bit of war intelligence out of a man as her curves would allow.

"You're crazy for crossing that river in the morning, princess."

"I got excited seeing you up on the dune."

"I scout there every day."

"But I don't *see* you every day."

"Do you *want* to see me every day?"

"I can't help but smile when I see you. I don't have much reason to smile, but around you, it is so effortless."

"I'm glad I can make you happy."

"My father's camp is so harsh. I don't like being out here."

"My mother's camp isn't much better. Winter can be brutal in our lands. No fire is big enough when you're alone in a tent at night."

"I find it hard to believe a general is alone in his tent at night."

"Well, believe it. You are lucky to be married, Atossa."

"I don't feel lucky. I feel cold. Darius never comes to me. We spend very little time together. In fact, I've probably spoken more to *you* than my husband the entire time I've been out here."

"I'm sorry. If you were *my* wife, I'd want to talk to you every day."

"Is that something you've thought about…being my husband?"

"Marriage is a good way to form an alliance, and prevent bloodshed. I heard my mother rejected your father yesterday. But their union isn't the only one which could stop this war before it got started."

"Too bad I'm already married. I don't think I'd mind being your wife. I have such a weakness for clever minds."

"You think I'm clever?"

"I think you're many things, Spargapeithes."

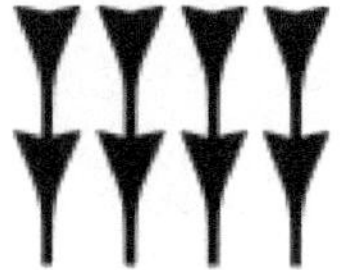

It took the Massagetae and their allies three days to pick up and move their camp a half a day's ride close to their burning grounds. It gave them much needed distance from the Araxes River and Cyrus' mocking flags posted in the sand. Darius had been tracking the move through various scouting reports. He was not pleased that the number of tents grew amongst the enemy. Tomyris wasn't running because she was scared, quite the opposite actually, she was regrouping. Her position was stronger now behind a difficult patch of dunes and open desert. The Persians would be exposed so long now before they could strike, it was not an enviable place to be. They couldn't even get across the river yet. Assembling the bridge was proving more of a challenge. No matter how many times Darius walked around the officers and barked orders to speed things up, the current of the river was next to impossible to properly navigate without killing men. Bridge building was an endeavor better suited to the warmer months. Right now, the winter was harsh and the water icy. Men couldn't stand in the water to properly bury a post worthy of bearing any mount of weight. Wood kept toppling, drifting downriver. One man drowned yesterday when he lied and said he could swim in the hopes of getting promoted. Or, at least Darius assumed that had been the motive. Ariomardus suspected sabotage because the man had been a Saka conscript, not from his own tribe, but a neighboring one known for their passive stance.

They had been a quiet people ripe for conquest and a quick victory. Ariomardus assumed that fight was hardly worthy of being called a battle, and gave Cyrus the false impression he could just walk through these sands and take people like a farmer in harvest. Darius noticed Ariomardus had genuine concern for the conscripts. He spoke their language, in more ways than one. They respected each other, without fear. Darius wanted that kind of effortless control. The way Cyrus ruled, it was a technique that worked in the past with smaller numbers, but large armies required a different kind of manipulation. Times were changing. If Darius didn't want to get left behind, he would have to find new ways to adapt, and he was hoping Ariomardus might unintentionally help him with that. This morning, the young lieutenant general beckoned for an early ride with the former Dahae soldier, roughly rousing him from a deep sleep. Ariomardus only got up with haste thinking Cambysses had run off again, and was eager at the chance of seeing Tomyris. It had been a couple of days, and he was feeling like he was missing her. His large black buck's training was coming along nicely, and he'd actually wear a saddle now so the brisk start to the day was more bearable. Ariomardus was a bit concerned with Darius' motives as the two trekked off away from prying ears and eyes along the river's edge, and back to a crest of a nearby dune where the foundations were being set for the observation towers.

"What's the meaning of all this, Darius? If you aim to kill me without witnesses, you didn't need to go to all the trouble."

"*Kill* you? I *like* you, Ariomardus! I consider you a friend. And I hope in time you will feel the same for me."

"We're *friends* now? How did that happen? We never speak to each other during the day unless Cambysses is in trouble."

"You are valuable to the army, and to me."

"How so?"

"The men like you."

"We are one in the same. The only difference is I have more blood on my hands than they do."

"Well, you also have connections."

"*Connections*? I am the least connected man you know. My tribe has been wiped from the face of the world."

"Your tribe may be gone, but I was referring to connections of a more…*personal* nature."

"*Personal*?"

"Queen Tomyris. I'm no fool, Ariomardus. She's moved her camp, and you know why, don't you?"

"She's a smart woman. I don't know why she does what she does. If you think I had something to do with that, you're mistaken."

"You can't learn to tell the truth until you learn to lie."

"What?"

"Lying might have kept you alive to this point, but you're not very good at it to a man who's already mastered the art. Speak plainly, Ariomardus. You told the queen to move her camp, didn't you? You told her of the bridges and the towers."

"I warned her to protect her people. I make no apologies. I've seen much death at *your* Persian hands. The Saka are my people. I'll never take pleasure in seeing their blood stain these sands."

"Cyrus thinks he can trust you."

"Cyrus is a wise leader. He knows better than to think he can trust anyone. Even those closest to him. Even his own family."

"Do you accuse me of something, Ariomardus?"

"You're a young man, Darius. You married a princess. You came from nothing and yet married a princess. How does that work?"

"A good man does not tell tall tales of what happens in the privacy of a woman's tent."

"You don't love Atossa. And she doesn't love you. Cambysses told me you've been married two years, and yet, no children?"

"What does love have to do with marriage?"

"Is it all politics with you Persians? Does *anything* mean *anything* to you people? Or is it all winning and eternal glory?"

"The masses will know my name, Ariomardus."

"Congratulations to the masses. I do not wish for the same."

"What *do* you wish for?"

"A quiet life. A family. Children giggling around me, and a good woman who loves me, despite what I've done. Sands for my horses to run, and no more war. No more blood on my hands."

"Sounds boring."

"I knew you wouldn't understand."

"Does she want the same thing?"

"*She?*"

"That good woman who loves you despite what you've done. The Massagetae queen."

"Tomyris doesn't love me. I'm her dead husband's younger brother. She can barely hold eye contact with me. I think I disgust her half the time we're together."

"I highly doubt you disgust *any* woman. Have you seen the way the harem stares after you when you walk through camp?"

"I care not for the opinion of the harem. They are all married wives and betrothed daughters. Persians are of no interest to me."

"You are loyal to a woman you have been charged to kill, and you wear her scar over your heart. The scholars back home would think that poetic."

"Remind me to never cross paths with these scholars."

"You know, you'll have to meet many people back in the capitals when we return for our victory parade."

"What makes you so sure there will be a victory here?"

"Some tribes put up more trouble than others, but they fall all the same, Ariomardus. Every one falls. You can't help it. I know your heart is in these sands, but that's where it's going to have to stay. Keep it here, bury it away, and ride on."

"I can't bury this away."

"What, do you like the pain then?"

"Pain is better than feeling nothing at all."

"There is pleasure in the numbness. Take it from a man who knows."

"You're nearly young enough to be my son. Don't speak to me of time, Darius. There's so much you don't even know that you don't know. It's almost amusing."

"Enlighten me."

"You know nothing of people. Nothing of loyalty or heart. It's not something to laugh at and throw away. It's all we are as people."

"Would you be willing to teach me?"

"Teach you what? How to be human?"

"How to be a good man. Teach me of this loyalty and heart. Prove to me it's not a weakness. And in return, *I* will teach *you* something. I will tell you how I read people."

"I am interested in this."

"I have a theory. People are like animals. You give me any person, *any* person from *any*where, and I can tell you what animal they are like. Go on. Test me."

"Alright. I'll play along. What animal am I to you, Darius?"

"You're strong, and smart, you're as dangerous as you are helpful. You're like that horse you try to tame. This huge black beast that is more trouble than it's worth, yet you keep at it all the same."

"You're trying to flatter me."

"Is it working?"

"Perhaps."

"Let me humble myself. Do you know what I think of myself?"

"A golden lion?"

"A goat."

"Ha!"

"Let me explain. Goats are small, compact, useful. They are brought everywhere. Everyone needs them. There's nothing they can't do, nothing they can't provide."

"Not exactly humble, but amusing. You got the small bit correct."

"Alright, alright, have a good laugh, but you'll see that I am right."

"What is Cambysses?"

"A rabbit. He's always getting out, running around and upsetting everyone. He's insignificant, and not good for anything. Cyrus though, he's a powerful bear. Slow and dangerous. A mighty force."

"That makes sense. And your wife?"

"Oh, Atossa, she's a falcon to be sure. Smart, talented..."

"Loud!"

"Yes! Shrieking even. Shrill, but smart. Unusually smart for being so small, and so pretty. Very careful, calculating, and cutthroat. Not unlike your queen."

"She's not *my* queen."

"Tomyris strikes me as an eagle. Deadly and unforgiving. She'll do anything to protect her own, which is why there aren't many like her around. A doomed predator for all their effort."

"Tomyris isn't doomed."

"That's your heart talking, Ariomardus, not your head. Just like that annoying advisor she has, always poking about where he's not wanted. That man's a snake. He'd just assume kill before ask a question. But an eagle can still kill him, so he hides in her shadows trying to make nice."

"And what about her son?"

"The boy general? He's a wolf puppy. Nothing worth taking seriously. The poor boy is going to end up hurting himself for pride."

"He's only a couple years younger than you, Darius."

"But he hasn't seen what I have seen."

"What do you know of what that boy has seen?"

"He hasn't seen what I have seen. He wouldn't do what I have done. When I was his age, I had already seen twelve Saka tribes fall. That boy still plays with a wooden sword for training I bet."

"He's a general. He has metal weapons. And when Cyrus orders us across the Araxes, you will see what that boy can do."

"You think I should fear him?"

"I think you need to take every one of the Massagetae soldiers seriously. You may have seen a lot of failures, but you have never seen Tomyris in a fight."

"And you have?"

"Yes."

"There's more to it than that."

"None of it concerns you."

"You know, this friendship of ours will work better if we trust each other, Ariomardus."

"Trust goes both ways, Darius. You can want it all you want, but pretty words mean nothing if you don't back it up with actions."

"You want to know what I'm afraid of then, what scares me about the Massagetae?"

"You're scared of them?"

"There's a mongoose in their camp."

"What does that mean?"

"Mongooses are people that undermine everything. They dig holes under the surface, weasel their way through the world, and then show up when you least expect it, once everything is ruined beyond repair. They knock the ground out from underneath your feet. Mongooses are small, and insignificant, so you don't pay attention to them at first, then they humiliate you."

"And you don't know who the mongoose is, do you?"

"No. I don't. And until I do, I don't know what to do about this war coming up. I don't know how to go about it. If I knew who the mongoose was, I could tell Cyrus with confidence when to ford that river. It's *my* damned word he's waiting on."

"*Your* word?"

"Atossa insisted I had this handled."

"Why would she say that?"

"She takes pride in the failure of those closest to her, in case you hadn't noticed."

"She is quite the mastermind. If her father waits for your word and you're victorious, you'll be a hero."

"And should we suffer a defeat, a setback, a falter even, I lose it all. I wind up killed in my sleep so the princess can marry up."

"Do you think Atossa has her eyes on another man?"

"I think she does. She's been distant lately."

"How can you tell?"

"A man can tell when his wife's eyes are elsewhere. Atossa and I have a formal agreement with one another. I help her, and she helps me. When one of us advances, we both advance. But she's been making more and more decisions without me. She goes missing for hours at a time, and doesn't tell me anything when she returns."

"You think it's another officer?"

"I've been asking around, but no one will tell me anything. The women know, but they look out for their own. No soul in the Persian camp will dare turn on their princess. They love her."

"If I knew who it was, or if I find out, I will tell you, Darius."

"Thank you, I'd really appreciate that."

"Can I ask you a question about this animal theory of yours?"

"You think it has merit, don't you?"

"Can a person be one animal, and then suddenly turn into this mongoose of yours?"

"Yes."

"Can an eagle ever turn into a mongoose?"

"Your queen isn't the shifty troublemaker I'm worried about."

"But she does scare you, doesn't she?"

"I'm not used to powerful women."

"Atossa is powerful."

"She is a lot of talk. Tomyris is talk *and* action. She's as dangerous as a man, as you or I, but prettier. Much prettier. I can see why you stare at her, but don't get too attached. We have to kill her soon."

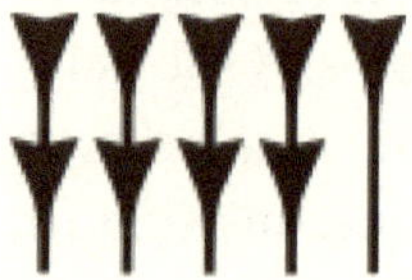

Tomyris' first night after moving the Massagetae into their new location was a steady stream of meetings. Some men didn't want anything to do with the Persian threat, picked up their tents and kept moving after paying their respects to the young queen. She couldn't be angry with their desire to protect their families from slaughter. Some men decided to send just their women and children away. Fathers and sons stayed. Spargapeithes was a big help in maintaining a younger army. His friends, and those who looked up to the teenagers remained in camp against their parent's wishes. Tomyris promised to look after everyone as well as she was able. She had secured allies in a handful of neighboring tribes, though they were all significantly smaller than her own. Skunkha was still sending runners out across the sands in the hopes of securing friends of friends for this noble cause. Tomyris was on the front lines now, there was nothing she could do about that. She wouldn't run, she wouldn't leave, but she did like fighting from her current position better. The Persians were going to be far from their resources and stuck with a river behind them to slow any potential retreat. The young queen didn't want to get ahead of herself though. Ariomardus told her he was coming from a ten-thousand-man army, and she was struggling to convince five hundred to make a stand. She wouldn't dare tell her men those odds. It wouldn't do anything to help morale, which was shaky at best. With the way the wind had blown today, all the smoke from the Persian fires and construction efforts had settled down into their valley, making the cold winter day hazy and the danger inescapable. Tonight though, the darkness helped alleviate the visible threat that was ever present during the day. Fantasies could be better entertained, like the delusion that the Massagetae could survive Cyrus' attacks. Tomyris didn't want to dwell on how many days she had left to her name. It was a heavy and somber thought to think everything around her would soon be gone. The people outside, her son, her horses, the laughter. All gone. Between meetings with her officers, she was dying for some relief, even it was only for her piece of mind and a line of lies, she needed Skunkha. The advisor though had his own mental hurdles to deal with. His father had come out of his tent and was walking between campfires while the young advisor was on his way to the queen's tent. Skunkha made a quick adjustment to his plans, and forcefully escorted his raggedy old father back to the outskirts of camp. Homarges hobbled as he walked with a cane made out of twisted driftwood from the Araxes River.

"I thought we had an understanding, father?! You can stay in the camp so long as no one knows you're here. You're lucky it's dark."

"I get restless keeping to myself all day."

"I don't care!"

"Do you remember when you were a boy, and we used to take our walks together in the morning?"

"Before the king called you in for the first meeting of the day, yes, I remember. What does that have to do with anything?"

"You used to be so excited to spend time with me. You'd rush in before the sun was up, and jump on me in my sleep to wake me up."

"I was a child."

"I miss those days."

"Alright."

"Don't you miss those days too, son?"

"Honestly, missing you comes in waves, father, and most nights, I pray for the gods to let me drown and be rid of it all."

"If you're trying to hurt me, consider yourself victorious."

"Don't expect me to believe someone as heartless and as ruthless as yourself could have something like delicate feelings which could be hurt by a mere handful of words. I could never hurt you. You have always been so preoccupied with yourself and your own betterment and ambitions to be concerned with me, or my effect on the world."

"I am proud of what you have done in my absence. You convinced Tomyris to move the camp."

"She didn't do this because of *me*. It was that Dahae soldier who sold his soul to the Persians. Cyrus' latest conscript. He urged her to move and warned her of the trouble coming for her. She listened to him because he said he is Sacephares younger brother."

"That's impossible. The boy was killed, wasn't he?"

"Ariomardus wasn't invited on the hunt that killed all the other men. I remember the argument that morning in camp as clear as if it were yesterday. Tomyris and I were eavesdropping from my tent. She couldn't sleep alone after the wedding and needed a friend. She wanted to go on the hunt too, but before she could go out and ask Ariomardus to join her out of spite for their fathers, he had run off on horseback and left. She never saw him again until the Persians came calling for him a couple weeks ago. She didn't even know who he was, it had been so long. I recognized him though. Ariomardus looks just like his father. They all had those light eyes."

"Greek eyes."

"Little Sparga has them too."

"Of course, he does. And he will abandon his mother just like all the other men in his family."

"Don't say that. Losing her son would kill Tomyris."

"But she'll still have you."

"Father, no. I can't have you pushing this every time we speak. I will *never* be king, alright? I will *never* marry Tomyris. I don't care what you think about it. I don't. Now, I have to go speak with her, can I trust you to stay in your tent?"

"If you want me to stay, I'll stay."

"Don't confuse my orders as an invitation to stay in the camp. If you want to leave, then by all means, pack up and get to walking. But if you stay, you stay inside. If word got back to Tomyris that you are here, and I didn't tell her…"

"She will find out eventually, son."

"No, she's got a lot to deal with right now. She's not as observant as she usually is."

"Women always find out what men hide from them."

"Don't speak to me of women as if you understand them. I was young when mother left, but I still remember what happened. I really have to go meet with Tomyris now, will you stay in your tent?"

"Yes, son. You have my word."

"Your word is about as useful as a bowl with a hole in the bottom."

"I'll stay hidden. Now go, speak to your queen, and be smart about it. I'm sure she needs you right now."

Skunkha felt terrible about walking away from his father, sitting all smug like in the back of his tent. How this man was still alive, Skunkha did not know. He had seen dead men look healthier than his father. There were scabs on the man's face and hands that appeared infected for weeks. His skin was discolored, and there was a smell of decay about him. Mongoose fur was on everything. Tunnels were surrounding the outcast tent. Skunkha even had the fur on himself and he hadn't even touched anything. He tried dusting himself off on his hastened walk over towards the queen's tent, but when he arrived late, she wasn't there. The advisor looked about to the horses, and her white mare was still tied up with the others. None of the small chiefs had seen her as Skunkha poked about with questions by the dinner campfires. Spargapeithes was coming in from his latest scouting mission, and Skunkha caught him by the reins. The boy was reluctant to oust his mother, but the advisor was like family, and so the prince nodded his head towards Tomyris' location. She was walking out to the burning grounds to speak with the gods. She never spoke to them in camp, but the burning grounds were a sacred place. Skunkha didn't want to interrupt her, but he was able to follow her golden firelight out and intercept her before she got too far. He wasn't the only one in the sands though, running after the queen. Ariomardus was trekking in the darkness without a signal to his name, and the two men reached the queen at nearly the same exact time. Skunkha wouldn't say a word around the Saka traitor if he didn't have to, and wanted Tomyris to dismiss him, but there was no such command on the tip of her tongue. She kept her pretty face expressionless; she was too deep in thought right now to be troubled by petty things like two men who disliked one another from a sixteen-year-old misunderstanding she knew little about. With her little torch she neared the flame near Skunkha to try and read his face and see if his intent was urgent tonight or if it could wait. His eyes shifted nervously when she lit him up, and she furrowed her brows. Skunkha half worried she could read his thoughts, but she reached over and began to dust him off. Pulling off some of the fur she examined it, and Ariomardus took it from her hand. He knew what it was, then snickered towards Skunkha.

"It's mongoose fur, Tomyris. You keep them in your new camp?"

"I don't keep mongooses; they ruin everything they touch. Skunkha, where did this come from?"

"I must have brushed up against someone."

"But you didn't *just* brush up against someone, did you? Some men spoke to me this evening, when they showed up *on time* for their meetings. They voiced concerns over a certain tent in camp."

"Oh? There're concerns?"

"You're my advisor. *I* shouldn't be the one telling *you* that your father has returned. And judging by the lack of surprise in your eyes right now, I'd say you already knew and chose not to tell me."

"My father is here, but I didn't tell you because I knew it wouldn't help anything. I don't know why he has stayed as long as he has."

"Why didn't you tell me Homarges had violated my order of exile? You are my advisor, and my friend, Skunkha."

"Can we not do this right in front of the enemy?"

"Ariomardus is not my enemy."

"Well, he's a Persian officer, and he is an enemy to the Massagetae."

"He is Saka blood, same as you and I. But both of you have interrupted my walk to the burning grounds. So, why is that?"

"We had a meeting arranged…"

"Yes, Skunkha, we *did*. But you were with your exiled father discussing equally important matters, I'm sure."

"Not exactly."

"You can go back to my tent and wait for me."

"Yes, Tomyris."

"Go, Skunkha."

"I don't feel comfortable leaving you out here alone with Ariomardus. Queen or not, you are still a young woman."

"Skunkha how many duels have I beat you in?"

"Well, over half. But…"

"I can handle myself. Besides, I won't be out here alone with him, I'll be with the gods. Ariomardus, why have you come? I moved my camp as you suggested. I uprooted hundreds of people. You said you'd see me when you had new information, what is it?"

"The bridges have been completed."

"What?! But they hadn't crossed the river. They were still setting posts. My son just came back from scouting a few minutes ago."

"Well, your son was probably just trying to keep you happy and not be the bearer of bad news. Or, he wasn't scouting at all."

"Don't assume anything about my son, Ariomardus. You don't know anything about him."

"He's my nephew. He may be your son, Tomyris, and I may be a stranger, but I was a sixteen-year-old boy once, you weren't. When my mother told me to go out at night…I wasn't going scouting."

"What do you think he was doing then?"

"Was he happy when you didn't pick a wife for him at the games?"

"There is a war about to rip open our world. Marriage isn't important right now. He is mature enough to know that."

"Perhaps there is a woman he has chosen for himself already, and he is too afraid to tell you who it is because he fears your disapproval, not only as his mother, but as his queen."

"That's ridiculous. My son and I are very close. He's one of my generals. He would never disobey my orders."

"You never disobeyed your father when you were sixteen?"

"You were at my wedding games. You know what I did."

"Exactly. Even if your son is nothing like my brother, he's like you. He didn't go scouting. If he had, you'd have already known those bridges are complete. Cyrus and the officers have them lit up with torches from one side to the other. They are a beacon on the river. No one could miss them. He moves tomorrow morning. What are you going to do, Tomyris?"

"I already told you. I'm going to fight."

"But will you be ready in time?"

"We'll have to be."

"Darius has insisted we have the men across the river by sunrise."

"The riders on horseback would reach my camp by midday."

"I can try and stall them, hold them back a couple of hours."

"I don't need you to risk your position for me. You're the best source of information I have right now. If I can't depend on my son, or my advisor…you must take care of yourself, Ariomardus."

"Are you worried about me?"

"Cyrus didn't get to be where he is in life because he houses traitors in his inner circle. He will find you out and test your allegiances. I won't have you dying for me."

"Who's to say I would die for you?"

"You're with me right now. That's a killable offense you keep repeating. Say what you want, but I know a man from his actions. Go back to your camp, Ariomardus. Make your preparations. I will make mine, and I'll see you tomorrow morning. Skunkha, go and round the chiefs. Bring them back to my tent but don't cause a panic. If you two will excuse me, I really need to speak with the gods."

Tomyris reached up and snuffed her own fire out. She handed the doused torch to Skunkha who was standing there beside her like a silent, scolded child. Ariomardus looked at the man for help as to what to do about the queen, but Skunkha would not help him. Both men simply had to do as they were told, and keep their questions to themselves for a better time. Skunkha was far more obedient. With his head down the advisor walked back to the new Massagetae camp with all haste in his step. Ariomardus traced his figure in the moonlight until he was well enough away across the dunes to obscure what the Dahae soldier had in mind. He was going to follow Tomyris to the burning grounds in an effort to speak to her in confidence, and urge her to avoid a slaughter. He couldn't stand the thought of seeing her dead in the sands, and no amount of heart or desire was going to defy the odds come morning. Five hundred were not even an obstacle to ten thousand. Skill could close the margin a bit, but numbers were numbers. The Massagetae needed to flee to save themselves. Ariomardus would plead his case on bended knee tonight if that's what it came to, but he hoped in private the young queen might come to see his side of things. She had conceded to him a couple of days ago, she very well might do it again. He was watching her face as she spoke earlier. She was second guessing herself and her choices. Her lips quivered, betraying her strong words. Tomyris had walked quickly to the burning grounds. Ariomardus wasn't as familiar with these sands as he wished he was, and got turned about in his efforts to track her down. How quickly she had gotten herself lost. She wasn't lost though, she was right where she wanted to be, on the edge of the ashen sands. Ariomardus couldn't interrupt her prayers. She was on her knees, hands up in the sky, speaking the nearly forgotten language of the elders used only during special times like births, marriages, and deaths. Ariomardus hadn't heard such desperate, heavy words in a long time. He hated hearing them now, from such a shaky voice. Tomyris sobbed in her pleas to the god of fire, Mehr, and the the goddess of water, Anahita. She asked for help from her father the king, and his father before him. She even put out a call to her mother, who had died giving birth to her. Ariomardus was in tears hiding on the crest of the hill. His sniffling betrayed him, and caused the young queen to startle in her demonstration. Her words became quiet, and she held them close to finish things off. She had gotten carried away in the freedom of the black night. Ariomardus didn't falter in his stance when Tomyris came towards him. The moon was behind her, so he couldn't read her face even in the dim light. He could only read her petite silhouette shifting in the sandy wind, and had to settle for that. All the warnings he had logically lined up in his head slipped away when she was close. He wanted to reach out and hold her close again, but felt unable to do so now. Somehow, it'd be wrong. They stood there in silence for a while until Tomyris ruffled around her waist to present the Dahae soldier with his golden knife again, and he cocked a half smile. The queen could see the shadows of his dimples, and the gleam on his teeth. His light eyes were hauntingly striking, and made her forget how to breathe for a second. He was rummaging around his waist too, and pulled out a matching golden knife in his possession.

"They are a pair, Tomyris. My father gave them to me before I left home. He said these knives can't stand being apart. They are like the gods Mehr and Anahita, always needing the other. So, please, keep yours, and our paths will be forced to stay together."

"If I die tomorrow, I want you to take the knife back."

"Neither of us are dying tomorrow. I won't allow it. You trust me?"

"I trust you."

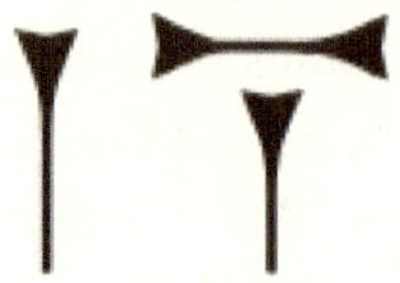

Two hours before the sun rose there was a ceremony in the Massagetae camp to speak to the gods en masse and ask them for their help against the Persians today. Five of the best goats from officers and chiefs were sacrificed, and their blood collected in great golden bowls for the rite of the soldiers. Tomyris and Skunkha dipped their fingers in the warm blood, and spread five lines down the face of every man fighting, directly over the right eye. They sprawled through camp, with more fires blazing than there were people. It was hot in the dead of winter, and the air heavy with the moisture of the morning and ash. Blackened residue coated the Massagetae's pale faces. Axes and spears were being sharpened to perfection. The archers tended quivers full of arrows, and every one took two bows with them, just in case. Swords were clanking and family sheaths were being brought out from tents for the first time in years. Mothers were crying, kissing their sons and husbands away. Sisters stayed strong, keeping the camp moving and tending to the feeding of the horses. Elderly men who could no longer run or ride were giving stern advice, words of wisdom, and sturdy pats on the back. Tomyris had led over skirmishes before, petty tribal clashes and rogue invaders, but never had she prepared for so large a battle. She had heard her father's stories as a child, but even those battles paled in comparison to what she was faced with now. Ten thousand Persian Immortals were about to come rolling over her sands, bent on victory by a callous and pompous leader. Her goals were that she was not annihilated instantly. If she died, she hoped she'd make an impression first, and possibly even convince some of Cyrus' forced Saka conscripts to come back in the defense of their own people. In the back of her mind, there was also Ariomardus' promise to her the night before, hours before really. He said he wouldn't let her die. But that's not how battles worked. They wouldn't be side by side. They might not even see each other out there. Ten thousand Persians. She couldn't even process what that would look like. How much ground would they cover? How would they come out? Would there be blocks of one hundred, lines of a thousand? And where would Cyrus be? Would he be sitting in camp, removed from all the carnage and simply waiting for a report? Or would be on the crest of a far-off dune, down by the river, in all of his pretty armor shining in the sun beside his children? Children. Tomyris came to her son's men last. The sixteen-year-old general turned to face his mother after finishing a rousing pep speech. The young queen dipped her fingers in fresh blood and let the warm liquid trickle down her son's face in five lines over his right eye. Her lines had yet to be drawn. Spargapeithes motioned for the bowl of blood in his mother's arms and she recoiled.

"No! A general must never touch the sacrificial bowl. It's bad luck. Are your men ready, Sparga?"

"We're going to make you proud today."

"Don't worry about making me proud, you just go out there and remember the war council's plans."

"If we do that, we'll never even swing a single sword?"

"Wars aren't settled in a single battle. No need to show Cyrus everything we're capable of in this first encounter. There'll be more battles after today. You and your men will have your chance."

"You're not just trying to keep me from getting hurt, are you?"

"I will always do everything I can to protect you as a mother. But when the fate of our people is concerned, a good queen needs to protect her generals as well. Hang back today. If everything goes according to plan, the deaths will be minimal for us and the burning grounds will be dark tonight."

"Is it true what the men say about the Persians being immortal?"

"No, Sparga. They wear armor and shields same as you and I. They bleed. They are just men. Being in Cyrus' army does not protect you from the god's will. Nothing can stop death."

"Is it true they number ten thousand?"

"To the best of my understanding, yes."

"They outnumber us twenty to one."

"The Massagetae can handle such odds."

"No, we can't."

"Yes, we can. We have to. The rest of the Saka in the northern lands depend on us stopping the Persians here. We can't fail. We won't."

"If you die today, I'm going to have to be king. You were my age when your father was killed. But I'm not you. I can't be king. I wouldn't know how to lead people. I wouldn't…"

"I'm not dying today, Spargapeithes. And even in the odd event that the gods did take me today, you would still have Skunkha, and you would not be alone. The people love our family. They would listen to you, and support you. You have nothing to worry about. When the time comes, everything always becomes very clear. Trust me."

"I love you, mother. Be careful out there today. I know how much you like a good fight. But this is serious."

"I'm well aware of what's going on this morning, Spargapeithes. I do not need a lecture from you on safety."

"Promise me you won't do something stupid and go after Cyrus. I've heard some of the other men talking. It's something your father did, break formation and go to duel the enemy leader one on one."

"I'm not my father."

"Promise me you won't go after Cyrus."

"I promise."

"And what about his children? You won't go after them, will you?"

"I have nothing against Prince Cambysses or Princess Atossa."

"Please don't hurt her, mother."

"Why are you so concerned over the princess, Spargapeithes?"

"I'm not. But some of the men have said that they'd like to take her hostage. I know what they'd do to her. They'd rape her. They'd…"

"Calm down. We're not taking hostages. No one is getting raped so long as I take breath. You understand?"

"If one of Cyrus' children were hurt, it'd justify a retaliation against me. Eye for an eye, like what Nebuchadnezzar did in Babylon."

"Khorasan isn't Babylon. I'm not Nebuchadnezzar. Nor is Cyrus."

"They call him Cyrus the Great for a reason, mother."

"Any man can tack on Great to his name, that doesn't make it so."

"No one calls you, Tomyris the Great."

"I don't need to feed a man's pride. I don't need my name remembered. I simply need to keep my people alive. Now, go take your men to get their horses. I need you to hold your line in the sand before the first Persian steps onto the battlefield. I want them to know we're ready. Massagetae don't run from their troubles."

Tomyris' face was hard and stern. Spargapeithes couldn't tell whether the authority that scared him most was that of his mother, or that of his queen. It was so icy, so matter of fact. The teenage boy nodded his head in understanding, and tried to mimic his mother's hard exterior. The blood had dried so fast on his face in the chilly morning air that he could feel it crinkle across the skin of his cheek. Stepping near the campfires warmed him, and the blood dripped down his face. His men were ready. Looking into their eyes, he fed off of their confidence. There was no doubt in their minds the battle would not go in their favor today. The morning would be glorious, and by the time the sun rose, the Persians would be questioning their decision to fight the Massagetae. Spargapeithes surged a fist into the air, and ran with a rallying cry through the tents and solemn family goodbyes. Other soldiers clanked their swords and axes against their shields. Spears shot up into the air. The hollers and wolf calls were echoing in the heavy morning. Tomyris insisted her son be the first line of showing on the sand dunes. This gave him satisfaction as a teenager, and allowed the young queen to talk over final strategy amongst her more seasoned officers back in camp. Their sabotage of the battlefield had been freshly completed. Large scale death would be avoided at all costs. On such short notice, playing dirty was their best advantage. Divers were in the river as they spoke. They wore special hides to keep them insulated and warm in the frigid temperatures. They hung to the bottoms of the three bridges, slathering the wood in heaps of collected animal fat and grease. Rope supports had been delicately frayed, and posts cut near through so they could not support weight. In the sands, lines of more animal fat and sagebrush had been buried in lines. Grease from campfires sat in bowls strategically throughout the dunes, marked with arrows sticking across the landscape. Tomyris had two lines of archers which would ignite these on the count of her whistle, or Skunkha's should something happen. The young queen and her advisor would ride down to the center of the battlefield preemptively, and wait for Cyrus to join them if he so chose to discuss terms of victory and defeat which were already fairly well understood. Capitulate or die for Cyrus, leave for Tomyris. Skunkha was very quiet this morning. Tomyris didn't like that he had more of that ruddy brown mongoose fur on his tunic.

"Your father wishes you well today, Skunkha?"

"He wishes us *all* well, Tomyris."

"Did he give you any parting advice this morning?"

"He warned me of Cyrus' victory marches across the dead bodies."

"So, your father both wishes us well and warns you of what will happen after we fail. He can't have it both ways."

"You know my father. He bets on all sides so he can never lose."

"But he *did* lose. I exiled him."

"But you haven't ordered him killed for coming back."

"Out of respect for you, and that's the *only* reason."

"If you respect me so much, why did you dismiss me last night?"

"What I had to say to Ariomardus didn't concern you."

"If the opportunity presents itself this morning, and you had to protect him or me, who would you ride for?"

"The opportunity won't present itself. But if it did…I am the Queen of the Massagetae. I'll ride and die for my people."

"Alright. I have my answer. Come here. I'll blood stripe you."

"I'll do it myself. Let's get our horses. I don't want Sparga out there too long by himself. That boy has a fire in his eyes that scares me."

"It's not the fire that scares you, it's the color. Those damn light eyes have always scared you. And I'm the *only* one who knows that."

Skunkha was upset, but Tomyris couldn't be bothered by feelings right now. She dripped the blood down the right side of her face and saddled up her white mare. Together the young queen and her advisor ran from the camp with great cheers behind them. The men were ready to march soon. Spargapeithes' detachment of soldiers were already posted on their sand dune when Tomyris and Skunkha came riding down into the red sands. The sun was just barely turning the sky pale and allowing the young queen and her advisor to see the smoke from Cyrus' camp. There was a thunder in the air, one which only a large sum of men could make. It was heavy, and Tomyris put a hand over her heart, feeling the shudder in her chest. Apparently ten thousand men were not light on their feet. The first lines of Persians rolled over the hills in shiny silver armor and shields. Blood red tassels danced on their helmets, and pale Saka faces were inside. Cyrus would use her own people against her. Skunkha looked over to his queen, bewildered. Tomyris scowled, but did not falter. The Persian officers were on horseback, scattered between the hundreds and thousands. It was like a blanket of metal coming across her sands. Ariomardus moved in formation as soon as he crested. He made sure there was a straight line between him and the young queen. Skunkha watched for a change in Tomyris' face, but nothing came. She was eagle eyed for Cyrus, who was brought in with his children on a palisade. Darius tethered their horses in his hands behind the opulent procession. To this, Tomyris did snarl her lip in disgust, and Skunkha straightened up in his saddle. The Massagetae were lining up behind their queen, loudly. While the Persians marched, Tomyris' army hollered and clattered, their horses whinnied in excitement. The Massagetae would not go down quietly, and it amused Cyrus. The Persians took their sweet time getting into position. Tomyris signaled her first whistle, and a group of several archers broke off to seemingly get lost in the dunes. After Cyrus came to the center of the battlefield and mounted his horse, Tomyris let off a second and third whistle together, and more archers departed. The old man chuckled, thinking her army was leaving her before the fighting had even started. The Massagetae's interests were merely represented by the team of Tomyris and Skunkha. Meanwhile, across from them were the Persian entourage of Cyrus, his son Cambysses, daughter Atossa, son-in-law Darius, lieutenant general Ariomardus, and three other gruff looking dark faced men in more armor than they could move in. Tomyris was unimpressed. While her and Skunkha's horses stood steady in the sand, the Persian's horses were not as sure footed, and anxious. Tomyris snickered, locked eyes with Ariomardus, and noticed him patting his matching gold knife on his waist. She reached down to touch the handle of her own, and cleared her throat. Skunkha saw both knives, and furrowed his brows. The sun was up now, piercing the red sands in streaks through the dark gray winter clouds. As the young queen opened her mouth to speak, Cyrus cut her off.

"I look forward to building my ranks with all your men."

"Safe to assume you are unwilling to leave without bloodshed then."

"It would be rude of me to deny my men the blood they came here for. However, if you would concede to marrying me…"

"I'd just assume marry your horse before you, *old man.*"

"Careful, *little queen.* Words are costly when armies are near."

"Then I swear on the sun, I'll give you more blood than even *you* can drink, *old man.*"

"You infuriating, disrespectful…"

"Save your breath for the battle. I wouldn't want you dying before you see what I am capable of."

"I will enjoy seeing you humbled, *little queen.* Today's blood falls in your hands."

Tomyris held her hands out for inspection, already blood stained from the morning sacrifice. Darius accidentally laughed, and Atossa shot him a death stare that could have paralyzed any right-minded husband, but this morning, he didn't seem bothered. Ariomardus smiled before turning away to follow Cyrus, leaving in absolute, vengeful, disgust. Atossa was quick to console her father, but Cambysses hung back reluctantly. He was all donned up in ceremonial armor, useless for fighting, but pretty to the eye. Tomyris knew there was no ill will between them, and bowed her head to him out of respect. If the old man would just keel over and Cambysses could take over, Tomyris was sure there could be peace between their people. But with her luck, the old leader wouldn't die for years and she'd be saddled with this war. Her men were cheering again in another wave of excitement seeing the Persians leave the center of the field. Tomyris spun on her horse, standing on the back of her white mare, taking a spiteful bow and riling up her army. Skunkha ran across the front lines and did tricks in the middle of runs. Spargapeithes and some of the other officers had their archers shoot up flaming arrows into the center of the impending battlefield. That was the final signal. The archers who had departed before the meeting of leaders now lit all three bridges on the Araxes River on fire, severed the ropes, and destroyed the posts. The Persians were none the wiser, but Tomyris could see the rising plumes of black smoke. Cyrus sent a runner, but the damage could not be reversed. Orders were barked, and men began to run. Horses fled in line. Tomyris whistled again, and traps were set. Lines of fire consumed the Persian ranks in blocks, sometimes trapping hundreds and killing tens and tens of soldiers on contact. The animal fat caught fast, and the grease stuck to the bodies so that no amount of flailing could stop their pain, and the river was way too far away to provide any dying comfort. Cyrus could be heard screaming. Tomyris had outsmarted him, and delayed the inevitable for now. The Massagetae roared in victorious cries and howls. More flaming arrows descended from on high. She hadn't lost a single man. The flames kept the Persians at bay, they only hurt themselves. The young queen looked for approval from Ariomardus, but he was nowhere to be seen until Tomyris looked amongst the fallen piles of armor. He had been thrown from his horse in the confusion of the fires lighting up lines in the sand. Without a second's thought Tomyris reared up on her horse and ran for him. She jumped through the flames and discovered the Dahae soldier had been cut in the neck by an arrow, not far from where she had cut him on the first night, they had crossed paths in the burning grounds. It was a bit ironic and a cry escaped her lips, betraying her queenlike objectivity. The fall had knocked Ariomardus unconscious, and he lied awkwardly limp in her arms and she pulled him into her lap. A thunder of hooves behind her left her unconcerned until the man put heavy hands on her shoulders. It was Darius. She didn't know what to make of him, if he'd kill her where she sat. For now, they had Ariomardus' health on the forefront of their mind. Darius motioned to help brace his friend's weight, and Tomyris wrapped her arms tighter around the injured man.

"We have aids in camp, Queen Tomyris. Please, let me take him."

"If he dies, will you honor me with sending a runner to my camp?"

"I'll come and tell you myself. But you shouldn't be here right now."

"He *promised* me we wouldn't die today. He wouldn't allow it."

"He's not dead yet. How did you even get over here? Did you jump through the fire or something?"

"Yes. Take care of him, Darius. But I've destroyed the bridges to your camp. You'll have to carry him across the river. There's a sandbar just upstream a little ways. The current is gentler."

"Thank you for telling me that. You should get back to your people. Congratulations on the morning's victory, Queen Tomyris."

"Congratulations on being a good man, Darius."

"You don't know what kind of man I am."

"If you weren't a good man, you'd have killed me already."

11

Darius was haunted by the words of the enemy queen. With the red sands on fire and skies gray with smoke, and a Persian defeat, there was much more the man should be focused on right now. The young lieutenant general couldn't help but indulge himself. What Tomyris said could have been a genuine compliment on his character, or just another mind game between political rivals. Blood stained his hands and clothes while he sat beside Ariomardus, unconscious on a cot of crude cloth in the makeshift healing ward of the camp. Since the Dahae soldier was such a high-ranking officer and one of Cyrus' favorites, he was set aside with a little more dignity. Many soldiers did not get the luxury of privacy, or a cot. Darius had his back to the masses, but he could still hear what was going on, the moans and groans of men cooking alive, their flesh white and roasting on their bones from the fires. The animal fat and grease that the Massagetae had used, in combination with the heat of the flames had melted the Persian armor and cloth to the soldier's skins. Damp sand was being used to cool them, but it was heavy and awkward for the servants to carry it up from the river. That was its own fight. With the bridges gone it was up to every man to swim his way back to camp, and many injured just weren't up to the challenge. Darius heard the gurgling and violent splashing of drowning victims. Horses returned without riders. If Ariomardus was awake he'd be herding those frantic animals, but he wasn't awake. His face was frozen in pain, brows weakly furrowed, mouth half open. He'd lost a lot of blood in the sand, and even more on the ride back. Thankfully Tomyris' tip about the river spared Darius the loss of his only real friend in camp, so far. He didn't know why she had done that, been nice to him. Surely it was out of concern for Ariomardus, but Darius didn't understand that either. They were strangers, and enemies, but also not. He envied the Dahae soldier, and didn't envy very many men in life. There was so much he still wanted to learn from Ariomardus, and emulate. Darius kept a firm watch on the bandage over his friend's wound. The blood wasn't seeping through as fast now. He'd have to wake up soon, and Darius would be there when he did, regardless of any other orders that might come his way. He nodded his head very sure of that, and sat up straighter in his chair. Ariomardus' wild black buck had navigated his way out of the battlefield fires and across the river by some sort of miracle to come and sit beside his human. Darius attempted to shoo the horse away, but the animal would not budge. Ariomardus' eyes flitted open with Darius verbally arguing with the black horse like he was yelling at another human.

"I mean it! You can't be here! You know you can't be here!"

"Darius?"

"Ariomardus?! You're awake! You're alive!"

"Where is she?"

"The queen is fine. She's probably well back into her camp right now. She's not hurt."

"My neck is *killing* me!"

"You got shot with a flaming arrow."

"Of course, I did. How bad is it?"

"You lost a lot of blood."

"Is that my blood all over you?"

"Mostly."

"And she's alright? Tomyris is alright?"

"She jumped through fire for you."

"I didn't want her to do that. I told her we'd get through this."

"And you kept your word. She was upset seeing you hurt, but I promised to get you back here to camp for help. The Massagetae destroyed all of our bridges but she told me about a sandbar upriver."

"I knew we could trust her, Darius. She's a good woman."

"She surprised me. She called me a good man out there."

"You *are* a good man, Darius."

"No one's ever thought so before. And I don't believe it still."

"You worry too much about the wrong things in life and not enough about the right things. If Tomyris says you are a good man, believe it. She knows a bad man when she sees one. Her life has been full of them."

"What do you know of her life?"

"More than I'd like to admit. She married my older brother. After he died, I tried to figure out how I could be in her life, and I was too young to understand being there would have been enough. I wasn't a good man; I was just an angry boy. I had to *become* a good man. It took me a long time. I asked about her everywhere I went. She was doing so well without me, I couldn't imagine what it would be like to come back to her, and see her, hold her."

"And is it everything you wanted?"

"She is so much better than me, Darius. I feel like such a fool laying here all bloody. I hurt her."

"Is it nice, though?"

"*Nice*? No, Darius, hurting the woman I love isn't nice."

"You *love* her?!"

"I think I always have."

"You couldn't have picked a better woman. You *could have* picked a better time, but that's life for you. What I meant was…is it nice knowing you have a woman who cares about you?"

"It is. I don't think I've had that in a very long time. Not since my mother, have I ever had that feeling of unwavering support. I can't figure out why she does it. She has everything in life. What could she possibly want to do with me?"

"I wish I could tell you, but there's so much about life that I do not understand myself. This morning, just turned everything around for me. I could have never thought Tomyris could pull that off. We have so many men in our army. All she has is five hundred, and they are not at all impressive. A couple of whistles and lines of grease, and we're struggling to recover over here."

"She's smart, like an *eagle*. Always has been. She is used to taking nothing and turning it into everything. I tried to tell Cyrus this, but he didn't want to listen."

"Perhaps you can try to tell him again? He's on his way over."

"Should I pretend to be unconscious?"

"No. It wouldn't do you any good. He likes you too much."

"Why?"

"Yet another question I can't answer. Well, I'll leave you two to it. I need to go and speak with my wife. I'm sure Atossa is not short on ideas after this defeat. I really am happy you woke up, Ariomardus."

"I'm happy to be awake, sort of. Thank you, Darius."

"I'll come and check on you in a little bit. Hello, Cyrus."

"My daughter is waiting for you in your tent, Darius."

"I'm going to speak with her right now. Ariomardus has just woken up, so be patient with him."

"A drink, Ariomardus? To celebrate your health."

"No, thank you, Cyrus. Saka don't drink wine."

"Ah, that's right. Should I get some milk for you then?"

"No, actually milk makes me sick."

"You must drink something. The healers said you lost a lot of blood. I need you healthy."

"Water is fine."

"Alright then. I'll have some sent over. How are you feeling?"

"I've felt better, but I will be out of this cot by nightfall. I promise."

"I like to hear that."

"It was good for me to be out fighting. An officer's life has never matched me. Getting my hands dirty feels much more…*right*."

"I think you will find that being an officer has its perks. Especially when you are an officer in *my* army. I was very worried when I was told that you had been cut down, and that *little queen* had you."

"Tomyris wouldn't hurt me."

"I have been told death is a rare mercy for their kind."

"Saka don't take hostages, if that's what you're getting at. They just prefer to be left alone. They're a simple, content people for the most part. Even when they do fight amongst themselves, it is nothing on the scale at which you fight, Cyrus."

"I can't tell if you mean to flatter or insult me, Ariomardus."

"I'm just stating the truth that I know. You have been killing and taking the Saka people for years now. You are a smart man, you know how to win battles, but this is different. Tomyris is different than any man you have fought against. She's a very smart, woman."

"She's still *just* a woman."

"But she's not."

"You speak very kindly about our enemy."

"She is not *our* enemy."

"You have lost a lot of blood. We will speak later."

"I want to be reassigned."

"What?!"

"I don't want to be an officer and Cambysses' personal guard."

"Then what *do* you want?"

"I just want to be a soldier, no rank, no attention."

"I'm sorry. But I can't do that. You're my best chance at winning this war and killing that *little queen*. And she *will* die, Ariomardus."

Cyrus peered down at Ariomardus lying in his cot. The old man sapped every bit of strength he had to squeeze the injured officer's hand, and make sure he understood what was being said right now. There would be no Persian defeat. One battle did not define the war. This was a setback, an embarrassment, but not a defeat. Cyrus was a great man, not a loser. He was a king of kings, a unitor of people and lands. Ariomardus was nothing but a pawn in the grand scheme of things, to be used when necessary and discarded just as quickly. Any changing allegiances would not be tolerated of acknowledged. Ariomardus showed no twinge of pain or fear on his face. A shallow threat from Cyrus was nothing compared to the crushing guilt he was already feeling for getting injured and having scared Tomyris. That was the last thing he wanted. This would shake her trust in him and his words, and if they didn't have trust, they didn't have anything. Then there was this searing, burning pain in his neck. He reached up and felt his shoulder and cot saturated in his own blood, and sighed. Beside him his black buck neighed in concern. It was amusing. This horse who would not be tamed now showed interest in his well-being. The black buck nudged Ariomardus' side for attention and pets. The Dahae soldier sat up and tried to get his strength about him. Across the river men were still hauling the injured and dying soldiers. Horses were scattered across the sands. Smoke was heavy in the air. The smell of hot flesh was sweet and stuck in his nose no matter how hard he tried to avoid it. Cyrus had left a cup of wine by Ariomardus' side, but he would not drink it or accept the kind gesture. Instead, he picked up the ornate vessel and chucked it towards the river, which only reopened the wound on his neck and a fresh round of blood to come dripping through his bandages. He laid back down and cursed himself, staring up at the shifting gray clouds above him. He was not in the burning grounds of his people right now, but he was in a land on fire, and the gods would surely hear him if he spoke to them now. He hadn't spoken to them in a long time, not since he was sixteen. He wondered if he should say anything now, if the god of the sun and fire would hear him, or care to listen. Mehr was not the most forgiving of gods. Tomyris spoke to him though, and he had blessed her with this victory this morning. Ariomardus smiled at that, and simply thanked the god for his swift judgement.

In the Massagetae camp there was no shortage of fears as the men raced back into their families to share the good news. No men had been lost. The worst casualty inflicted on their side was a young man who had twisted his ankle in the sands during the run out to the battlefield. Hardly worth mentioning, but Tomyris watched the boy all the same because he was in her son's detachment. Her riders had returned, the divers who had sabotaged the bridges weren't far behind. Runners came in to speak to Skunkha. News of a victory would surely build the Massagetae's numbers. The young queen watched her advisor closely. He was aware of her eyes on him too, and was very uncomfortable in his actions. Appearances and relations had to be kept up with the visiting chiefs. Tomyris and Skunkha made the rounds of handshakes and hugs. Many wives were eternally grateful for their husbands returns. As a widow, Tomyris more than understood. Spargapeithes enjoyed drinks in his honor with the other handful of officers. Fermented milk was flowing out of every sack, every pitcher, and every bowl. It was a lot of laughs, a lot of hollers, and a continuous round of cheers. Tomyris had a good mind to go and speak with Homarges on the outskirts of her camp and see what the old man and her father's advisor was up to, what his thoughts were, but she held herself back. She had exiled him because he couldn't be trusted. It had been her very first act as queen. She had survived this long without his interference. But she was also deadly curious about what he was here for. What he knew. He might have valuable insight. She didn't know, and it was the not knowing which killed her. Normally she'd speak with Skunkha about this, but because he was intimately involved, he was no source of comfort for her right now. She paced back and forth in her tent. She couldn't be out of the sight of the crowds for long. Her hands and tunic were still blood stained, a true sign of victory. The blood drips across the right side of her face were mostly smeared off from hours of running and riding in thick smoke. She sniffled, and smeared the ashen residue across her face further. The blood on her hands belonged to Ariomardus. She half expected to see Darius running for her camp at any minute, to tell her the bad news that he had died. He had to have died. The cut was too deep. Too much blood had been lost. Mid pace a shadow ran up to the back of her tent, and her heart dropped right out of her chest. Before she could even process how to be secretive about it, she just dropped to the ground to lift the hide tent in the back and saw a pair of dark-skinned hands crawling in. They belonged to the short and stout officer, Darius. He could see the young queen was visibly holding her breath, hands clawing at her heart and throat.

"He's alive."

"He lives?! He's awake?! He's alive?!"

"The first thing he did was ask about you."

"I'm fine. I'm fine. If he's fine, I'm fine. How is he?"

"He told me he'd be out of the cot by nightfall."

"That's good. That's good. Did you have any trouble getting across the river? Did you find the sandbar I told you about?"

"Yes, thank you for that. We've lost a couple hundred to the Araxes already and we haven't even done a final head count yet."

"I'm sorry. It didn't have to be this way."

"Cyrus wants it this way, and the old man always gets what he wants. Right now, he wants *you*…dead."

"I know."

"But that's not what everyone wants back in the camp."

"What do you mean?"

"Ariomardus has been speaking for days with the men. Many of the Saka conscripts are still fiercely loyal to you. I heard them today, seeing their friends wounded, it makes a man rethink some things."

"What sort of things?"

"What leader they fight for. I wouldn't be surprised if you don't start getting some stragglers creeping into your camp in the next few days. There're hundreds of men who don't want to fight for Cyrus. I even overheard one man rambling about how he was going to switch sides on the battlefield, but a fight never got underway. You set the fires off before any blood could be drawn."

"It was my plan all along. I don't want this war, Darius."

"I know you don't."

"But I'm not about to lose it either."

"You must know the odds don't favor you."

"I'm not stupid. I can count too. I underestimated just what it looks like to see ten thousand men all lined up in shining armor waiting to kill me though."

"I'd safely say over half don't want to see you die."

"But over half *will* follow orders to avoid being killed themselves. I don't hold it against the Saka in your army. I may be the leader they follow in their hearts, but ten thousand against five hundred, I know what I'm trying to do doesn't make any sense. But sometimes, you have to go through with it anyways. I will never bow down to Cyrus, Darius. I hope you're not trying to negotiate a ceasefire with me."

"I merely came as a friend."

"We are friends?"

"I respect you. I hope you can find it in your heart to respect me as well. Ariomardus is my friend. I admire that man, and I know you do too. In war, we must keep our friends close."

"And our enemies closer. Tell Ariomardus I look forward to seeing him soon. I don't know what I would've done if I had lost him."

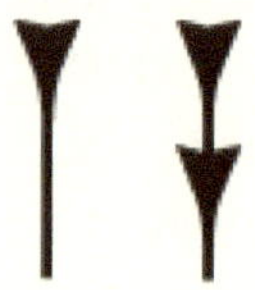

An early winter thunderstorm put an end to the fires in the red sands. For the Massagetae though, this weather was a sign of approval from the gods Mehr and Anahita. The balance of fire and water, sun and moon, man and woman had been maintained today. In honor of the small opening victory, a feast was being held in Tomyris' honor for her strategic thinking. Goats had been sacrificed, and were now roasting on spits in covered camps. It smelled amazing, and there was no shortage of cheer despite the muddied conditions. Nothing could dampen the united Saka spirit. In small groups of four or five, deserters from the Persian army had slowly made their way across the ashen battlefield. They were soaking from the Araxes River, and the rain. Since Darius had suggested to Tomyris that men might be coming her way, Skunkha was posted on watch with Spargapeithes holding double the scouting patrols to make sure no dirty work was at play. So far, it had been nothing but family reunions. Sons and cousins were returning to their people. Tomyris was praised a military genius which she would not credit for. In fact, the attention became somewhat somewhat suffocating that she had to excuse herself, and slip out of the camp to be one with the thunderstorm and the darkness. It felt to be cold. It calmed her nerves and settled her racing thoughts. The rain wasn't a violent torrent, more of an annoying, yet constant mist. The wind was cooperating, making the night bearable. Still, the young queen wrapped her arms around chest and perched herself on the edge of the burning grounds. It was black in front of her, black behind her. The dead laid quiet in the smoke which had once been, but no longer was. She cried. Unashamedly, unapologetically she cried. No one could see her or judge her here. She screamed to the gods, to her father for leaving her so young. She asked for help with Cyrus and his army, Homarges and his shady ambitions for returning, Spargapeithes and his choice of wife. She begged for the safety of her people, even at the expense of her own life. She wanted Ariomardus to be safe, whatever that might mean. A whistle came behind her head. Instinctively she ducked, and the golden knife in her waistband was withdrawn. She rolled forward in the sands, falling down into the burning grounds to discover a shadow off to her right. A dead man. A dead man with a knife in his back, a golden knife, matching the one in her own hand. Ariomardus' knife. She stood up to survey the sands. Another figure was encroaching slowly, hunched over, with an occasional moan. She opened her mouth to speak but the Dahae soldier beat her to it, and the young queen nearly tackled the poor man out of sheer joy. Thanks to the rain, he couldn't tell she had just been pouring her heart out.

"Ariomardus!"

"Ah! Careful with the hugging, my neck…"

"Oh no! I'm so sorry! How are you? Why are you here?"

"I followed that man all the way from camp. Cyrus paid him this afternoon. I just had a bad feeling about him."

"You killed him for me?"

"He was paid to kill you. I couldn't let that happen."

"You killed a man for me."

"I'd kill an army for you."

"That's crazy."

"You jumped through fire for me this morning, ran across enemy lines. You could have been killed. You *would have* been, if anyone aside from Darius came for me."

"Can we trust him?"

"I don't know, but aside from Cambysses, he's the only Persian worth his weight in gold over there. It's a rotten lot across the river."

"You should still be over there. You need to heal, Ari."

"Ha!"

"What? You need to take your injury seriously. You could get sick and die if you don't keep it clean."

"I'm not dying on you. It's just, no one has called me *Ari* since I was a little boy."

"Oh. I'm sorry. It just sort of slipped out. It's been a long couple of days for me."

"Don't apologize. I like you calling me Ari."

"You do?"

"And I like that you said *we* earlier. Like we're a team, you and I."

"I mean, you killed for me. I owe you."

"You're a queen. I'm no one. And queens don't owe *any*one *any*thing, not ever, least of all you."

"I owe you. You gave me information about Cyrus. You allowed me to be prepared, sabotage the sands, set up the bridges. This victory today is yours."

"And since when are victories celebrated alone in the rain at the edge of the burning grounds?"

"I'm not alone now that you're here."

"But why here? Were you speaking to the gods?"

"Yes. Shouting really. Not my proudest moment."

"And what did the gods say in response? This thunderstorm is quite vocal. They must have a lot to tell you."

"They said we're fucked."

"Oh, good."

"*Good*?"

"I was worried they were going to give us bad news."

"Are you trying to be funny right now?"

"Humor helps mask the pain."

"Are you really hurting that bad?"

"I've been better."

"Come back to camp with me. Those damn Persian healers wouldn't help a Saka man if their life depended on it. Fucking politics. I need to get you in front of a fire, dry off these wet clothes…"

"If you wanted to take me back to your tent so bad you could have just asked. I'd have gone willingly. No need to start a war for me."

"You really did lose a lot of blood, didn't you?"

"Is that what's all over you? *Me*?"

"I saw you fall. There was no way I could get to you fast enough to catch you before you hit the ground, but…I tried."

"What were you doing watching me in the middle of a battle?"

"Worrying. It's what women are best at, right?"

"Your lips are shaking."

"You said we weren't going to die today, but you almost did. I've lost a lot in my life, and most of it didn't hurt me. I don't remember my mother. Soldiers come and go. Alliances shift. Horses get injured. I can protect my son from just about anything. But you…you are your own man. I have no control over that. I know I shouldn't care, but I can't help it. I *hate* that I can't help it. Since I've been sixteen, I've been so used to being in control and handling things. This is all very new for me. And I don't expect you to understand or…"

"I *do* understand, Tomy."

"You do?"

"We have an odd way of crossing paths, you and I. Sometimes, I can't help but wonder if the gods don't have something to do with it. We were meant to come and go in each other's lives, and now I think we're meant to stay."

"You speak for the gods now?"

"Maybe."

"Well, there's a feast in my honor waiting back at camp. My sabotage would have been nothing without yours. You deserve a full belly tonight as much as anyone. Will you come back with me?"

"I don't know if I should. Besides, I'm not really that hungry."

"Liar. I saw the way your eyes lit up when I said, *feast*."

"My eyes didn't light up. Eyes don't do that."

"They do light up, and they did. I would know. I know all about your eyes. They're your brother's eyes, my son's eyes."

"What would your son and officers think, dragging me back into camp with you?"

"They would think you a good man for being loyal to your blood and not a sack full of coins in your hands."

"Your advisor hates me. He doesn't trust me."

"Skunkha has no leg to stand on right now. His father has come back to the camp, and he didn't tell me."

"Homarges is back?!"

"After I exiled him."

"I thought he'd be dead by now."

"I *hoped* he'd be dead by now. I almost went and spoke to him tonight, but I couldn't get myself do it."

"Good."

"You think it's right of me to keep pretending he's not just hanging on the outskirts of my camp, judging my every move?"

"He's no right to judge anything you do. And you are queen. You do not go to him. If he was any kind of man, he would come to you. Skunkha should have come to you at the very least."

"Skunkha's my best friend. I don't know why he didn't tell me. He has never liked his father, not as long as I can remember."

"He's your best friend?"

"He's helped me rule the Massagetae and raise my son."

"You know why Skunkha hates me, don't you?"

"I do not. And right now, I don't care to know. It wouldn't change anything. I can't keep living in the past when my future is about ready to be ripped right out my own two hands."

"No one is taking anything from you. Not as long as I'm here."

"Don't go making promises to me like that. You can't keep your word in war, no matter how good a man you are. I'm wearing your blood. You were limp in my arms just this morning."

"But I am alive in your arms tonight. Doesn't that count for something too?"

"You don't know how scared I was when Darius rode off with you."

"I'm sorry. I never wanted you to see me like that."

"But it happened all the same. That's what I'm trying to say. Just come back to camp with me tonight. We have tonight. Let's just enjoy what we have while we have it."

"Someone will notice that I am missing if I stay out all night."

"Wouldn't Darius cover for you?"

"I'd like to say yes, but I don't know for sure."

"Well, give him the opportunity to prove himself."

"So, this means we trust him now?"

"Yes. And I like the sound of you saying *we*."

Ariomardus was blushing, and pulled Tomyris into his chest to help maintain some of his dignity. She was quick to wrap her arms around him and squeeze him tight. He'd never been hugged like that before, like she was afraid to let go. She was afraid to lose him. He mattered to her. He hadn't mattered in a long time. Ariomardus kissed the young queen on the top of her head, and laughed at how soaking wet she was. She'd been sitting in the thunderstorm far longer than she was letting on, then again, so had he. The Persian soldier he had killed had been stalking her for better part of an hour after she left her camp. She hadn't gone straight to the burning grounds, but trekked down in the valleys of the dunes for more alone time. He was dying to know everything that was swirling around in that pretty head of hers, but now was not the time to go digging. She was right, it had been a long couple of days, and his neck was still burning like it was on fire despite the chill in the air. Back in her tent she had a poultice for his wound that only the Saka knew how to make, and it was a miracle cure for all sorts of ailments. Ariomardus was looking forward to that, and a warm fire he wouldn't have to sit at alone. He was also looking forward to being back with his people, his politics, and way of life. The Persians were so elaborate, so structured, and hierarchical. Everyone was trying to climb a social ladder, better themselves while turning on others. Saka could be like that too, but it was fewer and farther between. The Massagetae tribe especially, under Tomyris' guidance, had done away with much of that. They were equals for the most part, where even queens listened to women with no power whatsoever, and took it to heart. Tomyris was proud to walk Ariomardus back to her camp, and slip into the feast like they had both been there the entire time. They were given good cuts, full cups, and happy cheers. Ariomardus got heavy pats on the back for coming into camp, and was flooded with questions on how ridiculous the Persians were. Tomyris couldn't help but stare as her people accepted him with open arms, like it was second nature. He was Saka blood, the best Dahae soldier, but he had been gone for years. He wasn't gone anymore though. He was here, when it mattered. With any luck, he'd stay too. Tomyris wanted to believe what he said to her out at the burning grounds about the gods crossing their paths on purpose. She wouldn't dare question the gods. But Skunkha would, and he did as he tugged on his friend.

"What's Ariomardus doing here, Tomyris?"

"Calm, Skunkha. This victory feast is as much his as it is mine. *He* was the one who told me Cyrus had completed the bridges. None of your scouts told me."

"My scouts didn't go down to the river. That was your son's assignment. If you want to be angry, be angry with Sparga."

"I will speak with him later, once everything settles down. His mind is elsewhere at the moment. He seemed very concerned about Cyrus' daughter Atossa this morning."

"Why would he be concerned about her?"

"He's a prince. She's a princess. He begged me for months to host his wedding games, then on the day of, he changes his mind. He hasn't told you anything, has he?"

"No. Why would he?"

"You're as close to a father as he's ever known. A boy isn't going to come to his mother when it comes to girls."

"Do you want me to speak to him about it?"

"Don't make it obvious, and don't make it sound like I had anything to do with it, but I would appreciate you trying to find out whatever you can. I feel like I'm losing him as he gets older. I don't like it."

"You aren't losing him, Tomyris. He's just trying to prove himself. Remember what we were like at his age?"

"I do remember, that's why I'm so nervous. I got married, got pregnant, lost my father, lost my husband, inherited a tribe and exiled your father all in the span of three days."

"But you got through it."

"Only because I had *you* next to me."

"That's always where I'm going to be too."

"You're my very best friend, Skunkha. You know that, don't you?"

"I want to know that."

"But?"

"But you've gotten very close to Ariomardus, very fast. I just don't know where I fit into all of that. I see the way you look at him."

"And how do I look at him?"

"Like you love him."

"Is that wrong?"

"Do you feel it's wrong?"

"No."

"Then it's not wrong."

"You're my best friend. You're my advisor. You'd tell me if trusting Ariomardus was a mistake, wouldn't you?"

"I don't like him. His family and my family will *never* get along. I'll *always* keep my eye on him, but I'll *always* look out for you first."

"Thank you, Skunkha."

"Thank *you*, Tomyris."

"What are you thanking *me* for?"

"Putting Cyrus in his place this morning. I'll *never* forget that!"

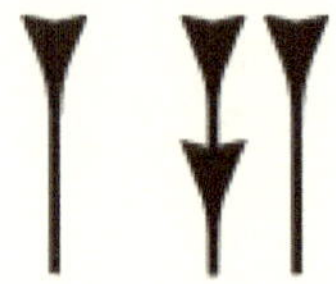

It was going to take days for the Persians to recover from Tomyris' humiliating sabotage. Pieces of the bridge and bodies had to be recovered from downriver. Not everything was salvageable but it didn't matter. Cyrus was not deterred. If anything, his hate was only renewed, and Tomyris knew the next time their armies met in the sands, it would be a very difficult day. She got lucky the first time around. She needed that win; however slight it might have been. It was already bringing in more soldiers her way. It was bittersweet to see these reunions. Long lost relatives were trekking in from the north. Some of the men weren't even Saka, but paler from the snow-covered lands. The Pazyryck were still horse people, but they wore furs and had tattoos of great beasts foreign to the sands on their arms and chests. Tomyris was a kind host, stern in decision and firm in her strategy. She had respect for the wisdom she carried of ruling for sixteen years. Some men don't even rule at all until they are old and gray, yet here she was in the war council meetings, able to answer every question with calm clarity and specific details. She had the numbers from Ariomardus, the caution from Darius. Skunkha had the parameters of the sands down to a fine art with the mapping of the dunes all drawn out on hides draped across the tables. Together, they had alliances secured. All the officers and smaller chiefs seemed to be getting along. There were a few light hearted jeers spun towards Spargapeithes' age and rank, but

Tomyris did her best to keep her son oblivious to what old men thought was amusing. The teenager was out on scouting missions three times a day at least, keeping the camp protected, and also keeping an eye on the Persians keeping an eye on them. The observation towers were like scars on the landscapes, large, unsightly, and in bad need of removal.

As much as the Persians wanted to keep a close watch on everything happening in the red sands, there was only so much surveillance that could be helpful. Posting one man in each tower led to blind spots. The soldiers kept falling asleep up there, and people were going missing. Not only was Tomyris welcoming men back to her side of things, but Prince Cambysses was also lost. Darius had covered for Ariomardus spending the night with the Massagetae by saying both he and the Dahae soldier were with the healers trying to help the wounded. While noble, that also left the prince unattended. Come morning, Cyrus needed to speak with his son, and there was no one to yell at. Atossa had made the honest mistake of walking into her father's tent while he was mid tirade. Rugs, beds, and pots were all being thrown about. The servants had been smart and fled. The princess came in searching for her brother to take their father's wrath like usual, but with Cambysses gone, Atossa got the fury instead. A strong slap to the face had her stumbling to the ground on all fours in disbelief. She hadn't been hit by years, and even then, it had been a tutor when she was twelve. In hindsight, she deserved the hit as a girl, but she didn't deserve it today. Cyrus killed the man for touching his daughter in such a way. There would be no such punishment this morning. Cyrus didn't even apologize. He was still angry, and quickly becoming winded, cursing in a language of the forgotten that Atossa had never been taught. She did pick out her mother's name in the confusion though and she crawled out the tent flap to sit and collect herself. She felt everyone staring at her as they passed by. No one would dare help her for fear of retaliation. Cyrus was a violent man. That was not news. Cambysses was always walking around favoring his head one way or another to hide black eyes and bruises. Servants hated working for the old leader. They often became maimed or scarred for life. Atossa started to cry on the entry rug. She didn't want to be so outwardly weak, but she had always been her father's favorite, and now she felt lower than an animal. She couldn't speak to the harem about this. The wives were either blindly adoring of every decision Cyrus made, or too scared to say anything even remotely against the man. The officer's wives were equally as useless. They so delicately depended on their husband's livelihood that they had to be obedient to a fault. A servant basically. She was a princess. She needed a genuine friend right now, a source of comfort and understanding. Her face was hot with embarrassment. She felt like her father's hand would leave a permanent mark on her dark-skinned cheek, shouting out to the world that she was no special. She was not important. And she never had been. She never would be. Destined to live her life in the shadow of a man. Atossa screamed in anger, and got back up onto her feet. She dusted off the infernal red sand from her skirts and marched to the nearest horse she could find. She stole an officer's horse who was with the healers and in no need of the animal. Or at least, that's what the servant had told her. Darius overheard his young wife's voice while he was sitting with Ariomardus amongst the wounded, and had to excuse himself in a hurry to go an investigate. Darius seemed more fond of keeping up appearances of a working marriage than Atossa did. While he knew she was visibly upset it just made him uncomfortable because he didn't know how to go about fixing it. He took the reins of her horse out to Ariomardus' tent on the outside of the camp overlooking the river for some privacy. The princess was adamant about staying on the horse for the duration of what would be a terse conversation.

"What's got you so worked up now, Atossa?"

"It's nothing, Darius. My father is just upset because that good for nothing brother of mine is missing again."

"Cambysses is gone?!"

"You're his guard, shouldn't *you* know that?!"

"I'm not his guard anymore, that's Ariomardus' assignment."

"But he's injured. That means it's *your* assignment again."

"It's not my responsibility to keep your brother from doing every stupid little thing that pops into his head, alright? He's a grown man, four years older than you or I. One of these days he should start acting like it!"

"Don't yell at me!"

"*You're* yelling at *me*!"

"He hit me!"

"Cambysses?"

"No! Not my *brother*. He's missing! Don't you listen?!"

"Who hit you? I'll kill them."

"You'll kill my *father*, Darius?"

"Cyrus *hit* you?"

"He's never so much as raised a hand to me before."

"You're his favorite. I don't understand."

"It's that damned Tomyris that's unsettled him. We should have been in and out of this desert already. Why can't she just die?"

"You've met the woman. Does she strike you as an easy kill?"

"I *hate* strong women."

"*You're* a strong woman."

"I hate myself sometimes."

"What's wrong? You're not speaking like yourself."

"What do you even know of what I am like, Darius?"

"You're my wife."

"And you're my husband. But I don't know the first thing about you. That was our arrangement. We help each other rise to the top. It's nothing personal."

"Do you ever wonder sometimes what it might be like if the marriage were real?"

"No."

"You said that so fast."

"Darius, you're an ambitious man. You have great ideas for the Persian empire. You want that power. I do too. It will fall into my hands one day, but as a woman, I need a man beside me who wants the same things. We want the same things you and I. We want the same power. We want Persia to be remembered through the ages. And we will live that life. We will make it so. It's just a matter of getting there. That's where we are right now. The struggle today makes it all worth it in the years to come."

"Is that all then? Power and glory?"

"We agreed on that. Has this war got you thinking something else?"

"I've spent a lot of time with the wounded lately."

"Why?"

"I don't know. I usually don't care about them. They're useless strategically speaking, but this time is different. The men, they talk about their wives and children a lot. The women come in on their knees, crying and kissing the pain away. It just made me wonder, what *you* might do if *I* was one of the men sitting in the sand, bleeding out on the battlefield. And I knew the answer right away.

You would not run for me. You would not cry, or even shed a tear. It would be a minor inconvenience to your day, but that is all.”

“What are you trying to say, Darius? I am not a good wife to you?”

“You would not jump through fire for me, Atossa.”

“What kind of crazy person would jump through fire?”

“Forget I said anything. The death in camp has made me weak of mind. Forgive me, princess.”

“You are forgiven. Just don’t do this again. Sympathy is not a good color on you, Darius.”

“I will continue to honor our arrangement according to the terms we agreed upon. I just hope that one day, you *do* find that man that you would jump through fire for.”

“It *could* be you.”

“But it won’t be, will it?”

“You never know what the future will hold.”

“You’re running to him right now, aren’t you?”

“Running to who?”

“You are upset. Your father hit you. Your brother is missing. You were running out of camp and you never even would have spoken a word to me had I not pulled you aside myself. You are running to the man you would jump through fire for.”

“I wouldn’t jump through fire for him.”

“Does he know that?”

"No."

"You're using him for comfort like you use me for power. Atossa, is there any man you would not use for your own benefit?"

"A woman must look out for herself in life."

"Ha!"

"What? What's so funny? You're not a woman. How could you *possibly* understand?"

"I may not be a woman myself, but I have seen other women, women in power. And they are nothing like you."

"Other women in power, you mean that Massagetae Queen? Don't you *dare* compare me to her!"

"I wasn't comparing. Comparisons require similarities. And you, dear wife, are the one coming up short."

"You *insult* me, and think you could be a source of *comfort* to me? You, Darius, *you* are the reason why you will die alone, with no woman running to you to kiss your pain away."

"I accept my faults, Atossa. Maybe one day you will be able to accept yours as well."

"I'm a princess. I don't have faults."

"Everyone has faults. Maybe princesses most of all?"

"Are you quite done?"

"There's a sandbar upriver. It'll help you cross easier. The current is gentler. Try to not be gone too long. I'll avoid your father until you're back. Be careful not to cross the Massagetae scouts. Tomyris has them out three times a day now."

"Thank you. But why are you helping me leave?"

"You're my wife. Why wouldn't I help you?"

"We *will* make this work, Darius."

"I know we will. Neither of us know how to lose, right?"

"Something like that. I'll be back in a little while. Do try and look for my brother while I'm gone."

"I hope I find him floating in the river at this point!"

"Ask Ariomardus to help you. He seems to have an unusual talent at finding people."

"He does, doesn't he?"

"Perhaps that queen you all admire so much has an idea where Cambysses is?"

"We don't *all* admire her."

"Our army has decreased in size. The missing men aren't missing. We both know it. You have your way about getting answers and I have mine."

"I know all about the way you get answers, Atossa. I haven't forgotten our night together in Ecbatana."

"Why would you bring that up now, Darius?"

"Why not bring it up? It was a very good night."

"For *you*. I was fourteen. I had no idea what I was doing."

"You did it well enough to keep me interested."

"Do you enjoy provoking me?!"

"Every chance I get. Go on now. Get your answers. Meet your mystery man. Enjoy him while you can, dear wife."

"What's that supposed to mean? What are you going to do?"

"I can't do anything…right now. I don't even know who this man is. But I will figure out soon enough."

"Don't hurt him! He's important. It would only cause problems."

"Wonderful! I *love* causing problems!"

"What is all this about? Lover's quarrel?"

"Hello, Ariomardus. My husband is in a bad mood again."

"How can you tell?!"

"You two need to find my brother."

"And what do we tell Cyrus in the meantime, princess?"

"I don't know. Not my problem. If you'll excuse me, I need to go."

"Darius? Do I even want to know?"

"No, Ariomardus. *I* don't even want to know. But we do need to tell Cyrus something to get him to calm down and give us time to find that useless son of his."

"He probably ran back to the Massagetae again."

"But we can't tell Cyrus that."

"Then tell him a horse and a goat are hunting a rabbit."

"My animal theory is serious. This isn't funny, Ariomardus."

"It's a little funny. Go on, get your armor and we'll ride around, see if we can't find Cambysses."

"I'm ready to ride now."

"No chest armor?"

"What's the point? An arrow can still slice my neck open."

"My wound hasn't even healed. Are *you* trying to be funny now?"

"It's a little funny."

Ariomardus pushed Darius, and the two wrestled about for a couple of minutes like brothers. Ariomardus pulled away first. His smile faded fast. The last time he'd done something like that was when he and his brother Sacephares were leaving home to ride for the Massagetae wedding games for Tomyris. Darius didn't understand the sudden change in his friend, and took it personally. The young lieutenant general was also still stuck in his head over the contentious situation with hie wife, and how they both had to accept the fact she was going to see another man right now. Darius wanted to kill her paramour out of jealousy. But it hurt, knowing Atossa would never be jealous over any woman he might become interested in. Ariomardus put a gentle hand on the young man's shoulder, the two nodded. Awkwardness abated. On horseback everything was simpler. The world moved different. Ariomardus was at peace, slowly drifting the searching circles closer and closer to Tomyris. The men crossed marks in the sand from Massagetae scouts, but Darius was more interested in tracking his wife. Atossa was nowhere in sight, lost between the valleys and crests of the red sand dunes. She wasn't lost though; she was perfectly found in the arms of young Spargapeithes. The two were sitting in the intimate shade of a single sagebrush. The plant was desperately clinging to the landscape almost as tight as the princess was clenching the prince's tunic in her fists, soaking his chest with her tears.

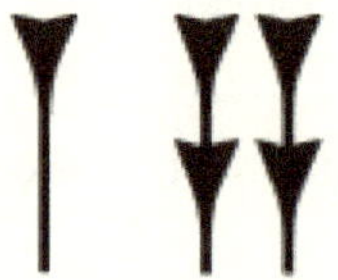

It had been five days since Tomyris upset Cyrus in battle. In that time roughly one hundred and fifty Saka conscripts had come back home to their fellow tribesmen in the young queen's camp. Another hundred had run in from the northern lands. Tomyris could boast some seven hundred and fifty soldiers now, all worth at least two to three Persians on average. But she had teenagers and grandfathers in her ranks. It wasn't a matter of heart, all the men's hearts were in this to the end, however long that might be, but they were getting anxious. The youth wanted first blood; the elderly wanted vengeance. She was doing her best to balance both requests while maintaining her steady heading. She hadn't spoken to Ariomardus or Darius for a few days. They had been near camp on scouting missions, or to collect the ever-wandering Cambysses, who did not seem well in the head as of late, but there had been no visits. Skunkha liked that, though the lack of developing information in the Persian camp made his queen uneasy. The reality of her sabotage was settling down hard on her shoulders. One trick with fire was well and grand, but she needed to follow that up with some promise. Some of the tattooed Pazyryck chiefs were getting restless coming all this way to sit in the sand and wait for orders. Respectfully, they would not act without Tomyris' approval, but she was also a woman, and a young one at that, unmarried. An alliance of this nature usually required stronger ties. Marriage had been heard around more than one campfire. Skunkha had heard it too but said nothing about it. He was still trying to deal with his traitorous father, and marriage proposals of his own. Wrongs to be righted, and the like. What Tomyris and Skunkha needed right now was a good sit down between friends, but the lines blurred so terribly anymore before duty and relationships. They were exhausted, in every sense of the word, and found humor where it ought not to be found. Spargapeithes had been trying to replicate a slight of hand trick his mother did with fire, swallowing it and forcing smoke out through his nose. Something had gone wrong with the milk he had drunken beforehand, and there were now burns all over his face. It wasn't too serious, no blisters. Tomyris did pull her son into her tent though for a closer look, and to apply a soothing poultice on the injury. Skunkha went and got fresh water to make the paste, and told the poor boy what he had done wrong, having seen Tomyris do this stunt for years. In fact, the two old friends had perfected it together since Skunkha was too scared to do it on his own. Spargapeithes was sat on the ground between his mother and her advisor while they reminisced of all their foolish childhood antics. It had been a few weeks since Spargapeithes could remember his mother laughing. Everything had been so serious since Cyrus arrived and put those observation towers up. Tomyris was studious in her attention to her son still, admiring his yet beardless face. She only saw her little boy as a toddler, even though he was going on seventeen and a general in war. Spargapeithes saw his mother's eyes glazing over and playfully pulled himself away, turning around so she could braid his long black hair. Normally other girls in camp would do this for officers, but for now, Tomyris would do. Skunkha sat back in his chair, a soft smile on his face.

"Tomyris, do you remember when you last braided your father's hair like this?"

"It was the hunt after my wedding."

"You were *so* angry he wouldn't let us go; I remember he swung back and hit me for laughing as you pulled on his head."

"You had a bloody lip for a week!"

"Ah, small price to pay, all things considered. I got off lucky."

"We both did. Had we gone on that hunt with the others…"

"You wouldn't have died. I'd have protected you."

"Everyone on that hunt should have wanted to protect me. But somehow, I know, you would have been the one to do it best, Skunkha. You're always looking out for me, and little Sparga here."

"I'm not *little*, mother! I'm a man!"

"Have you drawn blood in battle?"

"No. Only because *you* wouldn't let me."

"Have you married a woman?"

"No. Only because…no."

"Have you fathered a child?"

"No. But I *will*. I'll bear *many* sons and daughters one day."

"You mean your *wife* will. And you will be good to her. But you haven't done anything yet. You are a still a boy then. *My* boy."

"Yes, mother."

"Now go out in camp and see what the other officers have to say about Cyrus. I am interested what they say in my absence."

"About that…"

"Have you already heard something, Sparga?"

“When I was scouting the other day, I ran into Princess Atossa.”

“Oh! And why are Skunkha and I just hearing about this *now*?”

“You’ve been busy.”

“Nothing is more important to me than my son meeting with the rival princess. Speak, son.”

“She was very upset. Cyrus had hit her. She was arguing with her husband, that one guy, what’s his name?”

“Darius?”

“Yes. She and I were talking, and we wanted to set up a meeting between you guys.”

“Between who?”

“You and Skunkha, with Darius and Ariomardus.”

“Not Cyrus?”

“I don’t think Atossa thinks much of her father.”

“What about his heir? Cambysses?”

“I don’t think she thinks too highly of her brother either.”

“And did Atossa say when she thought this meeting would be a good time to take place?”

“That’s *kind of* why I came in here tonight.”

“Spargapeithes…for the love of the gods…don’t tell me you promised the princess I would go to a meeting *tonight*? You’re telling me *now*?!"

"I didn't want you to get angry!"

"Well, it's too late for that! Sparga, I have very important men here in camp waiting on my every word. I can't just…"

"Hold on now, Tomyris. This might be a good thing."

"What are you getting at, Skunkha?"

"This sounds somewhat important. Darius and Ariomardus might have information for us that we are in desperate need of."

"I thought you hated both of those men, Skunkha?"

"I do, with everything that I am. But I can swallow my pride for half an hour to get information that might help us win this war."

"Spargapeithes, what did your princess hope to accomplish with this meeting of hers?"

"*My* princess? She's married, mother."

"To Darius. It's a political alliance, son. Anyone with eyes can see that. There is no love there."

"That's right, Sparga. When two people love each other, everyone knows it. It's painfully obvious."

"So, does that mean you'll go meet them, mother?"

"I can't exactly not show up, now, can I? I'm outvoted. Son, go bring mine and Skunkha's horses around, will you?"

"I'm not coming with you guys? But, I'm a general."

"I already told you; you need to stay in camp. Listen to the men."

"Alright. If Atossa is there, will you tell her hello for me?"

"You really like her, don't you, son?"

"If it were possible for you to fix my wedding games and have her be my wife, I would be in debt to you for life."

"She's married. And Cyrus would never allow it."

"I know. But still. A man can hope, right?"

"A boy can hope. Men make things happen. Now go. Fetch the horses. I don't want to keep the men waiting. Skunkha…"

"You don't want to keep your Dahae soldier waiting, you mean?"

"Not now, Skunkha. This isn't the time to tease me. This is an official meeting. Where are my arrows and quiver?"

"I brought them to my tent to clean them after yesterday's hunting party. I'll go and get them. But what do you need arrows for? Neither of those men would lay a finger on you? Not a hostile finger."

"Atossa and Sparga went behind my back and Cyrus' back to do this. I don't trust the princess, Skunkha. I don't know her, but I know she is a powerful manipulator to pull this off. She acts in her own self interest and no one else's. To fool an old man is one thing, but she fools her husband and now my son. I have to pay attention tonight. You must help me read the men."

"What does that even mean?"

"You are my best friend. You know *exactly* what that means."

"No one in their right mind would ever lie to you, Tomyris."

"But I am still young in some ways. Perhaps, I let a pair of light eyes deceive me. It wouldn't be the first time."

"I'll be right by your side. Everything will be fine."

"I'm scared."

"What?"

"I've heard what the Pazyryck have been saying. They have been talking to my chiefs and officers. Swaying them."

"Tomyris, no. This is fear talking."

"Skunkha, I am no battle-scarred man. I am not my father. I am small. I am a woman. I am vulnerable in ways you are not. I…"

"You are smart, and you are clever. You kept every single one of your men alive versus a ten-thousand-man army that is getting smaller by the day. You are a queen. Don't you *dare* start doubting yourself. I will *not* allow it!"

"These men bled with my father, Skunkha. How can I possibly convince them to bleed with me, and trust me? They all say pretty words to my face, but the second I turn my back…my own son is making decisions without me. If Spargapeithes is doing such things, imagine what the other men could do."

"Your son made a mistake. He's young. I do believe like you, he is being used by Atossa and not smart enough to know. Don't hold that against him. He'll learn that lesson on his own. He's only sixteen."

"*Only* sixteen? What were you and I capable of at sixteen?"

"Do you want me to have a talk with him?"

"Yes. But later. We need to see how this meeting goes. Will you…"

"Will I what?"

"Will you try and be nice tonight?"

"For *you*…I'll try. But I make no promises."

Skunkha wanted to maintain a hard exterior, but Tomyris was genuinely unsettled right now and he could not help but want to help her though this. It was only a handful of times in their lives when she had admitted to him that she was scared, and each time she had every right to be. The advisor went over and wrapped his arms around the young queen. She settled into his chest, placing her forehead against his breastbone and sucking in deep breaths through clenched teeth. Skunkha ran his hands from around Tomyris' back, up to her shoulders and down her arms until he could unclench her fists with his hands. He was stronger than her after all. She squeezed him fingers in frustration, and he squeezed back, though he reserved most of his strength. This wasn't a contest, but a playful duel they did. He stepped back and her head fell, but she nodded, and muttered up something about the gods, but Skunkha couldn't make it out. Spargapeithes had returned with three horses, one for himself. Tomyris wasn't about to argue in front of her camp. All eyes were on her. She insisted she had to go look at something the scouts uncovered. A vague enough lie. She rode off on her white mare before any questions could be asked of her. Her son and advisor were close behind, flanking both of her sides. The Massagetae arrived late to the meeting. Atossa was already there on horseback, Darius and Ariomardus behind her. Spargapeithes was a nervous boy in front of his princess, but Atossa was a different woman than what he was used to seeing. She was presenting herself to his mother now, and no longer playing a damsel in distress. The pretty young woman's face was hard, and her jewels glistened in the moonlight. All the Persians glistened. Darius had his ax and sword ready for a fight. Ariomardus had a gold knife tucked into his belt. Spargapeithes recognized the knife, and looked at his mother. A matching golden knife. The teenage boy began to stare at Ariomardus with the hope the Dahae solider might look back at him, but no such luck. He was watching Skunkha. Tomyris' advisor was trying to pick a fight with Darius, shaky hand on his bow hanging around his back. Atossa scoffed. All the men were trying to turn this into a battle of their own. She was not interested.

"Queen Tomyris, it is a pleasure to finally have the chance to speak with you."

"If you don't mind, Princess Atossa, I will withhold my judgment on whether or not this meeting is a pleasure for me."

"You don't trust me, do you?"

"I know better than to trust a woman at face value. I know what we can get away with without a man knowing."

"I want to like you, Queen Tomyris. But my father insists that you and your people must submit to him."

"We've already been through this. I will not give my people and my lands to your father any faster that I will give him myself."

"Surely out of preservation, you would reconsider?"

"My people are willing to die to stay free of your father. As am I."

"My father is not a bad man, Queen Tomyris."

"Say that with confidence, and maybe next time, I'll believe you."

"Excuse me?"

"Your voice shakes when you speak to me. You are young. I understand. I was sixteen when I took over my tribe. You can't be much older than that now. You avoid eye contact. Your jaw is tight. Your face like stone. You don't trust either of the men behind you. Not really. You hate your father, but you want what he has. You think you can be better than him. You want to handle this on your own. Prove yourself. Prove to him you are a worthy adversary, a woman to pay attention to. But men will never pay attention to us as equals, Atossa. No matter what we do, no matter what victories we win. We will always be lesser. We will always have to fight twice as hard, be twice as smart, twice as clever, twice as cunning."

"You mean to lecture me, Queen Tomyris? You think you know me? I had a mother. I don't need your lessons."

"You *need* my lessons; you don't *want* them. There's a difference."

"I *want* this war to be over."

"Then tell your father to go home. Only death awaits him here."

"You mean to kill him?"

"Does that upset you?"

"I love my father."

"But he stands in your way. As does your brother. Both of which I notice are not hear speaking with me tonight, as they should be."

"I hoped we could come to some sort of agreement, as women."

"We agree that neither of us want you here. I will do everything in my power to see to it you go home soon, princess."

"You speak down to me."

"Queens rank above princesses. *You* are in *my* lands. I am your elder. I speak to teach you. It is important you understand your place. You're a smart woman, Atossa. Don't let your father's mistakes become yours. His goals in life are not yours. Be your own woman. Don't let the men in your life smack you around."

"What did you just say?"

"You heard me. Now go back to camp. We have a war to finish. Spargapeithes, Skunkha, let's go."

"We can't turn our back on them, Tomyris. Darius…"

"Skunkha! NO!"

"DARIUS!"

Skunkha had pulled his bow back, launching an arrow near Darius' face. The Persian was able to swerve and miss the attack, but in doing so had dropped from the saddle of his horse, and landed awkwardly on his back. The sands did little to cushion his fall. Ariomardus quickly jumped down from his black buck to run and grab Darius' horse before it charged away. Atossa was somewhat stunned and Tomyris wanted to believe it was just the shock of seeing her husband injured that caused this hesitancy to take action, but it was more than that. There was a brief moment where Atossa had a glint of a smile on her lips. Tomyris had seen it on wives before. Women who looked for an escape. The young queen didn't know anything about the nature of Atossa and Darius' marriage, but a princess and a top-ranking military officer was a smart, and advantageous political union. It might not have been anything more than that. When the princess attempted to cry, Tomyris knew there was no genuine emotion there, and asked her teenage son to escort the princess back across the desert towards her own camp. Skunkha was excused, and ordered back to the Massagetae with a coolness in her voice that Skunkha only very rarely ever heard towards himself. Tomyris also ordered he remove his quiver, and hand it over to her, that way any further attacks would have to be direct. Skunkha obeyed without protest, head down like a scolded child. As the meeting began to break apart and go their separate ways, Tomyris stepped down from her white mare, and handed the reins to Ariomardus so she could better examine the fallen Persian. Her hands were quick as they fell over all the problem points that she knew, bones and muscles. She held Darius' chin gently, and studied his dark eyes in the moonlight. The young man was moaning in pain, but she seemed satisfied enough with her survey.

"Darius, can you feel your hands?"

"Yes."

"Alright, that's good. How about your feet? Can you move them back and forth for me?"

"I think so."

"Can you lift your head?"

"No, not really. My neck is killing me."

"That fall knocked the wind out of you. I didn't see any broken bones. You might be sore, but you're going to be just fine. I'd like to take you back to camp to keep an eye on you. I have some things that will help with your pain."

"There are aids back at my camp. I don't want to cause any trouble with your people. I don't think they'd take too kindly to me."

"They won't even know you're there. I'll keep you in my tent. It's a much shorter walk to mine than yours. You're not fit to get back up on a horse right now. I can't carry you that far."

"You can't carry me at all. I'll be fine. I just need to wait here a few moments to regain my strength."

"The desert winds will cool you far below what is comfortable. Unless you want to freeze out here tonight, I need to get you back to my tent and in front of a fire."

"Cyrus will know that I am missing."

"I sent my son back with your wife. After speaking to her I know how good she is at lying. She will cover for you with her father."

"You don't know that."

"Yes, I do. Cyrus is the type of man who thinks a woman is only as important as the man she is with. Portraying *you* as weak portrays *her* as weak, and she won't give her father the satisfaction."

"How do you know so much about my wife? You're strangers."

"I was a princess once too, in the shadow of my father. She was lie for you out of benefit to herself. But it doesn't matter. You'll be back where you belong by the time the sun comes up."

"You sound so sure of yourself."

"I've fallen off my horse many a time. You don't get to know the tricks that I do without taking your fair share of injuries."

"Thank you, Tomyris."

"It's no problem."

"I just don't understand why you're helping me."

"I don't want this war, Darius. I never have. I know how hard it has been for the tribes around me. I know how many of my people will die trying to keep Cyrus away. If I could end this right here and now, I would. But I will not sell myself and my people so that way we might live. The Massagetae are nobody's prisoner, lease of all Cyrus the Great's. I don't think he's too great anyway."

"I owe you for your kindness and care, Tomyris."

"You owe me nothing but honesty."

"No, I mean it. Name your price."

"Should we be so unfortunate to come face to face in an upcoming battle, spare me and my son. I promise we will do the same."

"I owe your son no mercy."

"If you have *any* respect for me, Darius, you will spare my son and I will see to it he spares you as well."

"Those are your terms?"

"Those are my terms."

"Then I accept."

"You would make a far better king to the Persians than Cyrus."

"You don't even know me."

"I like what I *do* know. That is enough for me. Rulers are only people at the end of the day. We are not our titles. Titles come and go. They rest on anyone's shoulders, feed off of their minds until there's nothing left to feast on. First and foremost, we are people. We are flawed, and we are ambitious. We cry, we bleed, and we break. I think Cyrus has forgotten that. He thinks he is a title. He doesn't think he is human anymore. It is as offensive to me as it is to the gods. You are not like that. You are entirely human, Darius. My only wish is that you stay that way. Stay human, despite what your wife tries to do. Don't let her ambitious guide you. Be your own man, or she'll walk all over you."

"Atossa wouldn't…"

"Atossa already *is*. You two play a pretty game, but that's all it is, a game. I played it once, only very shortly. I hated it, and swore I'd never play again. Marry for love, or don't marry at all. I know not everyone can choose that for themselves, but I can, so I will."

"I *will* lead the Persians one day, and when I do, the Massagetae will remain safe and free for as long as you are alive."

"You shouldn't make such a promise to me like that. That is the pain talking. It's too good to be true."

"Not everything that is good can't be trusted, Tomyris. I am a man of my word. Just ask, Ariomardus. He'll agree with me, won't you?"

"I agree…that it is cold out here, and the queen's promise of a sit by the fire is too good to pass up by sitting out here making promises about the future none of us are in control of. We could all be dead by sunrise. You never know what could happen. We are not gods."

Tomyris looked up at Ariomardus who was avoiding her eye contact. He was a soldier through and through, no leader, no politician. He took orders well, but didn't like the responsibility of giving them. He would not get between the queen he admired, and the new friend he had acquired. Instead, he kept his head down, hands full of horses. Tomyris' white mare was struggling in his grip with the unwanted attention from his own black buck still in training. The young queen went over to remove the blanket saddle from her horse, and allowed herself to take the spool of rope from Ariomardus' horse, and craft a makeshift stretcher to carry Darius to her tent with. It was crude, but very useful and ingenious on such short notice. Together, Ariomardus and Tomyris were able to cradle the Persian officer onto the blanket, and walk him back to camp where Skunkha was successfully keeping all the chiefs and officers entertained with heroic tales of what had just happened. If you only knew the advisor's side of the story, this sounded like an epic one-man battle. It was not case, but no one needed to know that. Skunkha's credibility was only ever as strong as Tomyris' belief in her friend. Seeing as how she wasn't nodding her head in agreement beside him, the chiefs had a good laugh with him, and splashed their cups full of fermented milk together later into the night than they should have. Their inebriation allowed for the young queen to smuggle Darius into the back of her tent, which he was already familiar with, and get some much-needed aid for his aches and pains.

Tomyris drained a sack of dried herbs into a pot of boiling water. Ariomardus smirked at the old-fashioned remedy. The herbs were hard to come by anymore, but for a queen, he assumed, there would be some sort of exception.

"You laugh at me, Ari?"

"I just haven't seen anybody make this tea since my grandmother."

"Nothing works better for an aching body. The women in camp use it all the time. The men drink it too, only they think they're drinking something else."

"Clever."

"What a man doesn't know, can't hurt him."

"Sometimes it can."

"Is there something you need to tell me, Ari?"

"Cambysses is missing."

"Is that why the Persian scouts have been after my camp?"

"That's *one* of the reasons. Since the prince ran over here once before, there was reason to think he'd come to you for help again."

"I don't have him."

"I know you don't."

"But?"

"Not everyone in the Persian camp is so sure."

"You would speak well in my behalf, wouldn't you?"

"A good word can only go so far when Cyrus doesn't want to hear it. The king and the prince, well, you've seen it. They have a very troubled relationship. Darius and I, mainly me, are the prince's guard. If Cambysses goes missing…"

"*You* will suffer the consequences."

"Cyrus has a certain right to know where his heir is."

"I agree, but I don't have him."

"The red sands don't offer many hiding places."

"The Persian camp houses ten thousand soldiers, and a few hundred, if not thousand servants and aids."

"The Persian camp knows the threat is death if they harbor the prince without telling anyone. No one would keep Cambysses. They owe him no loyalty, nor does anyone else in camp. It's very unforgiving over there. No one looks out for each other."

"That's no way to live."

"You have such a different outlook on the world."

"I have to. Being different is the only thing that's kept me alive."

"I'm glad you're different. I wouldn't want you any other way."

"But?"

"Darius and I need to be back at camp in the morning, *with* Cambysses. Atossa can only lie so much. Cyrus has hit her once, there's no reason to think that it won't happen again."

"While I don't like the girl, I can't stand hearing she's abused. My scouts are already out three times a day. If Cambysses was near, I would know."

"Would you? I don't think he *wants* to be found."

"We *will* find him though, Ari. The man's not lost forever. He's not a foot soldier. He can't have gone far. How long as he been missing?"

"It's already been a couple days."

"You should have come to me sooner for help."

"I didn't want to have to come to you at all for help."

"Good to know I was your last option."

"I didn't mean it like that, Tomy."

"You need to rest. No one is finding anyone as tired and sore as you all are. Stay here, warm up, and help yourself to some tea."

"I don't need any tea."

"Please, Ari?"

"One cup, but save the rest for Darius. I won't drain you of your stores right before…"

"A war?"

"Cyrus will attack your people without mercy if he thinks you are holding his son hostage."

"But we're not holding him hostage? I don't hold hostages."

"The old man isn't about to listen to reason with his son gone."

"I'm going to go check on a few things. Will you promise me to stay here and keep an eye on Darius? Don't answer the tent for anyone. I'll be right back."

When Tomyris went to stand up, Ariomardus reached out and took hold of her hand. He wound their fingers together slowly, tightly, then brought up her hand to his lips and let them linger together in hold for a few seconds. His eyes were closed, dimples deep in his cheeks even though there wasn't even the remotest hint of a smile on his face. The young queen knelt down so she was eyeline with the Dahae soldier, and leaned forward so their foreheads touched. They breathed each other in, calmly, and let the golden flames crackles beside them. Darius had fallen asleep and was silent. Tomyris had to go, and Ariomardus reluctantly let her. She could see him musing over his own thoughts and troubles. They plagued him terribly, and he was only brave enough to let her know. She slipped out quietly to test the waters of her camp. In friendly conversation she prodded about the state of the war, and what her men thought of the Persians. She asked the women if they were worried. Her camp was prideful, maybe erring on the side of arrogance. No safe haven for Cambysses was here, she was sure of it. But the prince had to be somewhere, and he wasn't likely to be found wandering the sandy dunes all on his lonesome. Not in the right state of mind. But Cambysses wasn't in his right mind. He had been filled up with potent fermented milk of the highest order, and used for any secrets he might intentionally or unintentionally possess. Then he had been cast out, left to stumble in the red sands for who knows who to find. Tonight, it was Spargapeithes and Atossa, taking the long way around the dunes to find a distant sandbar in the Araxes River to say their sweet nothings to. Tomyris' son was holding Atossa in his arms, content with burying his smooth face in her perfumed black braids for all of eternity when a drunken shadow crossed the horizon. Atossa was frightened when the teenage pulled his sword and shouted commands. Cambysses answered incoherently in Persian. Atossa instantly knew it was her brother, and sighed.

"It's Cambysses. Lower your sword, Sparga. He's of no threat."

"You don't like your brother, do you?"

"No one likes him. That's why he runs away all the time. Spoiled."

"I could strike him down for you."

"You'd do that for me?"

"If it would make you happy."

"As much as I would like to be rid of that disgrace, it can't be done this way. But you are so sweet to offer. Something is wrong with him. Will you help me get him across the river? *Please*?"

The teenager was reluctant to cross the river. Doing so would put him in more danger than he had ever been in, and if his mother ever found out, she'd kill him with her own two hands. But Tomyris would never know. Spargapeithes reasoned with himself as Atossa was sucking the air out of his lungs with a long, passionate kiss. Her hands caressed his chest like a woman who knew what she was doing, and Spargapeithes had never been so close to a woman before. He let her do whatever she wanted to him, and when he was left gasping for air, looking down at her, he was sure he'd do anything for her. He'd die for her. Atossa was told to stay put and keep her horse hidden by the sagebrush at the river's edge while the rival prince rode up to his Persian counterpart lying face down in the sand. There was vomit beside him, and Spargapeithes nearly lost his dinner too, but was able to maintain composure knowing his woman was watching. Atossa couldn't have cared less, and she wasn't watching, but in the young general's mind, she was. Cambysses was unconscious, and covered in ruddy brown mongoose fur when Spargapeithes manhandled him up to lie across the back of his horse. He'd have to walk Cambysses across the river on foot, therefore soaking himself through with no proper explanation to give his mother when he returned home. Perhaps he would just miss her altogether. It was not entirely uncommon a practice, but it was since the war had begun. And after the night they had had Spargapeithes was nervous, but continued to help Atossa. Cambysses was dropped off in Ariomardus' tent to sleep off whatever had been done to him while Atossa attempted to convince Spargapeithes to come to bed with her, but he had to refuse. She liked him more because of that, and felt a twinge of guilt for using the boy. That was new for her.

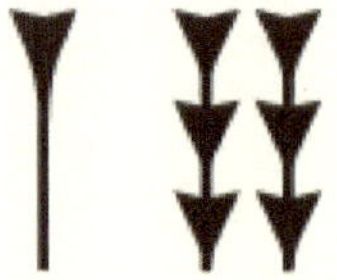

The whole of the Persian camp was in mourning today. No work was to be done; no scouting missions sent off. It was quiet, out of respect for the loss of Cyrus' most beloved wife Cassandae. Not only was she the mother to his children, but the only spouse he ever took seriously enough to actually love. She had been dead for eight years now after suffering a lengthy illness that had broken her husband. Cyrus had never been the same since, and every year since she passed it was like this. It was as if she had died all over again. The scab kept getting peeled off so it was to never heal. Atossa was barely a teenager when she had lost her mother, but she had been so sick for so long that the young princess didn't have the same love for her that her father did. The mourning day just made her painfully uncomfortable. Atossa usually spent hours with her brother Cambysses to pass the time between bouts of their father crying and screaming inside of his chambers. Today, it was a tent, and much less forgiving. This year, Cambysses was also missing, and Atossa didn't know what to do about that. Her lies had bought her time, but not a lot of it. Tomorrow Cyrus would be raging with a renewed hate, and the world needed to be ready. But right now, Atossa needed solace, and genuine concern. She had it in Spargapeithes, but couldn't bother the teenager again so close to last night. Her father's harem was being ridiculous, all primping themselves by the river's edge with perfumes and braids and fine silks. All of them wanted to be the next Cassandae, the next love, the next protected. None of them would be, but they tried nonetheless. Officer's wives help tie their clothes and hair, make tea and present offerings to the king of kings. It was humiliating to see the women so humbled. Atossa wanted no part of it, and crammed pillows over her ears to stop the singing. There were Persian songs mixed with Saka folk songs. None of them sounded like they were being performed with due diligence. Atossa was bitter, and knew her husband would appreciate her cynicism right now, but she didn't know if he was back yet. Carefully, the princess slipped out of her private tent beside her father's and back to where Darius was camped with the other officers. He was in fact back before sunrise as Tomyris had promised. His pain had receded since the fall the previous night but he was still in a sour mood. In an awkward effort to appear wifely, Atossa stoked a fire for her husband and the crackle of the golden flames startled him upright with a terrible headache.

"What are you doing, Atossa?"

"Checking to see how my husband is doing. Did the rival queen take good care of you last night?"

"My head hurts too much right now to tell if you are being serious or not. I didn't sleep with her, if that's what you want to know."

"I wouldn't care if you did. We don't owe each other that kind of intimacy. But I *would* like to know how you are feeling."

"I felt better last night. Whatever she gave me, it was good. I haven't slept that well since I got out to these red sands."

"Maybe we'll have to find out what she used."

"That won't happen. I can't imagine the two of you *ever* speaking to each other again. You disrespected her."

"She disrespected me first."

"She is a *queen*, and you are only a princess. We invaded *her* lands. She had the upper hand and you knew it. It was like listening to your father out there last night. None of those words were yours, and she knew it. This isn't her first conflict."

"You speak kinder words for *her* than *me*."

"Your behavior was disappointing last night. Did you…did you even *care* that I was injured?"

"I don't want you to die, Darius. You know that."

"No, I know you need me alive. It's all part of your grand plan to become Queen of Persia. You *need* me, but do you *want* me? Or could any officer with a high enough ranking be good enough to call you his wife?"

"You've never had so many protests to our arrangement before, Darius. What has gotten into you lately?"

"Even friends care for one another. Are we not friends, Atossa?"

"I'm sorry if my behavior last night upset you, but I can't go back and change what I did or what I said. I was under the understanding that when political rivals met like that, no harm was to be done to either side. The queen's advisor broke that understanding."

"You can be so naïve sometimes. We are in war. There is *never* going to be an understanding had when the threat of death is not lurking, if not glaringly obvious and present. We were all armed except for you."

"I noticed. Why does the queen and Ariomardus have matching gold knives?"

"I don't know. You'd have to ask them."

"But isn't Ariomardus your friend?"

"Yes, he is. That's why we respect one another. That's why he stayed with me last night, to make sure I didn't die in my sleep from the fall I had. That man cares more about me than you do and two months ago we were sworn enemies."

"You still might be enemies. He owes allegiances to that queen."

"He owes her nothing. He owes *us* nothing. He owes no one. He's very careful about those sorts of things. That is the beauty of keeping to one's self."

"Do you mean to upset me?"

"You were upset long before you got to me this morning. I know these mourning days always bother you. Everyone is crying and showing emotion you can't manage to show yourself. Cassandae was your own mother. Can't you at least *try* to put on a good show?"

"I knew coming in here and talking to you was a mistake. I'm going to go check on my brother and see how he's faring."

"Check on him?! Is Cambysses back?!"

"Yes. Sparga and I found him last night."

"*Sparga*? You mean Tomyris' son, *Spargapeithes*? You call him *Sparga* now?"

"He's shown me more kindness since I've come to this desert than you have shown me since I was fourteen."

"I know what kindness I showed you when you were fourteen. I remember it fondly. And if that little boy so much as *touches* you…"

"You'll what?"

"Atossa. You're using that boy, aren't you?"

"*Boy?*"

"He's *sixteen.*"

"He's a general. He has higher rank than you."

"He was given his position by his mother."

"Which makes him a prince. More worthy of a princess. Besides, I thought you trusted the queen's judgment?"

"He can't even grow a beard! He's still a child. He's never even killed a man."

"He said he'd kill for me."

"You slept with him, didn't you?"

"No. Not yet at least. But I will if I have to. He melts in my hands. You know what kind of power that is?"

"You're a horrible woman, you know that?"

"Tell me how horrible I am when I get you to be the King of Persia."

"Use who you want, Atossa, but leave Tomyris' son out of it."

"Why?"

"That's all the family Tomyris has. She loves that boy. If anything were to ever happen to him…"

"I don't want anything bad to happen to him."

"You'd jump through fire for him, wouldn't you?"

"I'm not having this talk with you again. I…"

"You would, wouldn't you? That boy, *he's* the one who's gotten to you, isn't it? The one you keep running off with."

"I don't run off with anyone."

"The queen knows."

"She does not!"

"That's why she sent you two off together last night. She knows."

"You're being ridiculous, Darius. I can't speak to you when you are like this."

"You're blushing! Why can't you look at me, Atossa? Why can't you just admit it? We're husband and wife, you and I. There shouldn't be any secrets between us."

"I don't tell *any*one my secrets, *least* of all my husband."

"That's fine. I know now. It's all fine. Have fun with your little general while you can. I don't have to worry about anything, not if Tomyris will be keeping an eye on things. You better hope you don't upset that boy, Atossa. I imagine the consequences would be…"

"Would be *what*? She wouldn't kill me. My father would tear this desert apart for me."

"Would he?"

"Of course, he would! I'm his favorite."

"Don't you think Tomyris would wage war for her son too?"

"Nothing bad is going to happen to Sparga. I won't hurt him."

"You already have. He has no idea what he's gotten himself into with you. Poor boy. I wish I could have warned him."

"*Warned* him! You really are the worst, Darius!"

"Then why did you come to me this morning on today of all days? You wanted comfort from your husband, but all I've been able to do is give you the truth. And we all know how much you hate that."

"My brother better be awake when I go check on him."

"Where even is he?"

"Sparga and I dumped him in Ariomardus' tent last night. But I don't know if he's still there. Wherever he is, I know he's somewhere disappointing the gods."

"Good old, Cambysses. I hate that man. What do you mean you had to *dump* him in Ariomardus' tent?"

"He was drunk on something, mumbling about the Massagetae."

"Mumbling about what, exactly?"

"I don't know. Names or something? Sparga said it didn't make any sense because the names were of dead men and exiles."

"That's interesting."

"No, it's not. He wreaked of sour milk and was covered in this ruddy brown fur. It got all over us too. Took me forever to get clean."

"Ruddy brown fur?"

"Yes! Do you want me to repeat every little thing I *said* and *did* last night after I left you?"

"No, spare me the details of you using that poor boy. I'm sure you did enough damage with your lips, not alone your hands. I know what you're capable of when you're desperate. Spargapeithes is a lucky boy. Go, check on your brother. I need to think."

Atossa wasn't used to be dismissed, but the way Darius had waved her off, it was clear she could make no final digs at her husband. She huffed as she left him, and walked angrily towards Ariomardus' tent on the outskirts of camp. She could hear her brother moaning inside. The Dahae solider was down in the river bathing. The princess was keen to take a quick observation and mocked her husband's voice when he had referred to Spargapeithes as a lucky boy. Tomyris was a lucky woman. Ariomardus was quite easy on the eyes with no clothes on. But Atossa couldn't think about that. She needed to check on her sorry excuse of a brother. When she bent down the entire tent had been fouled by vomit and excrement. Cambysses was not proud of himself as he rubbed his lazy eye hard enough to make it go straight again. This was what Atossa had been born after. This was supposed to be the heir of all of the Persian empire. A man who wandered around the desert like the village idiot and let who knows what happen to him. He should have died as a child and spared the world all this trouble. But death was heavy on her mind today and the princess tried to pull on any ounce of sisterly affection she might have held in her through her brief twenty years. She held her hand out, and Cambysses looked down at it as if he had never seen such a gesture before. Atossa's patience had never been noteworthy, and this morning was no exception. She snapped her fingers violently to get her brother to make up his mind about taking her hand or not. There wasn't really a choice. It was take her hand or get yelled at and then take her hand. The prince couldn't handle loud sounds right now, so he just placed his hand in his younger sister's and let her drag him out of the tent for some sun and fresh air. The wind was biting today, and absolutely frigid. She was wrapped in a blanket, staring out at the river. The corner of her vision could still hold a bathing Ariomardus in her sights. Cambysses could see him too, with battle scars to make a woman swoon, and muscles to make a man envious. The prince scoffed loudly, nearly vomited, and then groaned in agony. When a gust of wind blew past him, some of the ruddy brown fur from his clothing cam off and stuck to Atossa's indigo dyed blanket. She was thoroughly disgusted an began swatting at her older brother.

"Scoot over, will you?! Your filth is getting all over me!"

"If you just came to yell at me, why don't you just get it over with now and let me go back to sleep?"

"You don't even know what today is, do you?"

"What does it matter what day it is? We're still in this godforsaken desert. What else do I need to know?"

"It's mourning day for mother."

"All the more reason for me to go back to sleep."

"You're really unpleasant to be around, you know that?"

"Why do you think I keep running away?"

"One of these days father is going to understand how much better off we all are without you, and he'll let you *stay* gone."

"I hope those days are fast approaching."

"Don't you want to be King of Persia?"

"What man in his right mind would want that kind of pressure?"

"Men die all over the world trying to become king. Here you are with it promised to you and you don't even care. It's insulting."

"What about me *doesn't* insult you?"

"Right now, nothing. What even happened to you?"

"You know, that's the best thing about all of this. I don't know what happened to me."

"You don't remember *anything*?"

"I remember I was trying to make it to the Massagetae camp."

"And then?"

"Some dead looking man came out to me. Said he could help me."

"A dead looking man? And then what happened?"

"Then I remember being thrown onto the back of a horse and water sloshing up into my face. Now I'm here with you."

"You could have been killed."

"Would have been better than sitting here with you. You want me dead anyways, Atossa. You've poisoned me, hired men to kill me, locked me in trunks, burned me."

"That's what siblings do."

"No, it's not. I've never hurt you. I've never raised a hand to you or attacked you. I've never hired others to harm you."

"Why not?"

"What do you mean?"

"If I'm as terrible as you say, why don't you want to be rid of me?"

"We're family. We're supposed to look out for each other."

"You and I have never done that."

"*You've* never done that. *I* have. Why do you think you're father's favorite?"

"Because we share the same outlook. We're ambitious. Smart."

"It's because I've always taken the blame when you did something wrong. I always will. One of us needs to make father happy. Might as well be you. I'm not any good. Never have been. Never will be."

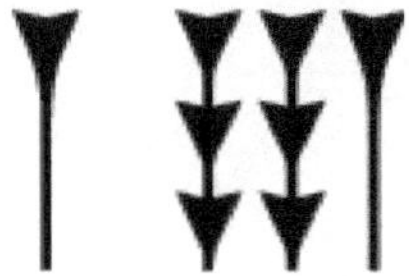

In the Massagetae camp the soldiers were bustling with activity. The officers were holding training sessions, running the men on horseback, shooting midrun, then teaching them how to fall and keep going. There were tactics on how to deflect a fatal blow, how to fight hand to hand if the weapons were lost or stripped, and how to commandeer another man's horse or cut his saddle and throw him off. The older men who had seen battle before bellowed from the crests of sand dunes down into the valleys, comparing techniques with other old men who had seen different battles. It was a great advantage to have so many different tribes of the Saka converge on this one point in the red sands. It wasn't only the Massagetae fighting here, it was everyone. There were men better with swords, others bow and arrows. There were men who threw axes, and flung daggers. In some cases, there were women willing to fight, and Tomyris took care to train them. Women fought different than men, not any better or worse, just different. They had some skill sets men didn't have. While biologically men could run faster, longer, and heave, women could manipulate and disarm. Tomyris' women were excellent horseman and archers, so she used their natural talents to help build up morale. Soldiers needed to stay back with the camp in case the Persians broke through lines or played dirty. The people couldn't be left defenseless. The young queen had a special unit of soldiers, mostly men, elected to stay behind for their brute strength. They could load horses and carts quickly if the need for evacuation arose. It was a very real possibility. Some tribal chiefs didn't like that Tomyris was holding a reserve in case she lost, but the Massagetae defended her at every turn. She had seen what happened when her father took all of the soldiers out of camp when she was a girl, and she was haunted by the screams the mothers and children made when the enemy rode in to have their way. Thankfully her father had chased them out before too much damage could be done, but that was still the day Tomyris learned the horrifying truth of rape with her own two eyes. She had only ever told Skunkha about that sight which darkened her thoughts. Usually she could put it away, bury it deep down inside of her, but the war brought it back up again. This time, that could be her struggling to fight underneath the heavy hands of an enemy soldier. Skunkha could see it was bothering his friend too, the way her stare went out into the distance mid conversation sometimes. The two were supposed sore with each other after last night, but they could never stay mad at each other for long. They were too entwined into each other's day-to-day activities. And Tomyris had made it that way for a reason. This afternoon while she let the women soldiers break for lunch, Skunkha came up to her to try and coax her out of the funk she had dropped into. She didn't want to talk, but she needed to, so she allowed herself to be walked to this tent on the outskirts of camp she had been avoiding for weeks. Homarges' tent. Tomyris rolled her eyes. She didn't want to go in, but Skunkha nearly manhandled her by the waist and carried her inside to see his ailing father. The young queen tried to maintain her authority, but Homarges had been like a second father to her. It was inevitable that she would revert to her teenage self, the last time she had seen him. She felt in her face as it snarled up. The old man could only chuckle.

"Take a seat, Tomyris, please."

"I'll remain standing, if you don't mind."

"That's fine. Your mother never cared much for the way I kept my tent either. You look so much like her as you get older."

"That's all very nice, Homarges, but I didn't come here to be social."

"I know. I asked my son to bring you to me."

"Well, I'm here. Speak. Say what it is you crossed the desert to say and let us be done."

"I talked to that Persian boy last night."

"What Persian boy? You had a Persian in my camp?!"

"The prince."

"Cambysses?"

"The one with the lazy eye that wanders."

"Cambysses. You had him?! They were looking for him everywhere! Do you know what kind of trouble you could have put us in by keeping him here?!"

"Easy now, easy does it. I didn't harm the boy."

"You shouldn't have done *anything* to him. You shouldn't even be here *yourself*. Apparently, the words, *exiled for life*, mean nothing to you. Or perhaps it's my word you don't respect?"

"Ah! The pretty face of your mother, but the direct boldness of your father. You are the best of both of them."

"Stop bringing up my parents. I do not live in the past."

"Perhaps you should?"

"What's that supposed to be? Wisdom?"

"A hard life lesson. You can try to run from the past all you want, but you'll never truly escape it until you die."

"This is maddeningly unhelpful."

"Aren't you the least bit interested in what I did with the Persian boy? What we said to one another?"

"I don't trust you as far as I can throw you, Homarges. Not that it looks like you would survive that throw. I've seen dead men look healthier than you."

"The desert can be a cruel and unforgiving landscape, especially when one has no one to turn to for help."

"I know another tribe took you in. You were too important to be left to the red sands and the red sands alone. And you only have yourself to blame for being exiled. If you were any kind of good or decent man, you'd have died that day with my father and my husband."

"That would have been easier for you, wouldn't it?"

"My life isn't used to easy. But on occasion I would appreciate it."

"Cyrus means to make a wife out of you."

"I already know that. I've refused him several times. No daughter of King Spargapeithes will ever belong to that man."

"If not Cyrus, then Cambysses himself. The prince likes you. He trusts you. He has nothing but good things to say about you since you protected him from his father."

"I will marry no Persian. That's not up for negotiation."

"A single woman can not make such selfish claims."

"It's not selfish. It's in the best interest of my people. I will not allow them to be Persian conscripts. I will not allow ten thousand immortals to rape my land and my people. I will not!"

"A marriage would prevent bloodshed."

"Blood has already been spilled, and burned. There is no going back now. I've said what I've said and I've done what I've done. I stand by my decisions, for good or for bad."

"A married woman would not be forced into such ultimatums."

"I am a widow. There is no Massagetae or visiting chief or officer that I feel the need to so desperately secure an alliance with as to suggest such a thing as marriage. I will not swallow my pride yet. It has not come to that."

"But if it does…"

"You have a husband in mind for me, Homarges? Is that why you insisted I get drug to you for? A proposal of sorts?!"

"Skunkha would make you a fine husband. He…"

"Father, no! You promised!"

"You must listen to reason, son! Both of you! With you Skunkha as king and you Tomyris as queen, Cyrus would have no chance but to defeat you in battle. It would give you better standing with the chiefs and officers. Bear a son for the sake of the gods! Bear *two*! You must think of the people!"

"All she *does* is think of her people! Every waking minute she is troubled with their preservation, and every sleeping second, she worries for their safety. There is no leader in these sands that cares more for their people than Tomyris. Father, you told me you had important matters to discuss with the queen, and I honored you that time. I didn't have to do that. I am her advisor and her friend, first and foremost. I am your son, second. You have done nothing but let me down in life, and I can't keep making the mistake that some day you will turn things around. Some people just can never be trusted. Tomyris, I'm so sorry. If I had known that this was going to…"

"Skunkha, it's alright. I know what it's like to want to think well of your father. It's natural for a child to want that. But you're an adult now, and you should have known better."

"If you want, I can pack him up and remove him from the camp for you by tonight."

"No. He's spoken with Cambysses. I can't have him wandering around right now. The old man is a liability. However many days he has left in this life, which granted, probably aren't many, I need to keep an eye on him. You and me, we *both* need to keep an eye on him. He will die here, and we will let him burn in our burning grounds. Until then, he stays in this tent, and speaks to no one but you or me."

"Understood, Tomyris."

"I mean it, Skunkha. I need to know I can trust you with this."

"You can trust me."

"I want to believe that, but you directly defied orders by attacking Darius last night."

"You are too easy on him."

"We have enough enemies across that river right now as it is. If we can make friends in high places, I'd rather ruin Cyrus from the inside out than the outside in. It's much easier the first way."

"Is that what that was all about?"

"No one likes Cyrus, and Darius has an eye for glory. Ari has already told me most of the Saka conscripts would turn to fight for me if they thought they could get away with it. We have to show them that they can."

"You play a wicked game, Tomyris."

"I play to win, Skunkha. Now, I have to get back to training. Can you check in on Sparga's scouting when he gets in? He should be back soon and I'm very interested in what he has to say."

"You mean, if he went to see *Atossa* again?"

"There's no higher woman in that camp than the princess. My son has no idea what he's doing, so we must look out for him."

"I'll keep an eye out for him."

"Thank you."

"I mean it, Tomyris. In more ways than one."

"I know. Oh, and Skunkha?"

"Yes?"

"Do something about these damned mongooses, will you? They're digging holes all over the place. If we don't watch it, the whole damn camp will be undermined."

"I'll see what I can do."

"Good. Come here."

"Come…"

"Give me a hug. You know I hate being mad at you."

"I don't like it any more than you do."

"Then you and me, we have to get back to trusting each other."

"I've *always* trusted you."

"You showed me last night that you don't."

Tomyris pulled away, and Skunkha felt stung. He wanted to explain himself, and why he went to shoot at Darius in the first place, but she was already walking away. Behind him, he could hear his father smothering a laugh, and the advisor had half a mind to go in and made sure that laugh was the last thing the old man ever did, but he couldn't do it. Instead Skunkha hung his head and sighed. He left his father's tent and tied thew flaps closed, then he proceeded to gather rocks and stones from the landscape and secure the tent to the sand. The old man had no strength left to him. There would be no grand escape attempt. With any luck, this might just be enough to send him over the edge for good. Skunkha was fine with that. He had settled with his father's death a long time ago, and really, being plunged back into childhood with him was worth than thinking he was dead. And at now of all times. He was losing his credibility with the queen and his relationship with his best friend all at once. Tomyris was everything to him, and if he lost her because of his father, there would be no recovery. Tomyris saw her advisor's craftiness in barricading his father. That action she could trust, but her friend would have to prove far more loyalty before things were squashed between them entirely. They just needed time, only time wasn't a luxury she had right now. She had training to do. The Persians were going to come back for her, and she needed to be ready. She wasn't confident she was going to make it out of this one, so in every lesson she taught her women, she tried to be vague about the outcome. Prepare for anything. Prepare for the worst even, because then if anything better than that happened, the women would be ready. The women had no wiggle room in preparedness. There was only being ready or being dead. Suicide was preferrable over being raped or made prisoner. All the women kept a dagger on them for just such purposes. Tomyris demonstrated a mock slit across the neck that would be so quick the little second of pain and realization of finality was nothing to be afraid of. The young queen had a way about her, a tone that the women appreciated. At this point. Tomyris could have said the sky was blood red instead of blue, and the women would have all nodded their heads in agreement. Tomyris wouldn't lie. The queen would protect them. She loved them, and they loved her. But even love had its limits. War brought out the worst in people, and played upon the sincerest of bonds with wicked cruelness. This was no better exemplified than between Cyrus and his children. Whereas Tomyris became hypervigilant about keeping her son Spargapeithes informed and protected, Cyrus took a much different approach. The old man was so dominant a force in his later stage of life that he kept his son battered on his hands and knees despite his physicality. Cambysses took a beating from his father for running away again, and Atossa was sat right there in the same tent to watch in silence. Eventually Cambysses passed out. Whether intentional or not, Atossa took a sigh of relief, then mentally tried to rally herself for her own defense. Cyrus looked at her wildly from underneath his white bushy brows. She couldn't ream him anymore, and she had always had a good handle on her father's emotions. But now, something was different. Something was eating at him from the inside, something she could not counter with all the sweet words she knew, and all the lies she could craft. He was unfixable. She gulped hard as the old man came in front of her on the cot, and caressed the side of her dark-skinned cheek. She tensed, waiting for impact that never came.

"I should have never hit you, my dear little, Atossa."

"These are trying times, father."

"That is no excuse. I have begged your mother for forgiveness every night since I struck you."

"And how did mother respond?"

"Had you been born a male, second, third, even *seventh* born, I'd have named *you* my heir before Cambysses."

"But I was not born a male. I am only a woman."

"*Only a woman.* Yes, that you are. And I have been reminded in deep thought of your mother, all that *only a woman* could do in life."

"What does that mean?"

"I want you to meet with Queen Tomyris, just the two of you."

"No guards?"

"She won't lay a hand on you if she knows what's good for her. And I want you to take something with you."

"A chest?"

"It's full of gold. Surely a queen would understand that some things, if they can't be settled in marriage, can be settled with coin. Your mother doesn't want me here in this desert. She has told me, frightening things. I must return home as soon as possible. We must end this war. If that can be done without battle, dear Atossa, perhaps you can be the negotiator. Be my favorite little princess."

"And what should I do if Queen Tomyris rejects this coin?"

"She'd be a fool to reject such a generous offer."

"Never underestimate the hate of a woman."

"Did your mother teach you that?"

"Mother was too sick when I was young to teach me anything. I learned that from someone else."

"The harem?"

"Queen Tomyris herself."

"You don't know the queen, Atossa. She couldn't have taught you anything. *When* could she have taught you this?"

"Last night, in the desert. I took Darius and Ariomardus with me to go and speak with her. She will not take your coin, father. All she'd do with the gold is melt it down into axes she'd use to kill us. Death is the only way out of here now…either yours, or hers."

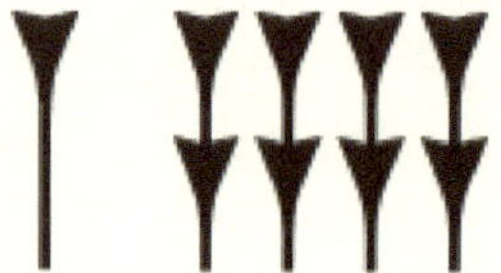

Cyrus' day of mourning for his wife Cassandae was coming to a close. Due to Atossa's lack of faith in delivering a chest full of gold coin to Tomyris to end the war, Ariomardus had been tasked with the uncomfortable chore. Darius was not yet healthy enough to get back up on a horse, so the Dahae soldier was trusted to go alone. Accepting the coin was understood that a submission would take place in lieu of a marriage alliance. Rejecting the coin meant further bloodshed. Ariomardus was very clear on the orders. What he lacked clarity in was the old leader's reasons for sudden withdrawal. The soldiers and officers had been told nothing of Cyrus' constant dreams of his dead wife pleading with him to leave the red sands. He was afraid of dying here, and rightly so. Ariomardus had seen unstable decisions made in battles before when old generals and chiefs became sick in the body. Cyrus might have had an ailment he was keeping to himself, but he was also sick in the mind. He'd drug everyone out here on the promise of eternal glory, just like the previous thirty-six tribes he'd taken. But the Massagetae were different. The challenges were entirely new. Tomyris would not and could not be bought. She was as intent on dying in this war as Cyrus was against it. The old man didn't know what to do about that, and Ariomardus could see that it was taking a toll on him. The Persian leader needed someone to talk to in confidence, but all anyone got was bits and pieces. Darius had thought of the coin. Atossa had rejected it. Atossa knew about the dreams of her mother. Darius knew the military prowess and statistics. Other officers in passing knew that winter was beating down hard, and the morale of the soldiers was slipping by the day. The soldiers knew their fellow Saka conscripts were fleeing in the night, nearly every night to Tomyris. Communication was very poor at all levels. No one said anything about what they knew to anyone else, and Ariomardus saw this all. He hovered around campfires and took late night walks to ease his mind and speak to the horses. Horses were such good friends to him. Much easier reads. Less complicated. If Ariomardus thought Cyrus would take him seriously about airing his troubles to the animals, he'd suggest it, but an idea like that might just throw him over the edge he was teetering on too. The Dahae soldier wasn't trying to make any sort of friendship with the old man. There was hardly respect for such a ruthless warlord as he was, but Ariomardus also took no pleasure in seeing a man become a shell of himself, and that's what was happening to Cyrus. He was berating his children. Cambysses bore the brunt physically, but Atossa took the emotional scarring. Whatever happened in this war, it needed to go on and happen already. The down time was brutal. Ariomardus loaded the chest full of coin onto the back of his wild black buck and road for the Massagetae in all haste. In his mind he came up with multiple scenarios about how to approach the young queen with this ridiculous and useless peace offering, but by the time he locked eyes on Tomyris, he'd forgotten just about everything but his own name. The way she smiled at him in the night, with her pale skin glowing in the moonlight, he'd never seen anything so perfect. It was a smile she had only for him, he was sure of it. Entirely disarming in the best kind of way. He could tell she was anxious to see him, and he let himself get a little inflated about that before realizing she was probably just interested in what information he might have for her on the Persians and the state of the war. Ariomardus took to unstrapping the chest in the dark, and Tomyris ran up behind him to place a lingering kiss on his shoulder.

"I missed you, Ari."

"You did?"

"So much can happen in a day sometimes. It seems since the Persians have arrived, days last weeks anymore."

"And are the nights just as long for you?"

"Unfortunately, they are not. Come, come with me inside my tent and warm yourself by the fire. It's too cold out here to talk."

"Hold on. I have a gift from Cyrus to unload."

"A gift from Cyrus? I'll put it straight in the fire then."

"I wouldn't do that if I were you."

"Come, come inside and we will speak of this gift."

"Alright. You seem rushed tonight? Is everything alright?"

"My soldiers are getting restless. Set that chest by the fire so I can see what it's all about. It must have taken a wood carver months to detail this."

"Cyrus was more interested with your reaction to what is *inside*."

"Gold coins…with…*his face* on them?"

"He's trying to bribe you, Tomy."

"The man must be in love with himself to put his face on coin. And so much. What is this supposed to mean to me? His coin is no good to me or my people. What did he hope to buy?"

"He wanted this to end the war."

"Coin in exchange for submission? Is he crazy?"

"I think he is troubled. Atossa said he's been dreaming of his dead wife telling him to leave the desert, or he'll die here."

"Cyrus is getting dreams from his dead wife? Perhaps he should lay off of the wine he's always swilling."

"Darius said that Cyrus wants the officers to be ready to march home, but he hasn't given the orders yet."

"Time is getting to the old man. It always does. I want nothing to do with his coin though. You should just take it back to him."

"Atossa thought you'd melt it down for weapons. She noticed our gold knives."

"The Massagetae have enough gold of our own for weapons and armor. I want nothing from Cyrus. It wouldn't be right. I won't submit to him. And I can't be bought with anything. Blood is the only way we are going to settle this. You be sure to tell him that for me. I don't think I want another negotiation with him."

"Even in battle you will have to see him again."

"That man's words weigh heavy on me. It takes me days to recover. At least in battle, I have the opportunity to die a warrior, and not be bothered by him anymore."

"It makes me sick to my stomach to think of you being alright with dying so young."

"I'm thirty-two, same as you. We are hardly teenagers."

"But we have a lot of life left in us, I think."

"I just want to be prepared, Ari. That's all."

"Then prepare to win. Prepare for a life…with me."

"A life with you? A Massagetae queen and a Persian lieutenant general? What a pair we would make."

"That's not what I had in mind for us."

"Then tell me what you see in the future for us."

"A Massagetae mother and a Dahae father. Just a simple Saka couple, living off the land and raising a family."

"I'm not a queen in your future?"

"Politics can be so complicated. It wears on you."

"And my son, Sparga?"

"He will be married, leading the people in your place."

"He would like that."

"But would *you* like it? Can you see what I see? A family in the dunes, little ones splashing in the river and giggling at our feet."

"I never knew you were thinking of these things."

"Does that scare you?"

"You think I scare at the mention of a man wanting simplicity and stability with me? Ari, I've wanted nothing more. I'm just surprised is all. I've asked the gods since I was young that I wanted a man who I could love and trust with everything that I am. And now, they have given me you, and my world is at war. Why would they do that to me? I just don't understand."

"Maybe the gods knew you could handle this."

"I'm glad the gods know what I can handle, because it's been so long since I could say the same."

"For what it's worth, I think you're doing amazing."

"You think too highly of me sometimes."

"Maybe, but you don't think high enough of yourself. You're a wonderful woman, Tomy, capable of doing so much good in this life. This war is just one part of you. It will not be all of you. You must take care of this, and move on. Just like a storm, this will pass."

"You are so wise. When you speak, your words calm me when I think I am coming undone. But then I think, loving you is like this war. I won't be able to come out of it the same way I went into it."

"Then don't come out of it. Stay. Stay with me. Stay in love."

"Can I do that?"

"You can if you want to."

"Loving and staying, that requires *two* people, Ari."

"I know. I'm not going anywhere. I'm not leaving you."

"You're not leaving? We are on two different sides of this war. You are so sweet, but I am so confused. You say this war is only for a short time, and that I need to move past it. You tell me to stay in love with you, that you'll never leave. War kills people. It takes people away. I can't move passed. All I know how to do is push through. Push through this war, push through life."

"Life and war are two very different things."

"Are they?"

"War is meant to be fought, not life. You shouldn't just be trying to push through life. That means all you're striving for is death."

"We all die."

"But it is not our *goal* in life. We are meant to be happy first."

"I am happy with you."

"Then hold onto that."

"I'd rather hold onto *you*."

"You would?"

"But you have to run back to Cyrus tonight and tell him I've refused him again. War first, life second."

"I don't have to run back to him tonight."

"Isn't he expecting you?"

"Yes."

"Won't you get in trouble if you stay with me?"

"What Cyrus doesn't know won't hurt him. I owe him no allegiance. I was born a Saka, and I will die a Saka, same as you. He will be no more thrilled to hear of your rejection tonight or tomorrow morning. Besides, it's not often I get to enjoy holding onto you. When I am asleep, it is constant, but when I am awake, the dreams must get me through. But the dreams are no comparison to the real thing."

"Then we can lie by the fire tonight, and you can hold me until sunrise. In the meantime, why don't you tell me all about these dreams you have of us."

"I don't know that you want to hear *all* of them."

"Why not?"

"A man's mind can be quite unforgiving. You are still a woman, and a queen. What I see isn't always…*appropriate*."

"You think I don't have those dreams too?"

Tomyris and Ariomardus spent the night talking by the fire. They covered all sorts of topics from childhood, and their families, to their biggest fears and goals. Sunrise came entirely too early, but Tomyris had soldiers to train and Ariomardus had to ride the coin back to Cyrus. The Dahae soldier was confident the war was going to go according to their favor, and the young queen did not ask for clarification of what he meant. She wanted to be blissfully ignorant for a little while longer, it was the only way to truly achieve happiness anymore. The war was no more or less solved than it had been a few hours ago, nor would battle be on the agenda for the day. But maybe tomorrow. The guessing game was wearing thin. Tomyris didn't have the manpower or strength to go charging against the Persians first. Such a move would be certain slaughter. No, instead she had to wait for Cyrus, who was now as she knew, severely ill of mind. As if fighting a renowned conqueror drunk on power wasn't enough of an opponent to have, now he was going mad. There was no way to predict what he might do next. Construction of the bridges had resumed, sure to reinforce what the Massagetae had destroyed the first time around. There were also guards posted at all hours of the day and night too, to protect from sabotage. Their fires were never snuffed out, and so Tomyris ordered her camp to do the same. It took a steady group of people now to do nothing during the day but collect wood for burning, and soak it in animal fat to try and make it go a little farther. Everything was a show now anyways. Cyrus knew he had the upper hand, but the young queen didn't want to give him reason to gloat about it. She was sure a battle was fast approaching. This idle time riding on everyone's minds would be over soon. When Ariomardus delivered the rejected coin, the old leader might just have his fill of this desert. He's too proud to walk away outright, but Skunkha repeatedly reminded his queen that that was always a possibility. Tomyris was leaning on her advisor again for sanity's sake. One could only train so much throughout the day without getting sore and exhausted. But the women were shaping up nicely. This afternoon there was going to be a demonstration to prove it, men against women in hand-to-hand combat. Weapons optional. No armor. First blood forfeits. There was no shame in not entering the mock skirmish. The idea was Skunkha's, and he insisted on being Tomyris' sparring partner.

Tomyris and her advisor knew each other's every weakness, both physically and emotionally. They had wrestled and fought, trained, and argued with one another for as long as they could remember. Sometimes blood had been drawn in scrapes or lucky cuts, but it had never been intentional, never with any malice to it. Today was a bit different. While the young queen and Skunkha circled round in a water compacted sand pit, Tomyris could see over her advisor's shoulder, where Homarges' tent had been unbarricaded. Full well knowing the dying man couldn't have put in the work himself, and quite assured that no one else in camp would provide aid, that meant only one thing. Skunkha had gone back on his word and helped his father again, against orders. Tomyris ran up to him, faked a hard right and socked Skunkha in the left of his rib cage. There was a teenage injury there from falling off of a horse while trying to learn how to ride while standing up and shooting a bow and arrow at the same time. Skunkha favored his left side, and was usually much more aware of an attacker making a move there. He had underestimated that his friend was going to pull such an underhanded move so quickly into the demonstration. If she was going to play dirty, then he would have to as well. Skunkha went to kick Tomyris' right foot from under her, knowing her right knee to be weak from a childhood injury she sustained while hiking in the northern mountains. The young queen was one step ahead of her advisor though, and jumped up out of the way, therefore taking Skunkha by surprise and landing with her elbow back into his left side. The pain was excruciating, and Skunkha dropped to his knees. There were some gasps in the crowd. Many chiefs and officers didn't think she would go so far, but the rules were first blood, and Skunkha wasn't bleeding, yet. Low murmurs and cheers began to hail the Queen of the Massagetae. They wanted her to win, to finish off the advisor. Tomyris saw her son, glowing with pride. He cheered the loudest, leading cheers even, and jumping up and down. Locking eyes with more than one of her recent Saka allies, she was given nods of approval. Tomyris flicked out her golden knife from her waistband, and dropped to her knees in front of Skunkha. He put his hands up as a means to say he was unarmed, and a strike as quick and as golden as lightning ran across his palm. First blood. The advisor sucked in a deep breath and the camp erupted in cheer.

Tomyris didn't feel good about this small victory, but she smiled for her people and bowed in their praise. Every single woman she had trained stepped up to volunteer for a demonstration of their own. Each of them had multiple men willing to fall at their feet, or get the better of the fairer sex. Some made explicit terms, others merely bragging rights. The people were consumed with showmanship, and the queen was left to help her advisor up off his knees. He didn't want to take her hand as assistance, and instead winced himself back into an upright position. He was still favored his sore left side when Tomyris repeatedly stepped into his path away from her. Finally, he took a deep sigh, and stopped resisting. She was angry with him, the scary, quiet angry that he feared most of all. A cold sweat began to form across his skin, and drip from the curls of his black hair down onto his pale face. She spoke through a clenched smile and forced whisper because others were watching their every move.

"Congratulations, Tomyris. You are still undefeated against me."

"Do you know why I cut your hand, Skunkha?"

"I don't need a reason. Rules are rules. First blood. I lose."

"I cut your hand so that way when you pick those stones up again to barricade your father's tent, you remember that you *never* should have let him back into my camp in the first place."

"That could have been anybody. You wouldn't know. You were too busy sleeping with the enemy last night to notice."

"How did you know Ari was with me last night?"

"You think I don't know who comes in and out of this camp? Sparga told me when he came in from his last scouting mission. Saw that big black horse running straight for your end of camp. Stayed there all night too. Didn't leave until you got up. I watched him. Big smile on his face, *almost* as big as yours. You hold him tight. I just hope it's worth it, Tomyris. I hope for your sake, he doesn't end up hurting you. Excuse me. I've got to go get this cut wrapped up."

When the Massagetae women were demonstrating their battle proficiency, Tomyris went back to her tent to think about what Skunkha had said to her. Looking out across her land, she could see clouds of black smoke from the Persian camp. Construction was in full swing, and a war was being waged. Cyrus wanted her lands and her people, but now his dead wife was telling him to go home. A conqueror never gave up without drawing blood first. The fires wouldn't be lit at all hours of the day and night if the Persians were preparing to leave. The Saka tribes had amassed for a war. If Tomyris didn't do something soon, morale would fall. Morale was about the only thing on her side right now. Behind her there were great cheers for the demonstrations, but her anxieties were screaming louder inside of her head. She would have to make a decision about whether or not to continue waiting for Cyrus to engage her, or to go and call him out on her own instead. When her son got back from his morning scouting mission, she would base her actions off of his report. She had explicitly instructed him to take a wider walk, and cut down to the river's edge to let the Persians know they were being watched. She repeated this several times to the teenage general in order to stress her desire to have the most up to date representation of her enemy's intentions. As important as this was, she was nervously awaiting his return, constantly scanning the sand dunes for signs of his horse cresting the hills. It usually didn't take this long to travel the course she requested him to take. She feared he might have slipped into some sort of disagreement, or physical altercation by making himself so well seen to the Persians. In reality, it wasn't trouble he had slipped into at all, but Atossa.

The Persian princess was decidedly unhappy with her familial and marital situation. The one shining detail about her being in the red sands in winter during her father's latest lackluster campaign, was the light eyes and sweet words of Spargapeithes. A sixteen-year-old general who didn't know anything about anything was Atossa's current crutch in life. Her want and desire to see him was becoming increasingly difficult to maintain. He had become a need for her to get through her day. Waving from a distance did nothing for her. She craved his touch, and withdrew from the harem's routines she normally performed as a necessary evil. The Massagetae's scouting paths were committed to her memory. She woke before sunrise, and traced the sun in the sky for when she needed to run from her tent, gather her horse, and trek across the sandbar in the Araxes River to see her young beloved. Usually, they waved and flirted from afar. But this morning, with Tomyris' new instructions to go down to the river's edge, Spargapeithes was greeted by his princess up close. She dropped from her horse and ran to him, making him smile from ear to ear. He hardly had the time to drop from the back of his own horse and tie him to the hearty stalks of a nearby sagebrush outcropping before Atossa tackled him and began smothering his face in kisses. This was new for him, and the teenage boy didn't know what to do with himself. It was all happening so fast, and he was excited, but he didn't know what to do, or where to put his hands, or if he should say something. Atossa knew what she was doing. She knew what she wanted, and she was going to take it. The princess was good at this, using physicality to manipulate a man. Spargapeithes was hardly a man, but he was close enough. It was endearing that he didn't know what to do. It made it easy for Atossa to use him as she wished. While she folded her body around him, in her lightweight, nearly see through dress, she took hold of the rival prince's hands and placed them on her where she moaned satisfaction in the boy's mouth. She knew he was enjoying himself because his body was stiff against her curves, and his lips curled into an impossible to erase smile. When she leaned away, she pulled Spargapeithes with her, and he followed her all the way to the ground until she was writhing in the sands underneath him. He still didn't know what to do, and to avoid the timely fumbling, the princess rolled over and pinned Spargapeithes into the ground to have her way with him. It didn't take long. From first embrace to straddle it was a grand total of five minutes. The prince had had the morning of his life, and the princess was deeply questioning herself. She always felt intense guilt after doing this. It was not the way a woman of her position should act, but she also couldn't help it. It felt good, but only for a moment. She stood up and was quick to dust herself off, shake the sand from her black braids and retie her dress so it sat squarely on her shoulders. Spargapeithes lied in awe on his back, still exposed and unwilling to speak. Atossa had half a mind to kick the boy to get up and respond, but she was also a little pleased she had been able to control the boy so well. Darius was not so inexperienced when she got to him the first time, and as a result the power dynamic between the husband and wife had always been uneven in his favor. This time, Atossa was in the lead, and she quite liked that. But she shouldn't like this. But she did. Atossa did finally give a swift kick to Spargapeithes while he lied there, implying he wanted another go around. Before she could berate the teenager however, a man cleared his throat behind her, and spooked her horse. Darius took the reins, and smiled with a knowing grin. He had come with a blanket for the cold, but shrugged this off and threw it at his scantily clad wife while Spargapeithes scrambled to get dressed.

"Atossa, why don't you wrap yourself up, you look cold."

"Darius! What are you doing out here?!"

"Ariomardus told me he saw you running off a few minutes ago. Said you looked a bit nervous."

"Ariomardus is never up this early in the morning."

"He is when your father comes calling for him."

"What did my father want?"

"I don't know. He wasn't asking for me. No one in your family asks for me anymore, especially *you*, my wife. A *boy*, Atossa, *really*?"

"He's not a *boy*. He's sixteen."

"And *you* are a twenty-year-old *woman*. You should know better than to think he would know what to do with you."

"I…"

"No, ah ah ah, little prince. This is grown talk. If I wanted to know how you liked fucking my wife, I'd have asked. Judging from the state of things…*you* had a very good time, and *she* did not. Atossa?"

"I'm actually quite satisfied."

"I know that's a lie. If it were true, I'd have heard you scream. I've made you scream many times."

"Not lately."

"That's because you won't let me anywhere near you."

"Don't think I don't know you get your pleasures elsewhere, Darius. You are hardly spend many nights in your tent alone. Why is it alright for *you* to seek comfort elsewhere and not me?"

"Because *I* do not bear the responsibility of giving this empire a legacy of legitimate sons, and *you* do."

"I will give you your son one day, Darius. Do not force that."

"I *have* never, nor *will* I ever force anything on you. But so help me, if you expect me to raise a pale skinned bastard as my own…"

"No baby will come from this. I will take care of things."

"Like how you take care of things after spending time with me back home? You're *not* home, Atossa. How do you expect to get those special teas from the healers for this?"

"I will handle this."

"In the middle of the desert you will handle this? You know, I'm not comfortable with the way you've been *handling* anything lately. Running off all the time. It was bad enough when I thought you were sleeping with a man behind my back. But now I see that it is even worse watching you with a boy right in front of me. What would your father have to say about all of this?"

"My father doesn't need to know everything that I do. Stop being so annoying, Darius. If I didn't know any better, I'd say you were jealous of Sparga."

"Jealous?! No. A man can't envy a boy. Look at him and look at me. Tell me you feel good about what you've just done this morning."

"It's not one of my finer moments…"

"Ah hah!"

"But it's also not one of my worst either."

"I swear on the gods, you need guards to watch you just like your damned brother! I *told* Cyrus! I *told* him it was a bad idea to bring you two out here. But he insisted. He said you two *needed* this experience. He would've listened to me and left you at home if he knew *this* was the kind of experience you were going to get. Fucking a boy in the sands, Atossa, honestly? You're better than that."

"Perhaps what is more troubling is what brought me out here this morning in the first place?"

"No. You're not turning this around. This isn't my fault. I didn't force you out here to jump onto the first boy you saw riding a horse."

"*You* befriended the rival queen. You've been in my father's ear against this war. If I didn't know better, I'd say you were even influential in the failure of our bridges."

"I had nothing to do with our opening defeat! I was as in shock at Tomyris' capabilities as anyone else. I haven't befriended her, but I *do* have respect for authority, and she has it as much as you might hate to admit it. Ariomardus trusts her, and I trust him."

"He's one of them! You can't trust Ariomardus!"

"I trust him more than you! You're fucking a boy in secret, Atossa! And you're covered in mongoose fur. Hey, boy!"

"My name is Spargapeithes. I am a general of the Massagetae…"

"You will quiet yourself and answer my questions. The fur came off you. Where did you get it? There're mongooses in your camp, yes?"

"Not that I know of."

"Then where does the fur come from; I wonder?"

"I don't know."

"I truly believe that. Is there anything in this world you *do* know?"

"You're not nice to Atossa. For a woman who is your wife, you…"

"I *really* don't want to hear whatever it is you have to say next."

"You don't love her."

"What do you know of love? One ride and you think you know her? She's been using you since she first laid eyes on you."

"You're lying! Atossa loves me! And I love her! I hope she *does* have my baby. Then I can marry her, and bring her home to meet…"

"Your *mother*? You think *Tomyris* would approve of this little situation? She would *kill* Atossa before she let you marry her."

"You don't know that. If I could just talk to her and explain…"

"Your mother doesn't strike me as a patient listener, boy. She's as wise to this manipulation as anyone, maybe even more so. Women know what lengths other women are willing to go to to win a war. Your mother isn't queen because she is stupid, or because she makes poor choices like my wife here. If you knew, if you *really* knew your mother the way the rest of the world sees her, you'd be scared to death and never have let my wife fuck you."

"I think this is the longest time I have heard you speak, Darius."

"And? Did you learn something, boy?"

"I did. It's no wonder Atossa ran away from you. I may be young, but I make her happy. And when I kill you in this war, I will make her happy for the rest of her life."

Darius took out his sword impossibly fast from its sheath. While Spargapeithes was trying to react by grabbing his own sword, he realized Atossa had taken it off of his belt while they were kissing, and tossed it aside. The princess attempted to scramble on her feet, and position herself in-between the two men, but Darius pushed her aside and into the sand. This act angered Spargapeithes even more, but he was unable to defend the princess' honor because Darius had run up on him, and crashed the heavy metal hilt of his sword into the back of his head. The teenager felt dizzy, and the ground give way beneath him. He faintly remembered hearing Atossa scream for him before he collapsed. Skunkha was riding over the dunes with Tomyris now. Since Spargapeithes had taken too long on his scouting mission, Tomyris naturally, and understandably had assumed the worst. She and her advisor could let their personal issues fall to the wayside when her son was in danger. Skunkha pulled ahead in the lead with his horse charging through the valley, but it was Tomyris' run on her white mare that had Darius dropping his sword in mid-air. Atossa scurried over on her hands and knees for it and clung it to her chest while she poured herself over Spargapeithes' limp body. His heart was still beating as she felt for it, but he was not awake. Tomyris was trying to assess the situation as she got closer. No blood was seen, so she was more than a bit confused, but slowly putting the pieces together. The princess and her son were intimately close. Darius was upset. It didn't take a genius to figure out what had happened, and she cursed up at the gods for allowing this. She could see a dust cloud of kicked up sand coming up from the dunes by the river across from her. Tomyris ran faster, but thankfully it was just Ariomardus, on his large black buck. He had come because he had seen Atossa leaving this morning, and had just heard her scream. He abandoned the guard of one of Cyrus' children for another. Ariomardus too, was able to survey the scene with relative ease while Darius began pacing and angrily muttering to himself. The Dahae soldier arrived to the awkward trio first, and tried to calm his friend down as Tomyris and Skunkha arrived. In a heavy Massagetae tongue, the young queen ordered her advisor to pick up her son and ride him and his horse back to camp so she could scold him later. The Tomyris came up to Darius, who was very reluctant to turn and face her. Before the young man could get a word out she slapped him, and as he reeled back from that to defend himself she already had her golden knife pressed firmly against his neck, tight enough to allow a few drips of blood to remind Darius of the way of things. Ariomardus sighed behind his fellow officer, but did nothing to stop Tomyris. The interference came from Atossa, who put a gentle hand on the young queen's forearm that was currently seizing her husband by the chin.

"It's my fault, Tomyris. Please, let Darius go."

"Your husband knows why I can't do that. We had an agreement."

"My husband has a habit of promising things to women he has no ability to see through. Please, let him go. I can explain everything."

"I don't need an explanation. I may be young for a queen, but I'm not so young that I can't read *you*, princess. You came out here and fucked my son, but you were sloppy, and your husband found you. Then, knowing my son, he said something foolish to Darius.”

“That’s exactly what happened. How did you know that?”

“Men are predictable, boys especially. Women less so, sometimes. I know you’re using my son, Atossa. But it won’t work. You won’t get anything from him of any value to your father’s war efforts.”

“What if I want more from your son than his value to this war?”

“You can’t play your games with me, princess.”

“This isn’t a game, Tomyris. Your son said he loved me.”

“He’s sixteen. He doesn’t know what love is. Would you like a little insight into the boy you just fucked this morning?”

“He’s not a *boy*! He’s a *man* now. I made him so.”

“*You* made him so? That’s funny. Because just last week this *man* of yours came to me with all the seriousness in the world and wanted to know what would happen if a horse and a goat mated. Is that what you want to bring back to your father as your choice of husband?”

“You don’t see your son the same way I do.”

“I would hope not. But this has gotten out of hand. I fear that there’s nothing more I can do without speaking to your father, face to face.”

“You mean…*now*?”

“Yes, while there’s still time to do something for you to avoid an unfortunate mistake. Trust me, I don’t want to do this. I doubt very much progress will be made. Your father doesn’t respect women…”

“No, he just doesn’t respect *you*. But I do, I *will*, if you let me handle this. I’ve done it before. I can do it again.”

"But *will* you? Because when I look at you right now, Atossa, you know what I see? You *want* this. For whatever reason, you *do* love my son. You were using him, and you messed up. This is war, and men die. You *know* this. Why did you do this?! You stupid girl!"

"Is it so horrible of me to like a man's affection?"

"No. But it was wrong of you to act on it."

"Have you never been in my position before, Tomyris? Have you never made a bad decision in trying times for love? *Tomyris*?"

"Fine. Take care of this. Or I will take care of this for you. Until this war is over, you are not to see my son anymore."

"You can't keep him from me! He's a general!"

"I'm his queen and his mother. Darius, take your wife back to camp and see to it she stays there. Ari…"

"I'll keep my eye on them for you, Tomy."

"Thank you."

"I'm just thankful you're mine and I'm not in your line of fire. Your son is lucky to be unconscious. I wouldn't want to be him when he wakes up. Try to take it easy on him though."

"Why?"

"*She* came after *him*. When a woman as pretty as that comes after you, there's not much a man can really do. I mean, look at what you do to me."

"What do I do to you?"

"What *don't* you do? Go on, ride back to camp. I think Cyrus is ready to make a move, and I want you to be ready for it."

Spargapeithes had been sulking around camp the past three days after his encounter with Atossa went awry. He was giving his mother the silent treatment, which she was not at all upset about, and only communicating with Skunkha with the occasional head nods and shoulder shrugs. As an advisor, Skunkha insisted that Tomyris remove her son's ranking for the time being until he could prove himself worthy of such an exalted title as general, but as a friend, he confided perhaps the boy needed a loss in battle to prove that for himself. It was not rare for generals to lose power in the Saka tribes for underperforming on the battlefield. Tomyris mulled this over since she already kept her son's assignment as far from the fighting as possible for his own protection. There was the option for her to trade his position in the sands with another tribal chief with more experience. Throw the young men down on the front lines. It was what the majority of officers had been asking for. A queen would make such a move, but a mother would not. That was the real problem, and Tomyris was not happy about it. But the prospect of battle wasn't as dangerous as it once was. The scouts said the Persians had been withdrawing slowly but surely by the day. Skunkha didn't trust it, and was upset about why the young queen was so dependent on word from Ariomardus to confirm such things her very own scouts had seen. But the mere mention of the Dahae soldier's name drew severe, close-minded criticism. Tomyris would not engage in arguments over Ariomardus' true loyalty, and Skunkha would not let the matter die. Still faithful to his position however, there was only one man in camp that Skunkha could trust to air his grievances, and that was his exiled father, still living in a stoned-up tent on the outside of camp. Skunkha waited until nightfall to make the walk out there. Many other tents had been moved so that Homarges could look and feel like the true pariah he was. Tomyris didn't even need to ask her people to do that. They too were unsure of why Skunkha would allow, and encourage such a thing. But family was family, and that was a tricky thing indeed. The advisor didn't even feel good about doing this, giving his father the upper hand even if only in conversation. But desperate times called for desperate measures. He looked down at his bandaged hand that refused to heal. It was infected now, and sorer than when Tomyris had first sliced him in her demonstration. Homarges insisted he was willing to share some of his poultices for his own sores with his son, but Skunkha refused, and his body shook in disgust.

"I tried to warn you son."

"I don't need a lecture, father."

"Then why did you come to me tonight?"

"I worry that Tomyris is holding the Massagetae back because of her love for the traitor Dahae soldier."

"And have you brought this to her attention?"

"She won't speak to me of him. She accuses me of being jealous."

"Well, it's not an accusation. It's fact."

"I'm not *jealous* of Ariomardus!"

"You have loved that woman since you were a boy. You have stayed by her side, lived life, and raised her son with her. It is only natural to want her to love you in return."

"Would a woman in love strike her man like *this*?!"

"You are my son, that makes you hard headed. Sometimes, we force the women in our lives to take drastic actions in order to get us to do what is best."

"So, you *agree* with Tomyris injuring me?"

"It's not what I'd have done if I was king. But I understand."

"If *I* was king, I'd trust my advisor over the enemy."

"She still speaks to you in confidence every day. You have not lost her. There is hope for fixing things still."

"Hope requires time. As long as there are Persians in the red sands, no Massagetae can have such a foolish thing as hope."

"Well, it's good the Persians are leaving then."

"Don't believe the talk in camp. I know scouts have said the Persians are fleeing, but Cyrus has taken thirty-six tribes in brutal warfare. He will not simply leave us alone after one lackluster meeting. We didn't even lose a single man that day."

"I have an understanding that Cyrus desires peace."

"Cyrus the Great desires *peace*?! You really are losing your mind."

"A chest full of gold coin came into this camp, and your queen rejected the offer."

"*I* told *you* that."

"And now *I* am telling *you* that Cyrus' daughter, Atossa came to me last night under the cover of darkness with a deal."

"You're lying!"

"If you go to Atossa before sunrise tomorrow and take that chest of coin, Cyrus will leave the sands forever."

"And that's it?"

"The Massagetae will be his, but he will allow you to remain in your lands in exchange for one hundred conscripts and taxes to be paid every year."

"Tomyris will never allow that."

"Tomyris isn't thinking clearly. You said that yourself. She is more interested in that Dahae man. So, let her be interested all she wants. Let her marry him, raise his sons and daughters. Cyrus will make you satrap of the Massagetae and you can finally get the respect you have always deserved."

"This actually might be crazy enough to work."

"Have faith in your father. I've only ever wanted what's best for you. And this is it. Don't spoil it, son. Take it! You've earned it."

"I have to meet the princess before sunrise. Where?"

"She said there's a sandbar on the Araxes. Do you know it?"

"I do."

"Then go. Bring an end to this."

Mongooses crawled all over the old man's lap like beloved pets. In the corner of the tent a pile of rotting meet broiled with flies and maggots. Skunkha was usually unnerved when his father gave the uneven grin he was giving the advisor now, but the potential to end hostilities was too good to pass up. Atossa wouldn't wait forever, and the Persians were leaving. He'd seen it with his own two eyes. He would bring that chest of gold coin back to Tomyris, and prove to her the error in her ways. Skunkha would be recognized as leader now, and her position as queen would be irrelevant. Perhaps it was what their friendship needed, a change in dynamic. Skunkha gripped his ailing father's shoulder's tightly and felt nothing but bone in-between his hands. Clothing cloaked the true condition of Homarges' sickness. He wanted this for his son, before he wasn't around to see it anymore. In a roundabout way, Skunkha would lead the Massagetae like it was always intended. The young man bolted from the tent, and haphazardly placed the stones back into place alone the hide edges. It didn't really matter the stability of the barricade. Mongooses had tunneled under absolutely everything, and were beginning to cause sinkholes throughout the surrounding camp. But Tomyris wouldn't be able to yell about that soon. By morning, she'd be powerless. Skunkha charged out of the camp without a word to anyone. Chiefs were confused, noting his direction was to the Persians, and brought their concerns into Tomyris who waved them off as orders in order to preserve her reputation. She couldn't very well maintain an army's support or respect if her second in command was running off behind her back, even though that's exactly what was happening. As much as she wanted to ride off after him, she had a meeting with her war council to tend to, and inform Spargapeithes that he was being moved up to the front lines. Still, the teenager said nothing to his mother, but a crack of a smile was on his pale face.

In the fractured remains of the Persian camp, nearly down to a tenth of it's former glory, Ariomardus still remained camped on the water's edge to keep an eye on the prince and princess. Cambysses was sleeping, and Atossa was assumed to be too, until the Dahae soldier caught her creeping out on foot to the sandbar in the river. It was safe to assume that she was waiting for her beloved prince on the other side, but far as Ariomardus could tell, there was no one waiting for her. The water was ice cold too, and very unforgiving so late in the year. She was knee deep for far longer than need be before a horse came over the horizon, and Ariomardus could tell it was Skunkha from the bob of curly hair on his head, even in the shadows. He contemplated interfering this rendezvous but decided to hide in the sagebrush instead, and learn what he could. Atossa had brought the chest of gold coin with her that Ariomardus had brought back to Cyrus after Tomyris' rejection. He hadn't spoken to her in three days but was still firmly under the impression nothing had changed the young queen's mind about submission. Skunkha took the chest and fled back into the night. There was next to no conversation. Whatever had just happened, it had been discussed about prior to this evening. Ariomardus went back to Cambysses' tent and riled the prince awake but he too was clueless as to what might have just happened. His father nor his sister had told him anything. Ariomardus then searched the camp for where Darius was sleeping. The man had two different officer's wives cradled around his sides. Ariomardus gave a swift kick to Darius' feet and startled the man awake. The women were ordered to leave at once. Darius was deeply confused as Cambysses welcomed himself inside his tent to be an eager observer. Ariomardus crouched down and spoke in a hurried whisper.

"I think something has happened, Darius. I just watched your wife give a chest of gold coin to Skunkha in the river. Tomy told me she'd *never* take the coin from Cyrus, she'd *die* first."

"Maybe she changed her mind? Why are you so worried?"

"What if something happened to her, Darius?!"

"We'll go take a ride, see what's going on. How long ago did this happen? Can we catch that rat of an advisor before he gets back to the Massagetae camp?"

"We can if we hurry."

Darius lunged forward and began to roughly clothe himself. Cambysses invited himself for the midnight ride as well, and followed both officers to where the horses were sleeping. What was left of the Persian camp was a small detachment of men in blood red tents. A feast had been held tonight to celebrate going back home. Men were drunk at sundown, which was why Darius and Ariomardus did not attend. Many officers took to their tents for the festivities which they felt like were a slap in the face to all the preparation and efforts spent out here in the most unforgiving time of year. Cyrus though, was a fan of grand speeches and flair. He loved to be loved, and was currently drinking himself into a stupor with men a quarter of his age, toasting the great victory to come. He knew what his daughter had done with Skunkha. The two had coordinated it, and told no one. Darius was beginning to fear for his own life and position as he rode out of camp with Ariomardus. But now was not the time to voice such things. Ariomardus was charging his black buck across the sands with unrelenting urgency. It was all Darius and Cambysses could do to keep up. Skunkha was nowhere to be found, and over the past few weeks there wasn't very many places he could go to hide from Ariomardus without him knowing. Darius and Cambysses split off to check the valleys and caves. There was no rival advisor anywhere. And he didn't seem to go to the camp either because when Ariomardus arrived to Tomyris' tent entirely out of breath, she was truly clueless as to what was going on. He gripped her shoulders tightly.

"Where's Skunkha?!"

"I don't know. Ari, what's wrong?"

"When was the last time you saw him?!"

"I don't know. A few hours. You're scaring me. What is it?"

"Skunkha took that chest of gold coin from Atossa. Cyrus is toasting your defeat *right now* in what remains of the Persian camp. I feared you might have been killed."

"So, Skunkha is missing with a chest of Persian coin and Cyrus is celebrating my defeat? I guess that's it then. Ari, can you do me a favor and go grab a goat from the pins for me?"

"A goat? Now?!"

"I need a sacrifice. I'll grab my blood bowl to mark the soldiers."

"You're going to try to prepare for war in the middle of the night?!"

"I'm not going to *try*; I *am* preparing for war. Grab me the goat and then you can run back to the Persians."

"No."

"No?"

"I'm not running back. I can't stand here knowing what I know, and just kiss you goodbye and hope for the best. I don't want to kiss you goodbye anymore. I want to kiss you goodnight, and good morning, and whenever I feel like it, until the gods rip me away from you."

"I want that too. But the gods can be cruel, and our parting might be soon, so, kiss me now…and then go get that goat."

Ariomardus let a wicked grin tear across his face before pulling Tomyris in hard for a quick kiss and sendoff. No one was surprised to see him running through camp tonight as he readied the officers with news of a battle. Most of the men were too excited to ask questions. There were clashes of swords and sparks of fire dancing through the night air. Babies were crying as mothers woke to ready their husbands. Children were running around taking advantage of the frantic, late night chaos. Tomyris brought out the sacrificial bowl, and held it high above her head explaining the latest developments. Spargapeithes was to take a third of the army, all volunteers, to go and raze whatever remained of the Persians to the ground. No hostages. No exceptions. Ariomardus cut the goat's throat with his golden knife and let the neck spill out the warm blood all over Tomyris' bowl and hands. The young queen was expertly quick in marking her soldiers tonight with the customary five finger drip down the right side of their face. Women were howling like wolves and chanting good luck songs for the war party. Spargapeithes wasted no time leading the men out into the darkness as soon as his mother marked the blood down his face, and kissed him with tears in her eyes. They would have words when he returned victorious. She was sure of it now. Darius and Cambysses took shelter in the sand valleys when the Massagetae and their allies ran out. It was safely assumed Ariomardus would not be returning to them, and if he was, Darius didn't have the time to wait. His wife was back in the camp, and even if they hated each other, and she did have Spargapeithes' bastard baby growing in her belly, the two had an agreement. Darius took hold of Cambysses' reins to run faster through the night. There was no way they could reach the camp before all hell broke loose, but they wouldn't be far behind. Skunkha was in the sand valleys too, and decided to stay there overnight in silence to see how things played out. He commanded his horse to lay on the ground with him for shelter from the cold winds, and listened anxiously to the war cries cackle around him. This wasn't at all what he was hoping would happen tonight.

The Persians were heavily inebriated when the Massagetae rolled into their camp and began to slash at what little remains of Cyrus' grand army of Immortals. However, it was also just what the old man had intended. Atossa was thrown from the main feasting tent onto her back, and kicked outside into the dark where Darius was able to follow her screams and forcibly pick her up to carry her to safety. Cambysses studiously followed his former guard in silence. Darius had made a promise to Tomyris not to harm her son, and as difficult as it was right now to listen to, the lieutenant general would not fight this fight. Officers were being startled awake to the sound of battle, but Darius did not run to give aid. Instead, he kept Cyrus' children safe in Ariomardus' tent down by the river, and asked the gods for a swift end to this ordeal. Atossa was crying into her husband's shoulder. She didn't think this would happen. Darius could scold her a million different ways for her naivety, but he kept his thoughts to himself, and just watched men fall to their deaths. Numbers had never been the reason for Cyrus' military advances. It helped, but the main reason he was so victorious was that even drunk off their ass, his men were battle hardened. They could fight better drunk than three Massagetae with all the training they had to their name. And Spargapeithes was running with volunteers tonight, no officers, and most men were his age or within a couple of years. They had no experience, and it showed. It was a slaughter. A Persian trap laid to the best of its ability. After fifteen minutes the worst of it was over, and the night became quiet again sans for the moans of the dying. No help was coming to either side. All healers had gone. Skunkha's curiosity got the better of him at this point and he crawled on hands and knees to the nearest crest of a dune and looked down at the blood red tents in horror. No Massagetae would be riding home tonight. All that remained of the virgin forces was Spargapeithes, tied to a tent pole on his knees, bleeding profusely. Cyrus was pacing in front of the teenager, clearly enjoying the turn the night had taken. Spargapeithes was offered wine, but the boy took a gulp only to spit it back out in spite. He was kicked in the side for that by a gruff looking Persian. Skunkha winced seeing such harsh treatment to a boy who was like a son to him. At this point, Cambysses and Atossa also came out of their hiding place by the river's edge, to see what their father was going to do. Darius was convinced Spargapeithes would be spared, not only because he was a prince, but because there needed to be a messenger to Tomyris about the defeat. Atossa was clinging to her husband in relief, digging her nails into his skin. She squeezed tighter when the ropes were cut and Spargapeithes was freed. The princess gasped, and it was all Darius could do to hold her beside him as the teenage boy was returned his sword which had been taken from him. One arm hung limp, so he couldn't swing it. Cyrus was in no danger. Skunkha was very confused what was happening. Spargapeithes stumbled as he turned to walk away, and was struggling to get a grip on his sword. He turned it, awkwardly. Darius had seen the move before, on injured men in battle. Proud, suicidal men. Atossa wanted to run to her prince, and was fighting, pulling, and tugging at Darius to let her go when Cambysses gasped. In the sand dunes Skunkha cried out. Darius watched Spargapeithes run himself through the gut with his own sword, and was dead by the time he hit the ground. Atossa wrenched herself free. Darius let go of his wife and ran his fingers through his hair, taking violent fistfuls and twisting at his skull. Cyrus was amused, and asked for a refill of his wine as he plopped back down onto his indigo and saffron colored carpets. The old, fat man fussed about his daughter, sobbing and lying on top of Spargapeithes' dead body. Meanwhile, up in the sands, Cyrus had sent soldiers off to catch Skunkha who had cried out, but they weren't going to find him. The advisor unstrapped the chest of gold from his horse and scattered it in the sands as he ran back to camp. The first stop he made was to his father's tent, to strangle the cruel man for one more ill-fated attempt at getting his son into power.

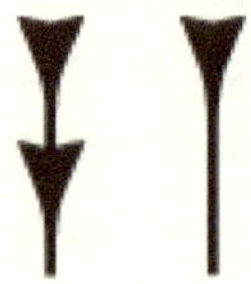

At sunrise no soldier had returned to the Massagetae camp. It was silently understood that they had been defeated. Over two hundred men had been lost. Ariomardus halfheartedly try to sell the idea that Cyrus was keen on taking prisoners from these sorts of battles, but his kind words were only met with tear stained smiles, whimpering limps of widows, and head nods from elderly fathers. The camp was holding together because Tomyris was leading by example. Her son had led the war party. Her son had not returned. If Spargapeithes had been killed, then the young queen needed to be smart about how she expressed her emotions. A mother was allowed to weep and wail, but a queen was not. This was Tomyris' only child, only heir. Her leadership might come into question even more than it already had by visiting tribal chiefs and lesser kings. She was not yet so old to not marry again and bear more children. The mourning period would be squandered by all this talk of the future. The bodies barely lied cold and yet already preparations needed to be made. On the horizon there were still fires in whatever remained of the Persian camp. Black clouds puffed into the pale blue sky. It would be nice to assume they were merely campfires for breakfast, but the clouds were larger than that. They were the size of pyres for disposing of a mass amount of bodies. Tomyris hoped she would get the honor of having her man returned her. Ariomardus insisted she would be given that much respect. She trusted him. With everything in her being, she took that man's word as truth. Skunkha had not been seen since the previous night. While the young queen craved an audience with her advisor for clarity, the claims that Ariomardus had made against him were damaging. Skunkha had spent the remainder of his night after the battle in his father's tent, beside his dead body. There were waves of delight and depression, relief and remorse. Skunkha was spinning, and half contemplated suicide to avoid the fallout that would surely consume him now that the sun had rose. He'd have to face his queen sooner than later, but it wasn't going to go well for him.

In the Persian camp the officers had sorted through the dead overnight, and built pyres for their soldiers. Two officers had been lost, and Ariomardus had run away, so Darius and the remaining two lieutenant generals collected sagebrush kindling enough for the morning. Four officers had taken eight thousand men and moved camp to the Jaxartes River, a few days ride away across the red sands. Cyrus was not done with the Massagetae. His children however, were entirely done with him. Cambysses worked with the servants to move the dead bodies of the Persian soldiers and pile them up on the pyres in equal weight distribution so the flames would burn through more efficiently. Atossa meanwhile had been trembling in and out of sleep for hours without a fire in the harsh winter night. She liked the feeling of shaking and uncontrollable shivering because the pain of knowing she had had something to do with Spargapeithes death made her sick to her stomach. She had vomited anything in her stomach from the past three days. Her body was as hollow as her heart, and she had ravaged the pretty black braids in her hair. She looked as though she had been attacked by a pack of wolves for all the clawing she had done to herself. Her dresses and skirts were torn, some shredded beyond wear. Darius hadn't even checked on her once to see how she was doing. She assumed that was because he thought this a fitting punishment for sleeping with the rival prince instead of staying loyal to her husband. From time-to-time Atossa would let out a blood curdling scream in a fit of rage. Cyrus took a drink of wine every time she did this. It reminded him too much of the tone of his wife's voice, who was also screaming inside of his head. But as the hours passed, he was sure his daughter would come around to her senses and be done with all this childish nonsense. The Massagetae were flies in their life, meant to be swatted at and disposed of. She would understand this too. Darius would help her. The old leader reassured himself as he sat on his brightly dyed carpets alone. The pillows and cot where Cambysses usually slept were abandoned. His servants were up to their arms in dead bodies, far too busy to dote on his morning needs. He hadn't stoked his own fire once since he'd been fighting the Saka people, and now, he was thinking about it. The thought of it disgusted him, and he threw his last cup of wine at his tent. The blood red fabric absorbed the wine like water since they were the same color. From outside, Atossa could see the stain growing on her father's tent, and decided to go inside to speak with him. She was all cried out by now, but still looked a mess. She walked with a bit of pride about that. Spargapeithes blood was dried brown all down the front of her, and caked into her hands.

"Father."

"Atossa. You need to get down to the river and clean yourself up. You look terrible. No daughter of mine should ever be seen by others appearing so, so…"

"A woman in mourning is allowed to be disheveled. It is preferred even, by some cultures."

"*Not* our culture."

"A princess should hold respect for her fallen prince."

"The boy isn't *yours* to mourn."

"He might as well have been mine."

"The only men you have to mourn are me, your brother, and your husband. Spargapeithes was none of those to you. You forget your place, Atossa. It would serve you well to remember who you are, and remember fast."

"Or what? You'll kill me?"

"*You* negotiated that deal last night. Do not think you escape blame for the carnage that followed."

"If I would have known Sparga was going to die, I'd have thrown that chest of coin into the river."

"You disgrace me with such thoughts. You're lucky Darius isn't here to hear you say such foolish things."

"You mean to shame me right now, father? To insinuate that I am *lucky* at this hour is a huge disservice to my heart. I am the most *unlucky* of all women in this desert right now, except for one."

"Don't tell me you feel *sorrow* for our enemy queen?"

"I can't imagine what it must feel like to be her this morning. She's lost everyone in her family, her parents, husband, and now son. She's lost a good portion of her army."

"Exactly! She is weak! Ripe for submission! It's right where we want her, dear Atossa, can't you see that?! There is no better time for us to make our kill strike!"

"You heartless, soulless man."

"Call me heartless all you want, but I have fought and won these battles my entire life. This is the way the world is, dear. This is my legacy to leave for you and your brother. This is how empires are made. It is messy, yes, and it is hard work, but it is necessary in order for me to provide you the life you are so accustomed to living. Do you think all women back home have the luxury of tearing their fine dresses apart as you have, without the promise of severe consequence?"

"What worse consequence is there to improper behavior than killing the man that I love?"

"You *loved* that boy?"

"I still love him. Death has not, and will not sway me."

"Are you trying to hurt me, Atossa? Are you trying to break me by telling me such nonsense?"

"It is not nonsense that I love Spargapeithes. I mean no effect on you at all. It is *my* heart, and *my* heart alone involved here. And it is *my* heart, and *my* heart alone that has shattered overnight because of your greed. When is it going to be enough for you, father? When is the killing going to stop?"

"You don't understand. Women *never* understand the ways of war."

"You honestly expect me to believe that? Tomyris is a woman. Don't you dare sit there and tell me that she does not understand the ways of war. She has proved more than a worthy opponent for you, oh mighty *king of kings*."

"If I didn't know any better, I'd say you admired our enemy."

"She's not *my* enemy. I thought she was, but I was listening to the wrong people. I was listening to you and the officers. Ariomardus is a good man. Many men like him have left your ranks for her."

"And you mean to join them?"

"No. Persia is my legacy. I owe it to them to right the wrongs you have made in your rule."

"You are not my heir."

"But you said I should be."

"But you aren't. A female can never lead Persia. The gods would not allow it."

"You don't speak for the gods. After what you did last night, I doubt they'll even listen to your prayers anymore."

"For the life of me, I really cannot understand why you are so upset. In the grand scheme of things…"

"My *life* is not a scheme, father!"

"I know. I know it's not. But you must be reasonable."

"Like you were last night?"

"What do you know of what happened last night?"

"I saw enough to know that you are a cruel, cruel man. You are not the father who raised me. You are not the one who used to sing me to sleep at night, and tell me stories of adventures. Mother took that man away from the world when she died. Ever since then, it's just been this hard shell of a man who looks like you, but has no heart, no soul. You are just empty, and dark inside. My father would never have done what you did last night. And I have loved you, and defended you, and stood by you for so long. I have championed your rules, and fought for your ideals. My entire life has been dedicated to your greatness, your pride, your image. I have wasted years I will never get back. I look upon myself and feel so ashamed for being so blind for so long. Father, how can you have made such a huge mistake, that the last person in this world that held any genuine love for you at all, can't even find a way to defend you anymore?"

"Are you quite finished, Atossa?"

"What is to be done with the Massagetae's dead?"

"What do you wish to be done?"

"Tomyris should be allowed to collect her men."

"And what of that of the body of Spargapeithes?"

"I will deliver him to Tomyris, personally."

"You will ride across the river and the dunes with a dead man strapped to your horse?"

"I have no trouble taking one last ride with him, across any terrain."

"You truly loved the boy, didn't you?"

"Yes."

"Then be swift about it, before I come to my senses."

"I can't promise how long this will take. Whatever funeral rites the Massagetae hold for Sparga, I would like to be a part of them."

"You're a grown woman. What you decide is your own business. But you should run by this by your husband first. I would like him to be your guard if you mean to spend time with the enemy."

"Tomyris won't hurt me."

"You're a little fool if you believe that."

"I believe she and I will be able to come to an understanding. Besides, Ariomardus is there, and he will look out for me."

"I wouldn't count on that. He was never loyal to us."

"He might not have ever been loyal to *you*, but I am not you."

"No. No, you're certainly not me. Your mother would be so proud. She was the only woman who ever questioned me so severely as you have this morning. I'm glad to see you finally found your voice, Atossa. I'm just sorry it had to come to this."

"You're not sorry. I've just made you uncomfortable. Excuse me. I'll see to it the servants bring you in more wine to sedate yourself."

Atossa walked out with her head held high. She had never left a conversation with her father feeling so empowered before. Hopefully, there would be more talks like that with the old leader, where he slowly but surely realized his time as the almighty had come and gone. Atossa would rise up, and take the power that was always meant for her. She only thought she was ready for that kind of responsibility before, but now she believed she could actually handle the life ahead of her. She didn't need a man to do this. It would have been preferred to have Spargapeithes by her side, but he would be with her in other ways. She rubbed her stomach, hoping to get physical validation in the weeks and months to come. There would be no tea for her to try and get her hands on. If the gods were merciful, they would allow her to bear Spargapeithes' child. The tiniest thought of becoming a mother because of him was what kept her from slitting her wrists the night before. In spite of her father's wishes, Atossa told no one of what her plans were for the day. Instead, the princess, in all her ragged, blood-stained glory, went to retrieve her prince's body and drag him to her her horse herself. Cambysses saw his sister proudly struggling, and offered to help her without any need for an explanation. She felt guilt swell up in her throat. He was right about her too. He had always been the more benevolent, conscientious of the siblings. She had treated him harshly for her father's approval, but no more. It took Cambysses and Atossa both to muster all their strength to heave Spargapeithes up onto the back of the horse. His body was stiff, and hard like rock. Much blood had been lost from his abdomen wound. Atossa had the prince's back facing up towards the sun to keep her from staring at the gaping hole in her beloved. While Atossa took to straightening Spargapeithes clothes on his body, Cambysses strapped him to the horse securely for a long ride to the Massagetae camp. Then he helped his sister mount her horse, and asked if he could join her. Atossa didn't know why he'd want to do that, but in the spirit of trying to be a more mature woman, she nodded in agreement, and trotted up to where the sandbar was in the river. While she was waiting for her brother, her husband came up on horseback, looking as if he had also invited himself along for the ride. She scowled as he pulled out Spargapeithes sword and offered it to her. He insisted a man always be burned with his weapon.

When Atossa rode into the Massagetae camp, the men flanked behind her. It was quiet, and not at all what the princess had expected it to be. There were women sewing holes in tents, cooking breakfast, and children petting the goats in the pins. It didn't look like a people in mourning. Atossa didn't know her way through these mass of tanned hide tents. Thankfully, a teenage girl who recognized Spargapeithes' body, Skunkha's niece, was kind enough to take the Persian princess' reins and lead her to Tomyris tent. It was unassuming for a queen, and also deathly quiet. Upon seeing the shadows in the late morning light, Ariomardus came out first, and then leaned in to whisper something to Tomyris. The young queen came out holding the Dahae soldier's hand. Atossa felt mirrored in pain looking at Tomyris. There was a sudden realization. But it was also not mirrored at all. Atossa had never had a child. She had never raised, and taught, and struggled with a child. She did not know what it was like to experience that kind of love, and so this loss was entirely foreign to her. The princess slid down, and Cambysses followed to begin untying his rival counterpart. In her shaking hands, still bloodied and stained from the carnage the night before, Atossa presented Spargapeithes sword to his mother on bended knee. Ariomardus left the women to help Darius pull the slain prince down to the ground for wound observation. In hushed whispers, Darius explained what had happened in the Persian camp. The feast charade, the massacre, all of it. There were no survivors. All the wounded had been killed. Over two hundred lied bloated in the Persian camp now. The bulk of the Persian forces were now lying in wait on the Jaxartes banks to strike Tomyris in her moment of vulnerability. Ariomardus corrected that last detail, noting Tomyris had never been more ready for war than she was now. The Massagetae needed to ride out to collect their dead, and the burning grounds were to be prepared for a celebration this evening. Darius was invited to attend, but he politefully declined. It wouldn't have been right for him to spend the morning burning his own, and the night burning his enemy. Darius still said enemy, and Ariomardus shook his head. It wasn't personal, just politics. Darius was still in the fight. These pleasantries with Spargapeithes hadn't changed anything. Not for him. But there was a change in Cambysses and Atossa. Tomyris knelt down in front of the young princess, and took her son's sword, which had once belonged to his father, Sacephares. Tears dripped onto the dried blood, and the young queen smeared them to feel the slickness again. Her throat burned liked fire, but for some reason a smile came to her lips. Atossa was confused. Behind the women on the ground, Ariomardus was barking orders like he had authority. Men needed to go and collect their fellow soldiers. He would ride out with them. Others needed to assemble and collect wood for the pyres, women needed to collect offerings to the gods. The camp was alive and well, stirring without the queen saying a word. Tomyris laughed away her tears, pulling Atossa in for a hug.

"You did the right thing. Thank you for bringing my baby home."

"How can you find the strength to smile, Tomyris? My chest aches."

"Sparga was such a kind boy. So light hearted. He would not want you to be sad. When Massagetae die, they are welcomed into another world by their friends and family who died before them. My son, he is meeting his father and grandfather for the first time today. He will be so happy to see them! I am warmed by the sight of the three of them together. And my mother, she will be keeping them all in line for me until it is my time to go and see them."

"I almost killed myself last night when I saw Sparga fall. But I stopped myself, because I might be carrying Sparga's child."

"It is too soon to know that. But if you are, I would very much like to be a part of your baby's life."

"I would like that too."

"Well, that's enough crying for one day! Come, we have a funeral to prepare for. You are staying for the burnings tonight, aren't you?"

"I wouldn't miss it for the world. Should I clean up first? Or…"

"You look perfect, Atossa. I'm sure my son would want to keep you looking just the way you are. Let the blood come off on its own."

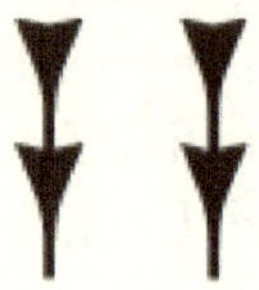

It took the Massagetae most of the afternoon to carry their dead back to the burning grounds. Most families took care to build their own pyres in the valleys where their ancestors had been burned for generations. Some of the visiting chiefs and tribal leaders paid personal respects to their soldiers, but not everyone could be afforded such niceties. Tomyris made sure to touch each and every man who had been killed. She placed a hand on their chest, and asked the gods to take care of them. She thanked them for following her son into battle and being so brave as to volunteer the night before. The young queen also promised that Cyrus would pay for what had been done to them, to the fullest of her abilities. While she was in no hurry to meet her soldiers in death, she wasn't exactly shocked at the possibility either. The final body she spoke to was that of her sixteen-year-old son, Spargapeithes, who Tomyris thought looked more like his own teenage father now than he ever had. But the most striking difference was that Atossa was on her knees beside his body, where Tomyris herself had once sat beside Sacephares. Atossa had loved Spargapeithes. There was true pain in her face as she wept, and clung onto his cold hands. Tomyris was a poor widow in her youth. She hadn't cried for the man who had won her, raped her, and died on her. She couldn't weep for a stranger. Skunkha had sat beside her that day to pull her through. Tomyris hadn't seen her advisor since all of this had happened. She hadn't sent a search party for him, not after learning of his betrayal. Power had meant more to him than their friendship after all. Good portions of her life had been nothing but a lie. But she couldn't wallow in her personal upheavals. Ariomardus was keeping watch on the burning grounds and the camp, making sure Cyrus wasn't up to anything in Tomyris' time of need. The desert seemed quiet for now, and he'd continually lock eyes with the young queen as he made his scouting runs on the back of his black buck, taming quite nicely given the circumstances. Tomyris snickered at how this winter was turning out, but her lips pricked into a snarl when she recognized a curly headed man heaving a body into the farthest reaches of the burning grounds. It was Skunkha, carrying the body of his father, Homarges. Atossa stood up beside the young queen, and looked out to see what it was that had gotten Tomyris so upset so quickly.

"I know you have every right to be mad at your advisor…"

"Please, Atossa, not now. My son is dead because of Skunkha."

"He didn't take the coin, Tomyris."

"Ari said he saw you and Skunkha make the exchange in the river."

"Yes, at first, he did take the coin. But when I was riding here with Sparga's body, I saw the coins scattered across the desert. Your advisor came back to you, Tomyris. He loves you; he always has. Don't blame him for wanting power. Titles corrupt a man like no other. My father knows that. He tried to exploit that to ruin you. You present my father with the greatest challenge of his life and he is not handling it well. Skunkha has lived his life in shadows, and at the first glimpse of sun he ran. Now he's preparing to burn his father. Let whatever else has happened between the two of you settle here."

"Would you be so quick to forgive a friend who wronged you?"

"I am standing here in your burning grounds at your mercy. I already know you to be a woman capable of a great many things. Forgiveness must be one of them.

"If Skunkha wishes to speak to me, he must be the one to step forwards first. A queen does not bow down to her advisor."

"He will come around soon enough. Will you offer your prayers to the gods in the name of his father?"

"I promised Homarges would be burned here, but I have no kind words to say on his behalf. Because of that one man's deals, I have now lost a father, a husband, and a son. He was behind them all, undermining them at every turn."

"Just like a mongoose."

"What?"

"My husband, Darius, he has this theory about animals and people. In every war there is always a mongoose, digging holes underneath everyone's feet while no one is looking. He is the secret master of all plans. No one can ever find him until it's too late. I understand now. Perhaps my husband deserves more credit from me than I have given him."

"Darius will be good to you, Atossa."

"But he will never be your son."

"No, he won't be. But as a woman, you will find that your heart can break and heal any number of times, even when you don't understand how or why. *You* can be broken and whole at the same time too. Pained, and yet still full of hope."

"That man of yours will be good to you too, Tomyris."

"You mean, Ari?"

"He's never lost sight of what he was fighting for. He has genuine care for people in a world with very little heart. I don't know how a man with so little to his name could be so kind."

"Material possessions and titles, money and glory, it's never been what's made a man. A good woman knows what makes the great men great, and it's not how many battles they won or how many scars they have. It's about how much they care for others. How much they give without worrying about receiving. They might be tough, and harsh on the outside, but they are gooey on the inside."

"I hope to learn that for myself one day."

"You will. Darius has the potential to be a great man one day."

"He says he has a lot to learn from Ariomardus before he can consider himself great."

"Then we shall have to do our best to see that our men survive this next engagement with your father."

"How do you know there will be more to this war?"

"Because I need Cyrus to look me in the eyes, and know what he has taken from me for killing my son. Only then, will this war finally be over."

"You know, my father thinks he has weakened you. I told him he was wrong."

"You will make a fine queen one day, Atossa. I look forward to hearing about all of the things you will accomplish."

"If I can be half as respected as you are, Tomyris, I will consider myself accomplished. Your son, even in our short time together, he looked at me with those light eyes like I was capable of doing anything. I just want to prove to him that he was right. Thank you, for coming to talk to me. I forgot how much I needed a mother."

"It's like my father used to always say, there's nothing like a funeral to make you feel alive. Our fight is not yet over. Come back to camp with me, and help me carry the women's offerings to the pyres."

Tomyris and Atossa spent the duration of the day working together as the oddest pairing anyone in the Massagetae had ever seen. A woman without a child, and a daughter without a mother. Two women with immense power, and none of the greed in their hearts to corrupt them. Rather than the death of Spargapeithes dividing them, draining them of spirit, it joined them, and renewed their vengeance for justice. Cyrus would not only have to lose this war, but he would have to fall, for good. Enough was enough. Atossa told Tomyris everything she knew about her father's plans for the Jaxartes River, to cut the Massagetae off from behind and slaughter them. Cambysses added to his sister's intelligence by warning the young queen of his father's ruthless tactics with his officers. A bounty had been put on Tomyris' head for anyone who could bring her dead body to Cyrus. The young queen took this information to her war council, and what remained of her couple hundred-man army. A trap would have to be set to pull the Persians into more favorable position. Tomyris offered herself up as bait since it was clear no one else was going to volunteer after what had just happened. Worried eyes wee cast about the tent, but no one said anything in difference to the young queen. If anything, they were encouraged by her boldness, and strengthened in resolve that this war would not drag into spring after all. The men would be home with their families soon enough for planting season. Life would get back to normal. But first, before anything could be handled with Cyrus, there were the funeral rites. Tomyris sponsored horse races and trick riding in circles around the collection of pyres. Some two hundred dead, and honorable souls. As day turned into night, grease from the campfires was poured onto the bodies and lit aflame in glorious, sky reaching, golden strikes. The Massagetae chanted and howled with vigor. They jumped through the fire, and danced in the heat of the flames. Tomyris taught Atossa the widow's dance beside Spargapeithes' body. Ariomardus stood back and watched at how good Tomyris was with the Persian princess. A part of him hoped that Atossa was pregnant with Spargapeithes' baby now, but Cambysses was still conflicted about the whole ordeal. The lazy eyed prince worried that if a pale skinned baby was born with light eyes, that Cyrus might have it killed, but Ariomardus seemed confident that Cyrus wouldn't be alive long enough to do that.

The mass funeral was over when the blackness of a cold winter's night consumed the burning grounds. Only the stars were lighting the way back to camp. Atossa and Cambysses were given a tent of their own beside Tomyris and Ariomardus for safe keeping. But at first light the Persian siblings were sent on their way to reunite with Darius and set the stage for the final battle. Skunkha could be seen skulking on the fringes of the camp, afraid of whether or not he was welcomed in Tomyris' presence anymore. He had no idea what she knew, but her stone faced expression towards him meant that whenever he did finally muster up enough courage to go and try to make amends, he would be met with the iciest of receptions. He deserved that much, he knew he did, but he also missed his best friend. He killed his father for her, that had to mean something. There were hopes Ariomardus might soften the young queen in the days following the massacre, but there was only so much a man could do. Tomyris was doing what she always did when she was upset, and buried herself in work. Ariomardus had become her advisor and together the two were constantly in one tent or another securing battle plans and drawing out strategies on hide canvases. Skunkha would listen to gossip around campfires from afar to stay informed. He couldn't stand being left out of something he so desperately wanted to fix. The people loved that he had stayed true to Tomyris, and were even happier still to know his father had been taken care of with not so many details said one way or the other. Skunkha dined with widows and his sullen niece, who was still incredibly beside herself at the loss of Spargapeithes. At every turn and every walk, Tomyris' eyes found themselves on her scorned friend. He was everywhere in the camp all at once, and while she wanted, and needed this rift mended between them, she would not rush to his side as a submissive. He had to know that. He had to know how this had hurt her. He did know that, but he was just at a loss for words. In the meantime, Ariomardus kept his hands on the young queen. He was her guiding force, her constant reassurance that she was doing the right thing. For every glance from Tomyris that was pleading to Skunkha to come to her, there was Ariomardus' glare for the advisor to keep his distance. No matter what, sparks were going to fly soon, and there was no clean way about going around it. Skunkha just needed to make up his mind.

Back in the Persian camp Darius was anxiously awaiting the return of his wife and brother-in-law. Cyrus had been kept thoroughly inebriated while his children were entertaining the enemy. Darius was a bit more gracious about it, but still awkwardly upset that the funeral games had taken so long. Atossa seemed to be in a much better place mentally, and even kissed her husband on the cheek to thank him for his patience in dealing with all of this. Darius looked stunned at Cambysses. The prince was equally taken aback by the change in his sister, but in a positive way for once in their entire lives. Perhaps talking with Tomyris had done her a bit of good. It was in Atossa's mind that while she was still riding the high in a recent surge of confidence, that she should try speaking with her father again and set some things straight about this war and his intentions. Darius steered his wife away from that though, with a troubled look in his eyes. Cambysses was left to go check on his father's curious condition while the princess allowed herself to be pulled into her husband's tent. She was half surprised it didn't smell like perfume, but Darius promised all of that behavior was behind him now. All that mattered was the agreement he and Atossa had made years ago when they got married. They would help each other to the top, and now might be as good a time as any to start taking those steps to leading the Persian empire, and forming it with their own ideals. It had been noted for the past couple of weeks that Cassandae was plaguing her elderly husband's dreams at night, warning him of his imminent death in the red sands. But Darius said in the past day since Atossa had spoken to him, that Cyrus was now seeing frightening images during the day. Darius had overheard a conversation the previous afternoon between the old man and one of his attending servants in all confidence. Cyrus was rambling about how he had seen Darius with four wings coming out of his back, soaring about the four corners of the known world that had been consumed in the name of Persia. Darius. Not Cambysses, not his son, and heir, but Darius. Atossa giggled in amusement that her father was finally losing his mind. Darius continued that he had tried several times to speak with Cyrus, and gauge his condition with his own two eyes, but that the leader had refused audience with him at every turn. Atossa leaned forwards and excitedly kissed her husband now, surprisingly herself as much as him.

"What was that for, Atossa?"

"You have just given me the best news I have heard in a very long time. It's finally happening for us, Darius! I told you it would! My father is under so much stress, it is starting to kill him. It is like a sickness that eats at him daily, and there is no stopping it."

"I was hoping you might be in a good mood when I told you this, but I didn't expect you to be this friendly. How did the funeral games go with the Massagetae? Safe to say they went well?"

"They were very respectful. Tomyris taught me a lot. You should've been there."

"It wouldn't have been right. I'm going to end up killing some of those men the next time I see them. It is easy to kill a man when you don't know about his wife and children back at camp. You're killing a scream; you're killing a sword. But I take no pleasure in killing a husband or a father."

"The time here in the sands has softened you."

"And what do you think about that?"

"I like you better this way."

"Do you like me enough to stay in a tent with me again?"

"Will there be room enough for us *and* your whores?"

"You're the only woman in my life, Atossa. I told you; I've put all of that other stuff behind me."

"Just because you have said that you have changed, doesn't mean I believe it. Two nights ago, I watched the man I love die. And last night I helped his mother burn his body. I am not ready to spend the night with you in your tent."

"We don't have to do anything. It would be enough just to let me fall asleep to the sight of you, rather than a memory."

"I suppose it would help project our marriage to the rest of the camp as being stronger than ever. It might make my father lose what little sanity he has left to his name."

"It's about time that old man started to fear someone again. It's been too long since he was uneasy."

"I just wonder, should we tell Cambysses about all of this?"

"Our plans have never involved him. Cambysses stands in the way of our goals."

"But he has been looking out for me my entire life, and I think I owe him a little bit of…"

"You owe him nothing, Atossa. He's not our ally. We leave him in the dark, just as we always have. It's you and me against the world."

"I guess."

"What is it? I don't understand. Being queen is all you have ever wanted, and now that you are closer than you've ever been to reaching out and taking power, you want to…slow down?"

"I don't want to slow anything. I want this war over. I want to go home where it is warm, and the water is clean. But…what would Tomyris do if she were me?"

"Tomyris is a queen because her father died. If she had a brother, she'd be right where you are. You can look up to Tomyris all you want but you will never *be* her, Atossa. And I'm just fine with that. I like you much better."

"You do?"

"You're my wife. Of course, I like you better."

"We are just political allies. We aren't *really* husband and wife."

"But what if we *were*? What if we tried to do this for real?"

"We have nothing in common but our desire for power. Darius, you've never once asked me a question about myself, or how my day was going, or…"

"Atossa, I know way more about you than you think."

"Prove it."

"I know that your favorite color is red, because of that one dress you remember your mother wearing in the summertime when you took that vacation to the sea as a little girl. And I know that you don't like to get up before the sunrise because you think that your hair looks prettier when it's been in braids for a few more hours. But your hair always looks pretty, especially when you think it's a mess, and there's these few strands that come down and bounce off of your eye lashes when you laugh. I also know that you hate the taste of red wine, but you drink it to impress your father. You prefer white wine, but only drink it alone in your tent, so I always keep a cup of it in there for you. And I know…"

"You know all of that about me? But how? I thought we could barely tolerate each other?"

"You didn't want me, but I've *always* wanted you. And not just because you're the princess. I love *you*, Atossa. I just hope, that one day, you'll be able to love me too."

"Tomyris told me you'd be good to me. The least I can do is be good to you in return. I'll stay with you in your tent from now on, and I'll try to give you those sons you've been begging me for since we were teenagers. It's time I begin to grow up and start accepting the life I have while I have it."

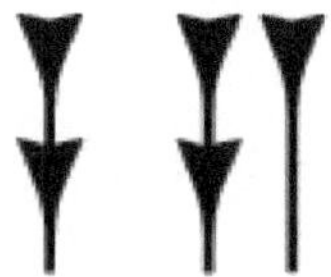

Defending the Massagetae camp from the Araxes River had taken a three day move in order to position themselves in the most advantageous location from the Persian attacks. Now that Tomyris knew that Cyrus had rounded about her to the Jaxartes River, the camp was in jeopardy once more. To move the camp to a safer place this time would probably take five or even seven days. A strike was easily assumed to take place before then. Everyone had warned the young queen that the next battle was breathing down their necks. She understood how much time it took to do things, but still, the camp needed to be moved. Any action on their part was better than just sitting there and waiting for the inevitable. Orders went out at sundown to pack up and begin the long trek out to an old camp location Tomyris hadn't lived in since she was a little girl. The elders knew the way, and would be the first ones out. A group of soldiers had to go with them though for scouting and protection. More soldiers had to sacrifice themselves to help the widowed women and children carry things. Tomyris' standing army, ready to fight at a moment's notice then had shrunk to about a hundred men, that was all. It wasn't enough, but it would have to do. They had the hearts of a ten-thousand-man army if that made any difference. They boasted they could each take out ten or twenty men on their own. It was an admirable lie. The young queen thanked everyone for their hard work in these trying times. Her voice was steady when she spoke, and nonnegotiable. This was no time for questions or hesitations, just blind obedience. The only person who seemed to have a problem with this was Skunkha, who was not adjusting well to being so left out of the loop when his friend made decisions. Since this move was occurring at night, out of an abundance of caution, the winter winds were quite unforgiving to those in threadbare clothing. Tomyris was in her tent distributing furs to those in need while Ariomardus stood out front to answer any concerns the camp might have. Skunkha had no interest in speaking to the Dahae soldier, but after casing and circling Tomyris' tent for ten minutes, the scorned advisor swallowed that last shred of his pride, and stood toe to toe with Ariomardus. Skunkha was tall, but the Dahae man was taller, and more intimidating with his light eyes and darker skin. Skunkha rifled a nervous hand through his curly hair and sighed.

"I just need to speak with her, Ariomardus."

"Tomyris is busy. Pack up your things and move camp. If you're already packed, be a *nice man* and help a woman in need."

"Be a *nice man*, huh? You mean to shame me?"

"You should be ashamed enough after what you did. I don't need to do anything to you. But if you mean to come here and upset Tomyris, then I will do something I can't undo."

"If you want to kill me then just get it over with. I can't deal with her hating me anymore."

"She doesn't want you killed. You hurt her, but you're family."

"And are *you* family now as well?"

"I am her protector and confidant."

"That used to be the position *I* filled for her."

"*Before* you betrayed her by selling the Massagetae to Atossa."

"I didn't keep the coin. The deal is off. If I could take back that night I would, but I can't. Nothing I can do can bring Spargapeithes back, or all of the other men. But I would like to apologize to Tomyris face to face. She deserves that. And if I'm to be exiled like my father, then so be it. But I want to hear it from *her*, not *you*."

"Your apology will have to wait until the camp has moved."

"Battle will consume us before we are settled."

"Then perhaps you can apologize to Tomyris by giving your life to protect her people?"

"You'd like to see me fall, wouldn't you, Ariomardus?"

"I hate seeing her cry, and you've brought so much unhappiness to her in the past few days. The old me would have killed you, and taken a tongue lashing from her later. But the new me…"

"You put her needs above your own. She has that effect on men."

"I love her more than I fear your head games, Skunkha."

"You don't need to fear me, Ariomardus. We're on the same side."

"Are we? Seems your allegiances shift like the wind anymore."

"No. That was my father's doing. I won't make that mistake again."

"If you really want to make amends, what would you say to her?"

"It's none of your concern. What happens between her and I is our own business. I'll apologize face to face, in private."

"But that's not going to happen for a few days, and as we both know, there are very high chances you might die between now and then."

"Why do you need to know what I would say to her?"

"I won't let you upset her further. Besides, if you mean to weasel your way back into her life, I'm not going anywhere. For her sake, it would be good if we could tolerate one another, or at the very least have some sort of understanding with respect. Tell me what you would tell her, and I might begin to trust you."

"I don't have a lot to say. But what I would say is that I was wrong to think that my father could ever change. All he's ever done is manipulate people by trying to tell them what they want to hear. But he left me years ago, long before the exile. We've always been distant. And what he wanted for me was never what I wanted for myself. I knew that. I just got distracted. Titles and glory can blind a man sometimes. I'm not proud of it, but it happened. Look, I loved Spargapeithes like he was my own son. I know he's your blood, your nephew, Ariomardus, but you must understand. I was with Tomyris when no one else was, and I have stayed by her side through everything. I broke having to watch her burn her son without me holding her. But she had you, and I am happy she has you."

"That was supposed to be an apology to Tomyris, not an appeal to get on my good side."

"You think I don't know Tomyris is standing right on the other side of this tent right now, listening to everything I have to say?"

"Why didn't you come to me about the coin and your father's schemes in the first place then, Skunkha?"

"Sorry, Tomyris. I should've. But you've been so consumed with everything lately. I was told Sparga was not to be harmed at all, only used as a messenger to deliver the terms. I wanted to give you the freedom I thought you wanted, to be rid of all of this responsibility."

"That is not your decision to make."

"But I will always be looking out for you. I thought that's what I was doing. Now I see, nothing my father or Cyrus said was true. Tomyris, I scattered that coin into the sands. And if there was anything I could have done to save your son I would have. Cyrus didn't kill him. The Persians didn't kill him. I saw it all. Sparga was released, and he fell on his own sword out of shame for the loss of his men. He died a warrior, Tomyris, not a prisoner. Your boy died a good man. I just wanted you to know that."

"You said you saw it *all*?"

"Well, most of the battle, yes, but all of the interrogation."

"Would you know the men that hurt my son if you saw them again?"

"I would have no trouble. Their faces are burned into my memory."

"Then be the friend I know you to be, and when this battle comes to us, you be sure those men end up dead. I don't care if *you* do it, or if someone else does it, but you make sure those men die, Skunkha."

"I would be honored, Tomyris."

"Ari was right though; you need to get moving."

"Do you really think going to the old campgrounds is for the best?"

"Cyrus knows we are here. The people aren't safe where he knows us to be. Therefore, I have to move the people out of his reach. There are other chiefs and lesser kings who have promised me they have allies in the area to help, we just have to get out there."

"And what will remain of our home here? Our burning grounds?"

"I am taking care of that."

"I've never known you to be one to run from trouble, Tomyris."

"I'm not running."

"Does that mean…you are staying behind?"

"I will give the camp time to move that they so desperately need."

"Tomyris, you can't stay back alone! That's too dangerous!"

"Sh! I don't need you scaring anyone!"

"But *I'm* scared. They'll take you prisoner and torture you."

"One person's suffering is better than the loss of an entire tribe."

"That's too heavy a burden, even for you. As your advisor..."

"Ari is my advisor now."

"As your *friend*, I must ask you to reconsider."

"You can ask me all you want, but I've made my decision."

"If you die, who have you named your successor?"

"Ari has the respect of the council. He is Saka blood."

"I can't believe you've let her do this, Ariomardus."

"It wasn't my decision, Skunkha. I'm no happier about it than you. But you believe me, if *any*thing happens to her, I will see to it *every* one of those Persians dies in these sands."

"*Every* one? Even your friends?"

"Tomyris is all the friend I need."

"Sounds lonely."

"You're one to talk."

"Good point. Well, if there's nothing more I can do here, can I at least ask for a hug, Tomyris, for old time's sake?"

The young queen came out of the tent from her not so obvious hiding place and hugged her advisor like she hadn't seen him in ten years. Ariomardus didn't watch, he kept his back turned and continued giving directions and reassurements to the people as they came up to him for guidance. Skunkha left the hug first, not wanting to spoil the moment by crying on his friend's shoulder upon struggling to attempt her decision to take on a suicide mission. No one was to know outside of the war council. If the people knew she was risking her life, most of them probably wouldn't leave, and insist to die in camp in a mass slaughter. Tomyris would not have a proud repeat of what had just happened with her son. If at all possible, she needed to avenge his bravery, and justify his courage. Cyrus would know that he messed with the wrong tribe this time, the wrong queen, and the wrong mother. More women came to her tent for furs. Tomyris handed them out until the pile was gone. It was bittersweet watching a line of horses and carts pull away into the desert, but it was for their own good as unforgiving as the weather was. A storm was rolling in, so the sky was heavy with chunky black clouds and abrasive wind. Visibility was choked off to a few feet because of the sands whipping around. Everyone was laden down with protective gear, golden armor and neck scarves. Caps and pointed hats were secured with ties tightly, and children were carried close to their mother's chests. The people would survive this war. Tomyris had done the right thing sending them away now while they could still be at some kind of peace within themselves. Her own inner turmoil need not be a shared experience. It was bad enough the war council pitied her, and Ariomardus kept looking at her like she was dying right before his eyes. But now Skunkha was in on it too, quivering lips and shaking his head in disbelief. She didn't need their approval to do this, it's just what had to be done, and that's all there was to it. The gods would be proud of her sacrifice. It was a highly noble thing to do, to give oneself up for the sake of the many. She was sick to her stomach just thinking about what Cyrus and his men might do to her. Scenes of that day as a child, watching and hearing the women get raped, she imagined she'd have to prepare herself for that. But she had her knife on her, the golden one matching Ariomardus. If anything got too bad, she'd just take it right across her neck and kill herself quick. She had heard from soldiers it was nearly painless because the blood spilled out so fast. It was a merciful kill, if there could be said to be such a thing. And if she was to be stripped of her weapons, she would just steal another. She would scrap and grapple, and claw her way into death. Tomyris would not die quietly, that was for certain.

By sunrise the camp had been cleared with the lone exception of Tomyris' tent. The young queen hadn't laid down but for an hour or two, and she slept virtually little at all. Ariomardus was beside her, formed around the shape of her body, with his heavy arm draped like a weight across her side. Thankfully he was a heavy sleeper, and Tomyris was able to slip out of his hold without disturbing or waking him. He was far less disarming when she stared at him with his eye closed. No light pierced through her sensibilities. No dimples taunted her insecurities. He was at peace, and she wanted nothing more than to keep him this way. He was going to be so upset when he woke to find her gone, but she could not bear the thought of seeing him disappointed as she said her goodbyes. It had to be like this, stealing herself away one last time, on her own. But she couldn't help but lean down and place a lingering kiss on his shoulder for her own enjoyment. Looking at Ariomardus lying in her blankets was the last sight she wanted to capture before running. Outside her white mare was already geared and packed for battle. All that was left to do was fight the storm and confront Cyrus. Oddly enough, the young queen had felt worse the day before than she did now. Now, she felt nothing. There was a hollowness, and a stillness inside of her. Her shaking had passed, the cold did not cause her pain. The nervous sweat had subsided. Tomyris' white mare was equal in temperament. Just another ride, just another storm, just another day. There was no rear back until the young queen crested the final sand dune before the bulk of the new Persian camp revealed itself on her side of the Jaxartes River. They'd already crossed. She saw the bridges and observation towers. Horns had been blown because they had seen her. Skunkha heard the faintest of those horns on the trek away from camp, stopped to look back, but full well knew there was nothing for him to see. He knew though, and hung his head in regret, wishing he was there beside her. Ariomardus stirred awake at the horns as well, but by the time he could throw himself together and race his black buck out to follow her, all he could do was watch. Tomyris went peacefully, riding her horse down into the camp with her hands raised in a nonthreatening manner. Darius rode out to meet her, seemingly in line with Cyrus' values instead of his own. He took hold of the young queen's reins and led her to Cyrus tent, where Ariomardus could see the old fat man roll out in his mustard-colored pajamas, his great beard flying about in the winds. He was annoyed. Even at a distance it was clear. As a prisoner, Tomyris was somehow still controlling this situation. But the power shifted quick enough. A group of twenty soldiers surrounded the Massagetae queen, and forcibly pulled her off of her horse. Darius took the white mare to the animal pins, and then returned to his blood red tent where Atossa was naked, and barely wrapped in a blanket for cover. The couple disappeared inside, and Ariomardus couldn't understand why they weren't more involved.

Tomyris was thrown to the ground of Cyrus' tent and all the soldiers were told to wait outside in case she tried to escape. Two servants tending to the old leader's breakfast were struggling to maintain a fire with the gusty wind drafts and tent poles creaking out of place. Cambysses was inside as well, rustling himself awake and trying to silently understand what was happening. He looked at Tomyris on her knees, unmoving, and not at all upset. Cyrus was content in front of her, cross legged on his fine carpets and smoking a pipe of some foul-smelling sagebrush combination he'd been forced to acquire out here in the red sands. It did nothing for him, and caused him to hack more than an old man should have. The servants rushed to him thinking he was suffering some sort of medical episode but he swatted them away, and then dismissed them as well so it was just he and Tomyris in the tent, with Cambysses as witness. Her weapons were quite visible on her belt. A long silver sword to one side, her golden dagger in front, and a golden axe tucked in behind. Cyrus had not prepared for her to come to him like this, a mere two days after her son's death, and in such a storm. As unstable as his mind had made him lately, he took the winds and bad weather as a clear omen from the gods that his wife was going to take him out of the desert one way or another. His wife, not Tomyris. Cyrus wished he had his wits about him this morning, or that he could still trust his daughter Atossa, and son-in-law, Darius. But all he had in confidence now was his son and heir, even that was a stretch. Cambysses couldn't take his eyes off of the rival queen. It was as if the young man was trying to communicate with her, but she wouldn't look at him. All Tomyris was staring at was Cyrus, nearly unblinking, trying to read a man who was coming undone the longer he stayed in her lands. If only she had the numbers and capabilities to outlast this man, bloodshed would not be needed. The tent shook violently from it's ties. One came undone, and a gust of wind took advantage of it and sucked the whole tent in its former glory up into the sky, twisting it about like a whirl of chaos. Carpets, toiletries, clothes, and papers went flying. Cyrus ducked for cover. Cambysses didn't run to help his elderly father. The soldiers posted outside were too busy chasing down the tents. The servants were paralyzed. Tomyris stood up in the gale force winds, thunderstorm raging, rain pelting the landscape like it didn't affect her at all. The gods had answered *her* prayers for assistance, not Cyrus'. Thunderstorms were *her* good luck charm, not Cyrus'. And this war was to be *her* victory, not Cyrus'. Tomyris walked slowly through the madness, came down to the old man's side, and taking her golden knife from Ariomardus, slashed a warning gash across the king of kings' face. He sat there in sheer horror, gripping his bleeding wound as it dripped onto his fine, mustard-colored pajamas that had been soaked in perfumes from a foreign land in the Mediterranean. He was living a life that had run its course. Tomyris would not kill him like this, without the world to witness. But he would die, and this was the first mark of death. Her knife had been poisoned with the juice of a rare flower that grew in the watery caves beside the Araxes. By nightfall his body would begin to fail him, while his mind was left intact to understand that there was no one who could help him. Cyrus' fate was sealed. Tomyris let the rain wash the blood off of her knife before she left the old man to cower in the scattered remains of his massive camp. Cambysses rushed up to her with the reins of her horse in his hands, and wished her success in the upcoming battle. She hugged the rival prince in all sincerity, and asked him to watch out for himself, but Cambysses merely shrugged. Death wasn't a punishment to him like it was to most. He looked forward to it favorably even, and was eager for it to embrace him soon. In a crack of thunder and crash of lightning, Tomyris' white mare bucked underneath her, and fell into a full run for home.

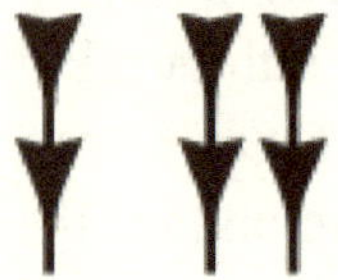

As Tomyris approached the red sands of her former home, there was nothing left for her. Ariomardus had packed up her tent and was gone, as it had been planned. The heavy rains from the storm had washed away any footprints she might have been able to use to track him. It was agreed upon that he would protect the back of the tribe as they walked out to their new campgrounds. The young queen hoped her people were sheltering well from the unforgiving weather. The rains were dying back though, and the wind was calming in this part of the desert. Tomyris rode down into a valley for a break from the winds, and decided to make a stop at the burning grounds so she could thank the gods for their help in the Persian camp this morning. She was still catching herself smiling from the ordeal. It was nothing anyone could have predicted, the way Cyrus' tent was torn up into the sky like that. You had to see it to believe it, and to hear it was something else. Cambysses was on her side still, but the young queen lacked the confidence to say for certain where Atossa and Darius' heart lied. They kept their distance from her this morning when it would have been nice to see them interfere. Perhaps that alliance had already shifted too. No matter. Tomyris had the gods on her side, and whatever they willed, it would be for the best. A good thunderstorm was always something to look forward to. It was the most clearcut, physical manifestation of the god's involvement. Mehr, god of the sun and fire, competing in eternal love with his counterpart, Anahita, goddess of the moon and water. You could not have one without the other. Some things just needed each other to work, it wasn't right to try and take them one on one. As Tomyris was musing her blessings to herself, she rounded the valley of the burning grounds, and saw Ariomardus sitting there on the crest of the dampened sands, forlorn and something of a broken man. His wild black buck was packed with her tent and their supplies. He was a dutiful man through and through, no matter how much it pained him. The young queen chuckled, and the sound caused the Dahae soldier to rear back with his golden knife and fling it into the air. Tomyris' white mare dodged the attack, and the young queen dropped down from her saddle to retrieve the weapon. She held it out in the mist, and slicked the sand off on the thigh of her pants. She was soaked through and through, but she knew why. What she didn't know was why Ariomardus had looked like he had been beside her the whole time. His black hair was whipped across his face and neck. He was not quick to look at Tomyris when she sat beside him, and offered him his knife back. She kept it out of reach at first, a sly game of speed, but the Dahae soldier was not in the mood. Tomyris assumed she had bad timing with her humor, and leaned into the man's side, carefully coiling herself around his stiff arm, and placed a kiss on his shoulder before resting her chin on his bicep. His light eyes were fixated on the blackened spots in the sands before them, where all the pyres had just stood a couple days ago.

"You left me this morning, Tomy."

"I'm sorry. I had to go take care of something."

"I know you did. But I…"

"But what?"

"Am I the dumbest man in the world for thinking I deserved more of a goodbye from you? A proper send off. All things considered, you were riding out to die this morning, and you just…left me."

"But I'm not dead. I came back."

"Why did you do it? *How* could you do it?"

"I couldn't stand the sight of watching you break. You are the most stable part of my life, Ari. You are the only thing that keeps me going anymore. Leaving this morning, I *was* prepared to die. And I had no words in me that would have done justice to saying goodbye to you. I can't say goodbye to you. Not this morning, or tomorrow, or someday when we are old and frail. I will never be able to find those words that can say that I am alright with losing you."

"I think what you just said was pretty good."

"It's different when I am holding you. The morning is behind me."

"And how did that go?"

"The poison you gave me should work. I slashed Cyrus' cheek."

"How were you able to get that close to him and leave without so much as a scratch on yourself?"

"How do you know I'm not injured? You can't even look at me."

"I take no pleasure in you seeing me like this."

"It's alright to be upset, Ari."

"I am usually stronger than this."

"We all have our moments when we are not proud of ourselves. But those moments pass, and we move on."

"For how much longer though? This war is ravaging my mind. I can't keep passing the days, preparing for myself to lose you."

"Is that what keeps bothering you?"

"You're the best thing that's ever happened to me, Tomy."

"Oh."

"I'm sorry. I know I can be a bit much sometimes."

"Yes, you can be a lot to handle, but that's also one of my favorite things about you."

"It is?"

"Most people only care about their own lot in life, no one else's. There is no way of fixing that kind of thinking. You can't make people care about others. Then there's you, *doing* too much, *feeling* too much, *saying* too much. It's because you *care* too much, you *love* too much. Life, people, they *mean* something to you. They mean everything. I hope, no matter what happens, that you stay like this. Stay *too much*, and don't you ever apologize for it."

"You're the only person I've ever met who feels like that."

"Well, everyone else who has ever told you that being *too much* was a bad thing is wrong. *I* am right. *You* are right, just the way you are."

"I wonder, just how long have you been waiting to tell me all of those things, Tomy?"

"For a while now. I can't stand seeing you doubt yourself."

"Well, now that I know that I have your support…"

"You'll always have my support, and my heart."

"You have my heart as well."

"And I wonder, just how long have you been waiting to tell me that, Ari?"

"For a while now. Thank you for coming back to me. How did you manage to find me though?"

"There is no more peaceful a place in all of this desert than the Massagetae burning grounds. Many wise souls live here."

"One day *we* will live here too."

"Yes, but not one day *soon*."

"Does that mean you have a plan for this final battle with Cyrus?"

"I always have a plan."

"You'll always have me too, Tomy."

"Good. I was counting on that."

"Of course, you were. When were you going to tell me all about this plan of yours?"

"I've been thinking on it for a few days now. I just didn't want to get ahead of myself before I knew how this morning was going to play out. The gods are on my side. I know that now. Cyrus is a marked man. All of his wrongdoings are going to weigh on him in these final hours. All we have to do is bait him enough that he makes his own fatal mistakes."

"Were you not bait enough this morning?"

"That was just a tease. That's all it was ever meant to be. I needed to make the battle interesting, something the old man will actually come out for."

"You didn't think he'd come out for the battle? He's too proud to stay away."

"No, I don't mean coming out to observe. I want that man on the field, I want him in the sands, in the thick of it."

"That's crazy. Cyrus hasn't swung a sword in battle in years."

"I hurt him this morning. I scarred his pride. The gods embarrassed him, ripped his tent right off the ground, exposed him to the error of his ways. He fears me now like he has never feared another. Cambysses and Atossa were telling me he has dreams now, of Darius ruling Persia. His dead wife Cassandae said he would die in my red sands. It's all coming together. The gods have made it so."

"I will ride with you through the end of days. Just tell me where."

"We need to meet up with the others, rally the soldiers and pull them up to the Jaxartes. Cyrus hasn't got much time."

"Hold on, there's just one more thing I want to do before we go."

Ariomardus looked down now for the first time since Tomyris had come up and sat beside him. He took hold of her chin in his freezing hand and kissed her hard enough to leave her gasping for air. It was what he had been saving for his goodbye kiss this morning, but now it was even sweeter because it wasn't soured with the prospect of death. The young queen clasped her hands around the Dahae soldier's neck and pulled him in for another, softer, deeper kiss. There would be more moments like this to come, but for now, they must be set aside. There was much work to be done and very little time to do it in. As Tomyris stood up Ariomardus observed her stature for injuries. She indeed had been graced by the gods to leave Cyrus' camp without so much as a scratch. She was somewhat impatient holding her hand out for him to take, wiggling her fingers with an innocent grin on her lips. He liked seeing her like that, without the weight of the world screwing up her face into all seriousness. Ariomardus took the young queen's hand and stood up, careful to tuck his golden knife back into his waistband, and jump onto his horse who was more than eager for a good run. Tomyris' white mare gave the black buck a worthy opponent across the red sands. The ground was made more firm with the rains and allowed a more competitive race between the young queen and her beloved advisor. The Massagetae camp were an easy enough find for them, and they were welcomed back with warm cheers, and frantic faces. The tribal chiefs and lesser kings which had been left in charge had taken refuge in some of the desert caves for the duration of the storm. As such, what should have been the progress of an afternoon, was cut in half. There was no way, and no more time that could be given to keep the people out of reach of the Persians. This was it. Tomyris needed too many men for battle. They couldn't be in two places at once, and many of the widows weren't keen on being separated from the men for a few days' ride. Massagetae didn't run from their troubles, they confronted them. As soon as Skunkha heard that he dropped what he was carrying and bolted for Tomyris. He scooped the young queen up in his arms and the two shared a heartfelt laugh between them. When the man set Tomyris back down on her feet she let her hands drift from his shoulders to his elbows, and held him there.

"I have something important to ask you, Skunkha."

"What is it?"

"Will you ride with Ari and I when we go to battle tomorrow?"

"I can't think of anywhere else I'd rather be."

"Good. Then gather the leaders. There's much to discuss!"

Every able-bodied man, and many of the women swarmed around Tomyris like she was a fire in a snowstorm. They fed off of her warmth, and her energy. She could not be extinguished. To every doubt she had a reassurance, every question an answer, and every problem a solution. She had been to the Persian camp; she had seen it with her own eyes. She had heard the men. She felt the tension. Cyrus had numbers the Massagetae couldn't rival in ten years' time. They had more weapons, more horses, more war carts. But the men were tired, and disloyal. There was no fight in their hearts, no urgency in their endeavors. An order barked was an order, and nothing more. There were Saka in those tents, and there would be Saka on the battlefield. Tomyris was sure if they exerted the right amount and properly applied show of force, that the soldiers would turn. Cyrus will be abandoned, not by all, but by many, by enough.

He is sick in body, and sick in mind. He has lost the faith of his family and children. He has lost the respect of his officers. The winter is breaking them. The land is working against them. The gods and the thunderstorm were a gift to Tomyris, and she insisted gifts like that were best not to be squandered. Every soldier tomorrow morning would be armed with a bow and arrows, even if they weren't archers. They would have knives, axes, spears, and swords. Everyone would be ready for everything. Bonfires would be lit tonight, kept aflame at all costs. The rains were going to be kept at bay for the battle. The goats for the sacrifice needed to be fed and prepared, washed and dressed for the sacred rites. This was no small matter. There would also be a feast. A feast of whatever they had. Nothing was to be spared. If they were going to the gods, they were going to go happy! The people swelled with Tomyris' speech. The young queen swelled in return. Ariomardus kept to her right, gripping her hand with immeasurable admiration for her strength. She sapped it from him, though she wouldn't dare say it. To her left was Skunkha, enjoying his return to exalted levels of respect and good favor. The curly haired man was the one who selected his three best goats for the sacrifice. After the fires were built early in the evening, Ariomardus slit the necks and Tomyris held the ceremonial bowl which overflowed with good omens. There was no bad thought to be had for miles. Whereas the Persian camp was scampering to make battle preparations for a cause they never believed in, the Massagetae were alive and well, dancing in flames, and singing songs. This was it. This is what everyone had come to the red sands for. This was where the final stand was going to take place. This was where it was going to stop. Cyrus would be stopped.

The Massagetae camp partied at all hours of the frigid, damp night. By sunrise, the skies had opened up, and pale blue was consuming the morning. The red sands of Khorasan were dark, ruddy brown, and dense for a good fight. Tomyris could see her breath as she woke up in Ariomardus' loving arms. He was already awake, staring down at her with all levels of affection a man could possibly possess, and smiling sweetly like a fool. He wanted to make sure that there was no repeat offense on the young queen's part, trying to fight a war on her own. She insisted she'd never do that again, and tried to pull away, but the Dahae soldier had a tight grip on her waist, and playfully wrestled with her underneath the blankets until he was on top of her, pinning her into the sands made damp and warm from their bodies overnight. He leaned down and kissed the tip of her nose.

"Is that all I get, Ari?"

"You'll get the rest after we win this war."

Tomyris rolled her eyes, lunged up and kissed Ariomardus passionately, biting his bottom lip to keep him in place a few seconds longer. He didn't want to pull away, but Skunkha was coming into the tent, carrying the bowl of blood for the face stripes. Tomyris was proud to dunk her fingers and mark her soldiers. Five lines down the right sides of their faces, straight over the eyes and everything. It scared the Persians, and the Massagetae loved that. They cheered and screamed, hollered and howled as they rode off on horseback. Only about forty people were staying behind today, and that was comprised of a small portion of the elderly, a handful of pregnant women, and all children under ten. Two twelve-year-old boys and an eleven-year-old girl came up to Tomyris for their blood stripes. The young queen would not deny anyone the honor. But before the brave girl was allowed to walk away, Tomyris handed the bowl to Skunkha beside her, and bent down to fix the girl's hair. There was a certain way to keep it braided and tied up so that way when one got stuck in a hand-to-hand fight, the girl's hair couldn't be used as a strategy against her. Tomyris went through a couple of quick combat tactics, and insisted there was no shame in running for help or cover. Skunkha always liked the nurturing side of his friend, and thought it was something of a shame she never had more children aside from Spargapeithes, especially a daughter. The former advisor looked back at Ariomardus, and smiled for the first time since meeting him. He knew Tomyris would finally have the chance to be the wife and mother she was always meant to be with Ariomardus. There was just this battle to get through first. The young queen took the bowl of blood back and marked Skunkha. Before she could mark herself, Ariomardus came up and dunked his fingers in the blood, striping the young queen himself.

"Let's go kill us the *king of kings*!"

      As Tomyris smiled the cold blood dripped onto her teeth and she tasted the sacrifice from the night before. It was going to be a good day. On the horizon, there was hardly any smoke rising from the Persian's camp down on the Jaxartes. Heavy fog was tamping down the red sands, but it would burn off with the rising sun soon enough. Tomyris let out a war cry, her white mare bucked up on its hind legs, and the charge was on. It sounded like thunder rolling across the desert. The Persians could hear it, and began muttering amongst themselves about how big Tomyris' army even was after the massacre on the Araxes. It wasn't about size today though, but heart. Cyrus came out from his tent in full battle regalia. The camp silenced seeing the leader in such fashion. Most of the metal armor didn't fit, and had to be adapted with ties and straps around his round figure. A brilliant helmet and grieves adorned his aging body. Atossa fretted about with worries to her husband that her father was delusional, but it was all just for show to appease the harem and appear loyal. Really, this was fantastic news to the princess and lieutenant general. There roles in life were about to improve tenfold, and Cambysses was resigned to his imminent death. The prince couldn't have been more at peace knowing his father was dressing for his last time this morning. No more berating lectures or beatings. No more fruitless lessons on etiquette or speeches about politics. Cambysses came up and kissed his father on the cheek before he mounted his horse. Cyrus was too consumed in paranoia to notice Cambysses hadn't kissed him in nearly fifteen years. A bandage was on the old leader's face, poorly attempting to soothe a festering, blackening wound from Tomyris the morning before. Cyrus rode out to the center of the sands beside the Jaxartes River with several officers including Darius in tow. Tomyris, Ariomardus, and Skunkha had already arrived for the final exchange of words. Cyrus was appalled to see Ariomardus so proudly defending Tomyris, and half choked on his own spit as he tried to scoff and present himself.

"Ah, *little* queen, what a fine day for the crows."

"I couldn't have said it better myself, *old* man."

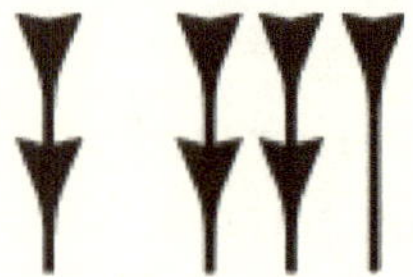

There wasn't anything left to be said. The horses were fidgety and the men wanted blood. Cyrus was the first to turn his back and walk away. The other Persian officers were quick to fall behind, leaving Darius sitting there with a gaping open mouth and sympathetic eyes. Tomyris stared at him, and the nodded to one another. Ariomardus mimicked the gesture. This war was going to be fought and won today, but the three of them had no ill will towards one another. Skunkha on the other hand was another story. The former advisor snickered, and this drew the lightning quick jerk of Darius' head. The Persian lieutenant general raised his hand and pointed his finger at Skunkha, insisting they would meet on the battlefield soon enough. Tomyris looked beside her, and noted a great lack of fear in her friend, but an almost wild intensity in his face, like a predator who enjoyed playing with his prey until the final moments of life were fully squeezed out. She darted a glance to Ariomardus, on the other side of her, and his lack of expression calmed her down. He was neither angry, nor excited. The seasoned soldier lied somewhere comfortably in-between. He wasn't fond of killing people, but he was good at it, and confident in his abilities. The Massagetae held superior position, and sounder judgement. The Persians had numbers, that was about it. Usually that was all they needed for a swift victory, but today was going to be different. Tomyris watched the enemy ranks as their officers' barked orders, pointing their swords in the direction of her own people. Her army was amassed haphazardly according to familial relations and tribes. The Persians sported organized formations, blocks, rows, and lines of men all gathered in fine detail. There were strictly archers on river's edge, there were spearmen and swordsmen. Tomyris' army had everything all at once, whatever the occasion might call for, they'd be ready. She also had women. Some of the grittiest soldiers were mothers who had just recently lost their sons in the massacre that had claimed Spargapeithes life. These soldiers were on the front lines with Tomyris. There was nothing in the world more fearsome to behold than a mother made childless. Some women had lost multiple sons. They screamed the loudest, bared their teeth like ravenous animals, and howled up at the pale blue sky growing bolder by the minute. The Persians didn't know what to make about that, but the Saka conscripts in their ranks could be seen turning.

The first charge was given by Cyrus. He didn't march with the front lines and columns, but held himself safely in the middle, with officers on either side. Darius was one of them, but he wasn't there by choice. In camp, Atossa went inside to distract herself in conversation with Cambysses who was drunk on red wine and half unconscious. Tomyris had not sabotaged this field of battle like she had before, but even the mere thought of fire line erupting in the sands like before, it had the Persians on edge. They didn't clamor and cram as they once did. Instead, there was cautious space, starts and stops in the marching, and odd maneuvers across the dunes. The Massagetae laughed at their enemy's paranoia, and hurdled insults and taunts as loud as their lungs would allow. Tomyris waited until the Persians were an arrow shot away before she raised her sword in the air and screamed for attack. All at once the sands came alive with the thrusting run of hundreds of horses. There were violent clashes of metal weapons and the inherent sound of twisted armor. Horses were downed by spearmen on foot, neighing in frightful pain. Women let out blood curdling howls. Tomyris and Ariomardus did well to keep a close eye on each other as they rolled through row upon row of Persians. The conscripts were already beginning to change sides. Sometimes whole divisions had turned on their former officers, in the name of their Saka blooded queen. The blood splashing up from the dead was a welcomed warmth to the chill of the morning. Tomyris had smeared it across her face to see better. All of her soldiers were giving everything they had. They weren't good for ten Persians a piece like their hearts said they were, but the efforts were as valiant as the gods. Her ranks ebbed and flowed by the second. Two men would be cut down, three more would change sides and come back home, one more slit open, four men would cross over. And it would happen, and happen, and it kept changing so fast Tomyris couldn't keep track of it. Families reunited; fathers died beside sons. Armor was torn off and bodies were stripped of weapons by the living to keep going, keep pressing forwards. Tomyris was leading the charge down one dune, with Ariomardus leading another. Skunkha was deep into the Persian lines ahead of them, pressing forwards for Darius in particular. The target knew he was being sought out. While the officers readied themselves to Cyrus' protection, Darius drifted out so his horse could move underneath him, and engage Skunkha properly. The two circled each other for longer than necessary before a Persian officer flung a spear at the chest of Skunkha's horse, and threw the man to the muddy sand. The impact was hard, and stunned Skunkha for a few seconds, but Darius obliged his rival to take this fight between them to the ground. Skunkha rose with a heavy chest, and a sore left arm, but he could still swing a sword. It wasn't the most accurate of fights, but death didn't need to be precise, just good enough. Darius spit, and laughed at how ragged Skunkha was, sand in his curls, blood across his clothes and golden chest piece. Darius egged Skunkha on, and the Massagetae man screamed, raising his sword high in a kill strike fashion. Darius dodged the hit, gasping for air at his luck of having remained unmarked, but Skunkha reared up from behind, slicing the back of Darius' exposed knee wide open, and sending the pain down into the sand, yelling like a fiend. The battle raged on around them, no one noticing the personal feud or paying special attention to it. Skunkha staggered over, placing himself atop Darius' wounded body. The lieutenant general crawled back in agony on his hands, begging for mercy. Atossa was with child. His child. None of that was for certain, but it was enough to keep Skunkha from pressing his sword straight down into Darius' exposed thigh where his armor had shifted. Skunkha assumed the child was Spargapeithes', and out of love for the boy he raised, he stepped back with frustrated anger.

"We will settle this in our own time, Skunkha."

"I look forward to the day we meet again, Darius."

Skunkha still needed to satiate his blood lust. All the while he and Darius were engaging one another, Tomyris and Ariomardus had been pressing into the Persian lines. Men were now scampering and drowning in the Jaxartes River as a means of escape. Some of the officers were yelling, begging, and pleading for a retreat. Cyrus was in a daze. He had never seen his army in such a state of collapse before. He was almost marveled at the site of it, and had no words. His hearing had gone out, and everything was muffled. He was sweating profusely in the cold. The poison and infection from Tomyris' cut was weakening his senses, dulling his sensibilities. His officers were beside him, screaming for orders, struggling to maintain the battle plans. They were yelling at one another, sometimes coming to blows, kicking each other off of their horses. Cyrus' own horse underneath him was unsteady, and half bucking to walk backwards. Tomyris pressed on. Cyrus locked eyes with her, and all around him the battle was like a fog, muted, and distant. There were tugs, pulls, pushes on his body. He was getting tossed about on his horse. Skunkha and the Massagetae were cutting down Cyrus' innermost circle of defenses. The officers were fleeing, trying to collect their men across the river and save face. Cyrus was abandoned. Darius watched from the ground. Ariomardus rejoined Tomyris a few yards off now. One of Tomyris' allies, a great white beast of a man from the cold mountains in the north, the tattooed Pazyryck tribe, shoved his ax into the chest of Cyrus horse and threw the old leader to the wet red sands down below. The horse was cleaved open in an elaborate bloody show of force. Skunkha was drenched in the red liquid, looking menacing and possessed as he stood over Cyrus. The old, fat man, king of kings, conqueror of worlds, left alone in the sands. Skunkha struck swiftly and without mercy, beheading Cyrus and spraying Darius nearby. The battle stopped. It halted almost instantly. It started in the immediate circle, a paralysis of sorts, and spread quicker than wildfire. Tomyris held up her sword and screamed in victory. Ariomardus rode up beside her, squeezing her in joy, and kissed her blood splattered face.

"Skunkha! Go on now, you give this old man his fill of blood. I've a sack here at my side just for the occasion! Persians, you are defeated! The Massagetae own these lands! You hear me?! This is Saka land! Saka land! Saka land!"

There were chants rising up from various parts of the battle strewn hillsides. Some of the Massagetae and their tribal allies had pushed as far as the river's edge, and were splashing in raucous laughter at their retreating enemy, all awkward and scared. Piles of weapons were abandoned where they stood, dropped in the sands for good measure. Some Persians surrendered, and begged to be made conscript, but the Massagetae weren't interested. The Pazyryck insisted they'd take some men back up north with them as slaves, but that wasn't any of Tomyris' business. She was done now, and a weight had fallen from her shoulders. She slid down to hug Skunkha, cram him into her arms and thank him for the justice he had served this morning. There were no words sufficient enough to express her gratitude. She laughed with tears in her eyes, and Skunkha did the same. They gripped each other's cheeks in their hands and laughed together. Ariomardus retrieved Cyrus' severed head from the ground, grabbed him by his matted white beard which he was always so fond of, and hung it in the air for all to see. Darius was up on at feet at this point, having removed the ties from his chest piece to quell the bleeding from his injury. He hobbled to Ariomardus' side, and received supreme satisfaction of taking a final look at his father-in-law's demise. Ariomardus nodded his head at his friend, because they were still friends after all of this, and Darius insisted he be the one to hold the sack open while Cyrus' head was placed inside. Tomyris scooped up the blood from the body with her own two hands, and drowned her rival's head in his own filth. That was for her son, and for her people. And now, she was done. With all of it. She took care to tie the bag, and handed it back to Darius.

"Do with it what you wish, Darius."

"The people back home will need proof of Cyrus' death. I'll arrange for his body and head to be brought to the capitals for mourning."

"Congratulations on your newfound freedom and titles. And please share my condolences with Atossa. I know there might not have been a lot of love or respect between the princess and her father anymore, but I know what she must be going through."

"I'll be sure to tell her. So, what awaits us now?"

"We will clean the battlefield of the dead. I will have our funeral games in the burning grounds, and then I will set my title aside for a new purpose."

"Might I ask who you intend to leave in charge of the Massagetae?"

"Skunkha."

"A wise choice."

"I think he'll do as well as king as any other."

"And what might become of *you*, Tomyris? I know Atossa will want to know."

"I very much look forward to a quiet life after this. Ari and I want to have a family together."

"That's wonderful! I'm so happy for both of you!"

"It's the first time I've been looking forward to something in a long time. It feels good."

"This will all feel good soon, Tomyris. You'll see. Once Atossa and I are in charge, the world will be a much better place."

"You have your work cut out for you, but I wish you well. I wonder though, what might become of Cambysses?"

"He will lead the empire through a period of mourning for Cyrus. After that, I'm not sure what use he'll be anymore."

Tomyris gave a knowing nod. She understood what Darius' sly smile meant. Ariomardus wrapped a heavy arm around the young queen's waist, and pulled her tightly into his side. She didn't watch as Darius hobbled away carrying the sack full of Cyrus' head. She didn't want to see any remnants of that old man ever again. It was bad enough she was going to have to live with the memories of this war, and what it had taken from her. But there was still the promise of what lied ahead. A future with Ariomardus. A life unburdened with rule. The night before, Ariomardus had mentioned that he wanted to visit the place where is mother was from. She was an Aspiciae, a Saka tribe which had been decimated for a few years now. The lands were said to be a wasteland, but not altogether unlivable. There were grasslands for horses and a river not far away. It was a much more temperate climate than where the Dahae or Massagetae lived, a good place to raise a family. He had fond memories of visiting his mother's family when he was a boy, but hadn't been back there for far too long. Tomyris was drunk off of Ariomardus' stories. They sounded almost too good to be true. And the way he lit up when he spoke, it captivated her. She drew closer to him than humanly possible, and never wanted to leave. Even now, cold, soaked, and bloody, she had this picture in her head of little feet running through waist high grass. Spargapeithes hadn't been a toddler in so long, she missed the way he used to giggle. The uncontrollable fits of joy he used to have. She wondered if she had children again, if they would be like him, happy, with the light eyes. Gazing up at Ariomardus, she had no questions a life with him was going to be everything she wanted and more. He would make a wonderful father, stern, when need be, and soft all the other times. The children would learn horses from him, and fighting from her, or a bit of both from each. It would be an adjustment for sure, leaving the Massagetae behind, and not being needed all the time, but she would still be needed in other ways. She was fond of the way Spargapeithes used to cling to her tunic when she was cooking by the fire, eager to taste everything there was to be had in the desert. There for a while, Skunkha's full time job was keeping Spargapeithes from eating everything in sight! Skunkha would make a good king too. He had the mind for it, the head for rule. The people loved him. How could they not? The mighty slayer of Cyrus!

Tomyris wriggled in Ariomardus' hold and she turned so her back was against his chest, both arms wrapped around her waist, fond of caressing her stomach, where she had his golden knife tucked safely. Tomyris reached out, and gently tugged on Skunkha's sleeve in front of her. He hadn't stopped staring at Cyrus' body since he killed him, but for Tomyris, he could do anything. She carefully smiled for him, signaling approval, and watched as he took a deep breath.

"Sheath that sword, Skunkha."

"I killed him."

"You did good."

"I *feel* good."

"The people will be honored to have you lead them."

"I hope I make you proud."

"You already *have* made me proud."

"I made sure to kill those men who helped torture Sparga. One of them is over there, the other, well, his pieces are somewhere in that general direction."

"Thank you."

"Are you going to be alright, heading out on your own after all this?"

"I think I'm going to be just fine. Ari and I will find a way to make peace with everything that's happened."

"When you get settled, you must be sure to come and visit me."

"We'll visit often. The children will need to know their uncle!"

"Children?!"

"Should the gods will it! You should know, I'm not cutting you out of my life, Skunkha, nor whatever children Ari and I bring into this world. You are my best friend. You always will be, even if we don't see each other every day anymore. On the bright side, you'll finally have the time to find yourself the wife I've always wanted for you!"

"A king must have a queen, right?"

"You will have your pick of the finest women. There will be no shortage of potential wives at your tent when you get back home."

"I don't know anything about being a husband."

"You will learn quickly. It's about being a friend, first and foremost, and you are one of the best."

"I am happy for you, Tomyris. Even if that wasn't clear before, I really need to say it now. I am happy you are happy. It's all I have ever wanted for you."

"I know."

"And Ariomardus?"

"Yes, Skunkha?"

"Take good care of our girl."

"I will. No more battles for us. I'll do my best to keep us at home."

"I would like to see that home one day."

"You will always be welcome, Skunkha."

"Thank you, Ariomardus. Now, if you two will excuse me, I have to get down to the river, and wash Cyrus off me. What a beautiful day it is, isn't it? Just gorgeous! Not a cloud in sight. Just blue. So much blue. I've never noticed before just how pretty the sky can be."

        *   *   *

Ten years after the events in the red sands of Khorasan when Cyrus the Great was beheaded and immortalized, the Persians returned to settle the score. Darius had made well on his promise to Tomyris to let her live in peace under his rule. But Tomyris hadn't been queen in years, and there was no love loss with the Massagetae king, Skunkha. Darius the Great, as he was known now, walked with a permanent limp from the Battle of Jaxartes. Skunkha still kept the sword in his tent as a souvenir of his great victory. Unlike the first time the Persians descended upon the Massagetae, there was no swell of support from the dwindling Saka tribes. There was no heroic stand or show of force. Darius took great pride in killing Skunkha, and acquiring the Massagetae, finally closing that painful part of his past for good. Atossa was happy as well. She didn't dare make the journey as she had when she was younger. No need to go back and open old wounds. Besides, the queen was busy at home, raising her strapping young nine-year-old son, Xerxes, who was a spitting image of his father, Spargapeithes. Paler skin, striking light eyes and all. Darius raised the boy as his own, along with three more sons that were undoubtedly of his own blood. Atossa had done well on her promise to be a good, loyal wife to him. They had celebrated a renewed phase in their relationship after leaving the red sands, and never looked back. Atossa's promise to Tomyris about keeping Spargapeithes' son in her life was honored only once. Upon word of Cambysses' convenient death, a mere seven months into his rule as king, Atossa gave birth and Tomyris was allowed to visit the Persian capital of Ecbatana. The former queen came with her husband, Ariomardus, who needed to help his wife around as she was very pregnant with twin boys, Kurtun and Kavaz. The Saka couple stayed for one night only, and asked the gods to protect Spargapeithes' son. After returning home, Tomyris and Ariomardus lived a peaceful life of obscurity, as far away from politics and conflict as possible. They raised their boys to be daring, brave, and they raised their daughter Zarinaya to be just as strong. Throughout their lives, Tomyris and Ariomardus remained inseparable, dying within hours of each other in their old age. Their family laid them to rest on a single pyre in the abandoned Massagetae burning grounds, now lost to time.